UNFINISHED

=============

Finding yourself among a lifetime of miles
and the ***JFK 50-Ultra-Marathon***

A Novel

Brian Burk

ISBN-13: 9781729573136

Dear Dad,

When you passed from this earth on April 5, 2018 the world lost a man named Richard Paul Burk. I lost a dream I held onto for most of my life. I hope you knew that I always loved and respected you.

When I try to put into words our relationship it reminds me of two travelers starting at a common point and although they appear headed in the same direction the course of time caused each to drift away from one another.

At one time, I believed the path that you were following would carry and guide me during my travels through life. Unfortunately, this path never seemed to stand up to the rigors of life. Early on our roads had many intersections, many opportunities to travel through life together. For whatever reason, those intersections were less traveled until eventually they became like abandoned off ramps which disappear into the overgrowth of time. Looking back, it seems life's challenges, personal demons, distractions or the weight of expectations always kept our paths apart.

For all the good intentions, for all the dreams, all the desires, our roads never seemed to come together. Eventually the void became so great that it could only be bridged for a fleeting moment in time.

Now that you are gone, forever unable to be reached all I can do is wonder. I've come to grips with my role in this relationship and I've accepted yours. I'm heartbroken that our relationship never became what I believe it could have been.

I love you, and I hope you finally have peace.

Forever your son,

Brian

ACKNOWLEDGMENTS

Thank you so much to my family and friends who helped me edit Running to Leadville and this book. Without your help and encouragement these stories would remain captive within my mind and my computer hard drive. Michele Burk, I Love You. Jessica Beets and Anthony Burk, my kids, I love you and I'm so proud of you guys. Chris Beets, thank you for taking care of my little girl. Al and Rosie Diedrich, thank you for welcoming me into your family all those years ago, and for raising such a great daughter. Jeff and Kendra LeMasters, my favorite couple. The Run4Life 24-Hour team...what an awesome bunch of runners and friends. George Nelsen, for getting me into this crazy ultrarunning world we share. Eric and Josh, I always wanted brothers to grown up and share life with...I feel I got close the years we got to hang out together. Laura Nevin, thank you for being a good friend and for all the pizza stuff. Brian Lesh, thanks for the kind words and input on the story. Bryan Staffy and the crew at Run-N-Tri Outfitters, thank you taking care of all my running needs. Chris and Jane Chrisawn, it's a good day to have a good day. Anne Brown, Carol Colby Carraher, Joye Cano, Cara Rogers Hendrickson, Cheryl Cain, Steve Speirs, Kimberly Ratcliffe, Lyndsey Bryant Foster.

And my furry little Miniature Schnauzer girls, Chelsie, Hanna, Carly and Emmy Lu. My life feels empty at times without you by my side, but I look forward to the day when another little four-footed girl steals my heart. Thank you for teaching me how to be a better doggie daddy and person.

Just as the JFK 50 Mile course weaves through historic Western Maryland, the event itself weaves its way through the lives of generations of race participants.

For half-a-century my year has rotated around America's oldest and largest ultramarathon footrace. From a 12-year old in canvas sneakers --barely beating the time cutoff-- to a 24-year old post-collegiate winning in a course record time, to the event's director (now in my 60s) for the past quarter-century-plus, the JFK 50 Mile has literally been my life.

To so many, it is much for than a footrace. It is difficult to explain the magic of the JFK 50 Mile, but Brian Burk "gets it" and catches the true flavor of the JFK 50 Mile in his novel "Unfinished."

Enjoy the journey!
Mike Spinnler

JFK 50 Mile
Finisher 1971-73, 1975, 1977, 1982-83, 1984, 1987-88
Race Winner 1982 & 1983
Course Record Holder (5:53:05) 1982-1994
Race/Event Director 1993-present

For more information on the JFK 50: https://www.jfk50mile.org/

A Life Forever Changed

Chapter 1

From the shop floor, he heard his name broadcast over the public-address system. “Paul Richards, please report to the Shift Supervisor’s Office.” A steadfast worker, he prided himself on being self-sufficient, self-motivated and a low-maintenance employee. This extra bit of attention bristled at his desire to go noticed only for his hard-working habits.

A mid-shift page to the Supervisors Office, the “head shed” as some called it, could only mean a few things. None of them seemed good at the moment. A bad run of product, a request for overtime, or some petty workplace issue seemed to be the likely reasons. Paul shut down the spinning machine he had been massaging all shift to keep running. He removed his required personal protective equipment and made the long walk from the shop floor to his supervisor’s office.

The downside of working the spinning process was the always present acid mist that hung in the air. Paul’s clothes were littered with small burn holes and were constantly falling apart. The upside was the constant demand for the fibers he spun, which in the long term meant job security. With a pregnant young bride at home, the reliable source of income was a blessing. Paul’s sense of professional self-worth was anchored in his ability to keep his machine on-line a “shift leading 95%” of the time. With the success of the business he was making the same amount of money and in some cases more than those of his peer group who went to college to become lawyers, engineers or professional business managers.

All around him the floor buzzed with motion. It had been a good year for Pennsylvania Rubber Works of Jeannette, Pennsylvania. The company had seen remarkable success in producing a line of sports equipment the likes of tennis balls, footballs, basketballs, and soccer balls. The demand for soccer balls kept the company racing to meet the oversold status for the hottest sports craze that was sweeping the nation. With the increase in sales, the spinning line was running near full capacity.

Weighing heavily on Paul's mind as he made his way upstairs was the impact this downtime would have on his monthly production numbers. The higher spinning yields drove higher profits for the company all resulting in a higher profit share for his take-home bonus. He hated to be away from his machine, if even for a few minutes.

The atmosphere felt still and strangely different once he stepped into his boss's office. Something just wasn't right. On the other side of the room stood his boss, a first line operations manager with 20-years' service. A self-made man cut right out of the sun baked and sweat stained tobacco fields of Richmond, Virginia and molded in the management trainee program of his employer. Although his no nonsense image intimidated many, Paul found his boss caring and kind. Paul respected that this man was very demanding of his employees, but he was also very fair and honest. He demanded that everyone give a day's work, stressing that the more money the company made the more it would benefit every employee. Paul liked this attitude and felt comfortable working for him. Today the look on his boss's face caused Paul to feel uneasy.

Two other men stood in the opposite corner of the small office, each had their backs to the door when Paul entered. The sound of his shoes on the hardwood floor alerted them to his presence. The two men turned around and faced him but their eye sight was directed toward the floor. Caught off guard with the extra audience, Paul slowly looked around the room trying to gauge the environment that he had just entered.

"Well I must have really screwed up to get called off my machine. Not sure what I've done Mr. Harver. I'll fix whatever issue has caused you to call me up here." His comment did little to break the tension in the office. The clock hanging on the wall with its metronome tick was the only sound that could be heard in the now silent surroundings.

"Paul, you are one of my best employees. No, you ARE my best operator Paul," Harver commented as he made his way closer to his employee.

"Oh, this must be serious Al…what have I done?" He paused to clear his throat. "The only thing I can think of is the shop football pool…I know it's wrong but the pot is only $25.00. Is that worth my job? And the guys, we all have a little bit of fun with it."

"Paul, no come on man…I'm in that pool too," Al replied.

Al took a few more steps and reached out. "We had a call from the hospital, it's Susan."

Before his boss could get any more words out Paul spoke up.

"Is she okay? Has something happened, to Suzy? I must get there...will you let me go. Please I have got to go. To be with her."

The taller gentlemen in the corner of the office wearing a black three-piece suit, a white shirt, red tie and highly polished shoes finally spoke up. "Paul, we will help you deal with your grief anyway we can. If you need time off to deal with funeral details, expenses, you name it, the company is here to help you."

"What? Funeral? WHAT ARE YOU TALKING ABOUT." A now irritated Paul cried out.

With both arms reaching out for a man he knew was having his world turned upside down, Al tried to fill in the gaps within the message that was just delivered.

"Paul, something happened to Susan," she... He paused to regain his composure. "She passed, I don't know all the facts. They wanted us to tell you and to get you over to the hospital as soon as possible."

Paul fell to his knees, crashing onto the hardwood floors of Harver's office. A strong man now reduced to a wreck of emotions. His eyes teared up, his breathing labored. "My Suzy, gone...no way you are wrong, she can't be. You hear me, you are WRONG.

The air fell silent. No one moved.

Pauls' voice broke the silence with four simple words, "What about the baby?"

"It's a boy Paul...he is fine. There must have been complications, with labor, Susan did not make it. Your boy is alive and well. Come on let's not waste anymore time. Let's get you over to the hospital."

The two men left the office and moved fast through the shop. A few of Paul's co-workers noticed the commotion as the pair rapidly left the building via the side entrance and got into Al's truck for the drive to the hospital. The world was ablaze with motion. Al piloted his broken down and rusted out blue Ford F-150 through the narrow city streets. Paul sat quietly trying to process the information that had just been relayed to him. His wife a fit and healthy 24-year-old woman was now dead? Suzy was never sick a day that Paul knew her and now his active and vibrant wife was gone. The news was overwhelming and difficult to process, his love, his best friend and his wife was no longer alive. No longer part of his life.

His mind then focused on one thought, how did this happen? How did Suzy not make it yet the baby survived? Panic hit him like a runaway rail car. His wife and best friend was gone. He was alone in a world that he found challenging to navigate. And now he was a single father. There was a logjam of thoughts collecting as the truck zoomed through city center and into the hospital parking lot. In seconds, the two men were inside the lobby and rapidly moving towards the elevator. Paul entered the elevator, stepped to the back and stood there quietly. As the heavy stainless-steel doors slammed shut Al noticed Paul did not look so good, his face pale and blank, his eyes fixed and empty. He looked like a man who had just processed that his life had taken a dramatic shift on its axis and would no longer be the same.

Al's responsibilities ended when he got Paul to the attending physicians office. Al who had been through some loss of his own asked Paul if he wanted him to stay. A normally very private man who believed your family life should remain in the parking lot and not to be mixed with work, said he would like it if Al stuck around. The two men stood quietly in the uncomfortable office.

In the dim lighting Al noticed the framed certificates and Medical school diplomas that hung around the room. Behind the broad walnut desk were book cases full of medical journals. Quietly he wondered how many hours of study and thousands of dollars of tuition were invested in this doctors' career. As well qualified as this physician must be, Al knew no amount of schooling, no understanding of the human anatomy or featured medical case studies had prepared the good doctor to deliver the news that was forthcoming.

Within minutes an older man wearing the traditional physician's white lab coat, light blue shirt and black polyester slacks entered the room. He looked tired. His face was flush. A pair of weary blue eyes hid behind an emotionless gaze centered on a round face and a full head of gray and wavy hair.

"I'm sorry to keep you waiting. Paul, I'm sorry. There really is no easy way." The doctor began to speak. He explained that the baby's placenta had pulled away from the womb, that there was a lot of bleeding. Suzy had hemorrhaged and that the baby nearly drown in a combination of blood and embryonic fluids. The words continued to flow although Paul could process very little of the information presented him.

"Did you try, did you try to save her?" Paul asked.

A tear ran down Al's cheek as he tried to steady himself and remain quiet as he could. He knew no more emotion needed to be added to an already tense situation.

In his reply the doctor tried to comfort the grieving husband the best he could.

"Yes, Paul we did, we tried everything. We just could not control the bleeding, deliver the baby and save your wife. Paul I'm so sorry. We tried everything."

When there was nothing left to say, no questions to ask no alternatives to speak of, the three men sat quietly in the doctor's office. One man in complete shock unable to truly understand all that had just been revealed to him. The other two unsure of what words to say next.

There was a knock on the door, a nurse entered and slowly walked in. "Paul I'm so sorry, I know there is nothing that can help make this easier, but if you would like to see your son, I'm sure he could use his fathers' touch. Have you thought of a name?"

"What? I guess I should go see him. Suzy wanted to name him..." Tears rolled down Paul's cheeks, his eye swollen and red.

"Kyle, Suzy would have liked that."

\- - -

18 years passed since Suzy left behind a grief-stricken husband and a new born baby infant. An outsider would think that such a tragic event would form a bond that would link the father and son together in a reciprocal support group. Just the opposite had happened. The years passed under the cloak of lost dreams, dependency, financial burdens, a failed career and a depreciating sense of place in the world. Paul Richards found it impossible to move on settling to relive the loss and wallow in a world of perpetual grief and ever-increasing dependency. While the little boy grew physically he needed the love and warmth of his father. What he received was guilt, strain and the emptiness of a life paying ransom for something he had no responsibility over.

As Kyle matured he learned to compartmentalize his sadness and at times the overwhelming guilt over his mother's death. For much of his life, he felt isolated and separated from his father. At the same time he also felt love and affection for the man. He understood it was hard on his father after losing his wife. He was also well aware that his dad lost a really good job because of the demands of childcare. Numerous times throughout his life he had been told that school hours did not coordinate with shift work. Kyle didn't know how to deal with something he could not do anything about. To try to relieve some of the stress he grew up determined to be good boy and a good son. He worked hard to get good grades in school, and keep up after his chores around the house while his father worked two jobs to pay the bills. Kyle painfully understood the fact that the bills hardly got paid because of the low paying jobs his father had to take to tend to the needs of a child.

"If only your mother had lived, I would not have to fend for both of us." A statement Kyle was painfully used to hearing.

Kyle tried to be a source of pride for his father, doing well in school, and staying out of trouble. This seemed to have the opposite effect. The more demands put on a single parent, the more it drove the two apart. Finally, the only conversations the two were having was on what would go on the shopping list for food, if Kyle needed to be picked up from school or sports and whether his father needed to pick up more beer for the weekend.

A boy growing into a young man understood his father was dealt a heavy blow losing a young wife, having a son to raise on his own and the loss of a job that gave him a sense of pride. With a maturity level beyond his years Kyle understood his father's life was a hard one, yet he loved him and only wanted to be part of making his dad's life better. Intermixed within the trappings of life it hurt him to be the point of so much rejection.

It had been clear for years that his father blamed him for his mother's death. It was clear that his father's life took a turn when he was born and it was clear that his dad had a tough time dealing with it. Kyle became aware early on that his father was drinking to get away from his own "adult" torment. The trail of Budweiser beer bottles around the house would surely testify to that.

"I feel like I'm only working these crappy jobs to keep food and clothes on our backs, that is not what I dreamed about." An endless supply of guilt-riddled words attacked Kyle's self-worth. If these words did not blame him for causing his mother's death, they pointed to the fact that to take care of him his father had lost out on his dreams. This verbal abuse caused great sadness in the boy's heart and haunted him.

Kyle felt lost, unvalued and alone.

The two lives came to a crashing point on the eve of high school graduation. Excited to be passing through one stage of life the young man was trying on his Navy-blue cap and gown. Reluctantly he asked his father if he could get a new pair of shoes. Kyle didn't think his worn out running shoes, the same ones he had used for his final Cross-Country season would hold up for his walk across the stage. This simple question unleashed an explosion of emotions, rage and anger. A firestorm Kyle was unprepared to weather.

"Good Lord Kyle...I think they're fine, I don't have the money to buy new shoes for you every time you want them. These minimum wage jobs only pay so much. I've got to work four hours to buy you a new pair of shoes." His father's anger grew more intense and more savage feeding off the very vortex of energy that it was unleashing.

"I had to give up a job where I could make twice as much as I make working two jobs, because I needed to tend to your every need."

Normally Kyle took everything in stride, tonight those words hit home. The impact hit him hard and square in the chest. For most of his life the young boy had done without. Clothes, toys, food and school supplies had all been a limited commodity around his home. Now on his big night, on the night he would graduate from high school in the top 5% of his class, he would have to walk across the stage in a pair of worn out, dirty and grass-stained shoes.

"Just this once I wish I could have something nice, I'm graduating high school Dad, and you don't have the money or any time for me." He collected his thoughts, "you always have money for Budweiser. You always have money and time for your beer." Kyle replied half under his breath but loud enough to be heard.

"What did you say?" His father asked.

Instantly Kyle recognized the gravity of his comments. After weighing the implications of his rebuttal Kyle simply wanted to avoid another falling out where he would be reminded of his lot in life. He desperately wanted to avoid being reminded that his birth had caused his father so much pain.

"Nothing," Kyle replied.

"Oh, it was nothing, you think I drink too much. I guess you're a big man now that you can talk to me like that. Yea your mother would be so proud."

"Don't talk about my mom, she would have loved me. You have never loved me, or accepted me. I more than anyone am sorry that she died. It was not my fault. That's all I've heard from you my entire life, that her death was somehow my fault. She was my mom." Kyle replied with tears in his eye and hurt pouring out of his heart.

The room went quiet for a moment until broken by the coldness of his father's voice.

"She was my wife and she is gone. She left me and I lost everything to take care of a child. I gave up everything I had to raise you and I got nothing in return. I drink so I can get up in the morning...and if you think your big night is going to change that. IT WON'T, she isn't coming back." His father left the room and walked out of the house.

Kyle could no longer hold up under the weight of a lifetime of rejection and the barge of hateful comments that had been tossed his way. His soul was crushed, his heart was torn open and he wanted to run away. He desperately wanted to be in the presence of someone who accepted him and loved him the way he believed his mother would have.

In a fit of anger and disappointment, Kyle collected a few of his belongings and tore out of the house.

2012 Olympic Team Trials

Chapter 2

"For 23-miles I've felt great, for 23-miles I've kept this dream alive and NOW…it's coming apart. My legs are letting me down!"

Kyle remained in contact with the lead pack of male elite runners from the very first stride of the qualifying race in Houston, Texas. This race, the United States marathon trials, would determine who would represent the United States in the Summer Olympics. For most of the day, his dream was well poised just a stride or two out in front of him.

History would prove that this race would be one of the fastest qualifying standards ever posted. The elite men in the field included the elder statesmen of the team, the 2004 silver medalist, Meb Keflezighi and the young blonde-haired rock star of American long-distance running, Ryan Hall. These two provided the country her greatest shot for an Olympic gold medal in the marathon in London, England later that summer. For much of the day, the two thoroughbreds had been glued to each other's hip and now it was time for someone to make a move.

Kyle like so many other hopefuls simply wanted to remain in contact with the lead group. Running a strategic race Kyle wanted to be part of the show, but he also wanted to have enough gas left in the tank at the end of the race to make a dash for his place on the team. His ultimate goal was to be one of the three men that would qualify to make the trip to London.

Leading up to this sunny January morning in Houston, Kyle had done everything he could think of to make a run for his Olympic dreams.

Through long years, against staggering odds, with marginal talent and in the face of some skeptics who thought it was beyond his reach, Kyle pursued the dream.

- - -

Just nine months prior Kyle packed up his dusty and sun-bleached red Jeep Cherokee and made the long drive cross country to Mammoth Lake, California.

Kyle knew if he was going to successfully accomplish his dream he had to push himself and run with the best. He also knew that the best marathon runners in the country lived and trained in Mammoth Lake. The 3,000-mile drive was the first step. Getting invited into the elite group came relatively easy compared to finding a place to stay on his limited budget. Actually, showing up for his introductory workout with the likes of Deena Kastor, Ryan Hall, and coach Andrew Kastor would prove to be the hardest thing he had ever done.

Much to his surprise, the elite group was welcoming and Coach Kastor was demanding but easy to work with. Today his talents would be measured against the standard of elite competition. At his first group workout, as the new guy, all eyes seemed to be glued on him. The rookie as some called him, the virtual unknown from small-town West Virginia who came to train with the best. Sure, he had won a few local races with impressive times and placed an impressive second in his first big city race at the Cleveland marathon, but little else was known about this new face in the crowd. This new guy seemed to come out of nowhere with some impressive times and talent only equaled by his drive.

On a cold and bright morning, Kyle joined a small group of six others gathered just a few minutes after dawn. Standing among such a talented field, Kyle instantly wondered what he was doing there. He first recognized Hall and Kastor.

It seemed like only yesterday, with a million of others around the nation, he was sitting on his couch watching the dramatic finish to the women's marathon in Athens. Kyle caught up in the drama, was glued to his television set as the United Kingdom's hopeful, Paula Radcliffe, suffer another epic melt-down on the marathon's biggest stage. In the end, he cheered out loud to an empty room as Deena Kastor wearing the red, white and blue won the Olympic bronze. The memory of Deena entering the Olympic Stadium of Athens "Spyros Louis" would forever be a defining moment for U.S. Olympic sports, and for Kyle. Today she was standing right next to him. Today he would put his legs up to the test of an Olympian.

The run started off at an easy pace which allowed some small talk to be worked in as the athletes got into the rhythm of running together. Within the pack the chatter soon turned into a question and answer session directed towards Kyle. Someone asked about his background. Another wondered what brought him to Mammoth. Another quizzed him on the races he had run and his finishing times trying to gain some insight into his competitive potential. Then came the question that everyone wanted to ask but most were too polite to bring up.

"So, Kyle, why do you think you can run at the Olympics, I mean at the world-class level?" A random voice from behind the pack asked.

Kyle took a deep breath in between strides then answered. "To be honest, I guess I'm really trying to figure out if I can."

During that initial run, he found out that he fit right in. It's one thing to drive across the country, it's another thing to run at the elite level. Once he had demonstrated that he had the talent, that he had the legs and the lungs to run at their level, the group welcomed him into their talented fraternity.

What surprised him during his time with the Mammoth Lake Track Club was that he had the ability to match the pace of lead horse Ryan Hall. Kyle made the drive west to test and refine his physical talents. What he found out was that he was more than capable of hanging with the best. He also discovered that running fast was one thing, racing fast was another. He found out rather quickly that he needed to learn the art of racing at that level.

- - -

After 21-miles the lead pack of four made the first move. Kyle knew it was time. As the pack pulled away he pushed his left foot hard into the ground to match their acceleration. The first foot fall landed easy, already running a 5:05 pace he was surprised at how easy it was to shift up into the next gear. His legs felt powerful and light with every muscle fiber working in near perfect rhythm. His arm swing matched his breathing, his breathing matched his footfall, and like the precision interactions of the best Swiss watch, everything was timed to perfection.

The crowd that lined the streets that morning knew that the defining moment of the race was about to be played out in front of them. The lead pack of men began catching and passing some of the slower elite women. The roar was deafening in places around the course. With over a million people watching the national broadcast on T.V., the crowds who came out knew they would be a witness to something special. Inside Kyle believed this was the time and the place to prove he belonged on the world stage as a marathon runner.

"Four of the best are right in front of me, I just have to hold on to them," Kyle flatly reminded himself. He knew he just had to remain in contact, a great showing at mile 21 meant nothing. To be running strong at mile 22 was nice. You may get plenty of airtime on the national broadcast while running with the big dogs.

Olympic dreams are achieved if you can finish in the top three and he knew the time to put on the big move was going to be coming up soon.

At mile 23 with less than three seconds separating the top ten men. Kyle was right where he wanted to be.

With less than three miles to go, the only thought that broke his concentration was when he allowed himself to be in awe of the elder statesmen of the group Meb Keflezighi, who was leading the run for the Olympics. That slight deviation only lasted a micro-second. Then it was back to work.

With two miles to go, it came. The move.

Meb was the first one to kick, Ryan followed. This forced the men in the lead pack to answer the call or fall from contention. Kyle knew this would be the move that separated the three that would vie for Olympic gold against the world's best. He also knew the consequences of not being able to hang with the upper crust. If he fell behind now he would sit at home and watch the race on the television just like the rest of the world.

His brain told his large muscle groups to fire, to run faster, to pour on the coals. But something happened. Something he was not ready for, something his worst dreams were made of and something he feared with the very core of his life. His legs did not respond.

"It's time… Damn it, it is time let's go." Kyle demanded that his legs pick up the pace but try as he might it was all he could do to keep up the pace he was presently running. In the span of one stride, his body went from running fast and easy, almost effortless to now struggling to hold onto what elite speed he had left.

"Not now…come on legs" he asked again almost pleading with himself to answer his own call.

"This can't be happening, I ran with Ryan all summer and into the fall. I matched his workouts, I ran his kicks, I was there for the long runs and at times I beat him at his own game and NOW I can't get my legs into an upper gear. RUN KYLE RUN!" He pleaded with himself.

Try as he might to coax more speed out of his now heavy and lumbering legs they simply would not respond. Where once his breathing was effortless now he was beginning to feel the accumulative taxation that running at an elite level would impose. Instead of finding the next gear, his body struggled to hold onto the five-minute pace that felt easy just a few strides ago.

With great fear Kyle could feel himself slowing down. His body would not respond. There was no high gear, no extra stride length and there was no promise of a top three finish as the lead guys pulled away with every failing foot strike. As his speed fell off, the flickering light of his dream began to fade. Then something more ominous hung over his head.

As the Olympic dream began to fall out of his reach he likewise began to die inside. Where once confidence and strength had been his anchor, now feelings of failure, demons of past disappointments, and the hurt of failed relationships began to rise to the surface. He had let himself down, his body was failing him, and his dream was now just another disappointing event that would haunt him like so many others before.

Kyle crossed the finish line in 10th place, seven spots removed from the finish he thought would redefine his life.

Returning Home

Chapter 3

Kyle returned to his adopted hometown where the small-town streets felt as comfortable as they did familiar.

The stores were the same. The people walking the sidewalks seemed to move in and out of the same routines they had before he left. Kyle walked down the main street of Berkeley Springs, WV, the road that connects the interstate highways of Virginia and Pennsylvania. The two-lane blacktop thoroughfare sees near constant traffic as a continual stream of cars and semi-trucks roll through town. This morning Kyle noticed a group of older gentlemen, the locals refer to as “the breakfast club,” walk into a nearby restaurant. Not to be mistaken for the hit movie of the 1980's and pop culture fame, this club is a collection of pensioners from the Sicilia mines. Their ages ranged from the hipster in his early 60s to the less youthful senior member who was 78. These men spent their lives moving untold tons of silica sand from out of the ground to the processing plant just up the road. Now, they meet daily to discuss the state of the world, their grandkids and the rivalry between Kyle's favorite team, the Cleveland Browns and the recently more successful team from Pittsburgh as Kyle sarcastically calls them.

As Kyle walked past the Black Cat diner, one of the small-town shops and eateries that line the town center, he noticed one of the older gentlemen make eye contact with him and wave as he passed. Kyle remembered seeing this gentlemen in the same spot the day he left for Mammoth Lakes. He wondered if anyone he knew would recall his crushing failure on the streets of Houston.

Kyle next approached a two-story brick building on the west side of the street. The building has been a fixture in Berkeley Springs for nearly 200 years. In that time, the storefront housed all kinds of retail establishments and it was rumored that it was once a front for selling moonshine out the backdoor. Today the building was home to "Run Berkley", an independent running store owned by Kyle's' high school cross-country coach. Prior to his trip out West, Kyle worked in the store and rented a room above the retail space. The running store was his home and today he hoped to be welcomed back.

Kyle entered this store a thousand times before but today, somehow it felt different. In the past he walked into the retail shop as a hopeful Olympian, today he felt like a washed-up former athlete who failed at reaching his dream. As he walked into the store, he was surprised to find that the shop was very busy for a Wednesday morning. As Kyle scanned the room it appeared that four or five customers were checking out different displays in the small retail space. Two were getting fitted for shoes. He could see his former coach, Jim Holt bouncing back and forth between customers ensuring each got his special attention to achieve the best possible shoe fitting. In one corner was Leann, Jim’s wife. She was busy showing a customer the latest running shorts specially designed for long distance runs. Two other customers milled around the shop. With such a large crowd in the store Kyle thought about exiting stage left before anyone saw him. In an instant, his plan failed when Jim’s always attentive hearing picked up on his footsteps and looked up to greet his new customer.

"Oh, it's Kyle Richards", Jim said out loud so that the entire store was sure to hear the commotion. Jim broke away from his customers, stood up and walked towards the door. "Ladies and Gentlemen....you have no idea how lucky you are..." Kyle looked at Jim with an uncertain and cautious gaze. "Today A TOP TEN AMERICAN marathon champion has returned to Berkeley Springs!" Jim said with extra vigor.

"Oh, please it's just me, Jim....please. Save that for the guys on the podium."

Everyone in the store looked towards the door and began to clap as Kyle tried to fight off the extra attention. "No please, I'm not a big deal, placing top 10 is nothing to be proud."

Kyle could not get the rest of the words out of his mouth before Jim spoke up. "Stop selling yourself short...top ten in all the nation. Kyle be proud!"

One of the women who was getting the personal shoe fitting got up and walked toward Kyle wearing miss-matched shoes.

"Kyle...I watched every step of the race. I ran with you that day, you so inspired me. Really all of us. We're sorry you did not get the finish you wanted but you won for all of us here in little old Berkeley Springs. You put the runners of Berkeley Springs on the map. For over 20 miles you hung with the big dogs. Congratulations. We are proud of you and We Love You."

"Yes, we love you, Kyle." A voice called out from behind the display rack of Garmin sport watches.

"Thank you all, really thank you," Kyle repeated. "Really I wish I could have done better but I gave it all I had. It wasn't..." He stopped short of completing the sentence.

Jim walked forward, "Kyle it's okay. Live in the victories you have achieved, not in the failures. That is someone else's voice, not yours. Understand me, Kyle?"

"Yes, sir...loud and clear. Thank you, everyone." Kyle sheepishly replied.

After a few minutes of attention and a few requests for

autographs, the store was empty again with just Kyle, Jim and Leann.

"Kyle can you believe that lady bought two pairs of your favorite brand of racing shoes just to have you autograph them, you're famous," Leann commented.

"Yea, crazy. I'm sure their collector value went down once I signed them." He chuckled.

Leann asked, "So, what are your plans now?"

Jim stopped what he was doing to pay special attention to Kyle's answer.

"Well, since you asked. I hope to get my job back and to lay low for a while."

"When will you start training again, maybe you should get into one of the marathon majors, Boston, NYC or Chicago?" Leann asked very excitedly. "You could earn some prize money and there will be other Olympics trials." Leann tried to soften his disappointment on not making the U.S. team.

"A major, no I think I'm done...I put so much time, effort and money into making the Olympic team that I'm not sure I can get up to that level again and maybe I just don't have it. Maybe I'm just not good enough." Those words hung in the air.

"Hey, that's enough...sure you're down right now, but that's him talking not you. I believe in you." Jim stopped and corrected himself. "No, Leann and I believe in you. You need to get all those negative thoughts out of your mind. Those thoughts were put there by someone else. You're elite, you are special, you have talent and you are a person of value. Never let anyone, ANYONE tell you otherwise." Jim sternly held court.

"Have you heard from your father?" Leann's soft voice asked a very difficult and complicated question.

"Only once since I told him I was moving to Mammoth Lakes to train for the Olympics."

"Only once?" Jim cautiously asked. He was pretty sure he knew the answer. Years of being a fixture in Kyles life taught him the repeating patterns of a man still living in the self-imposed pits of grief.

"Yes, only once and is was not a call for good luck before the race. He called a few days after my disappointing finish. I expected he would call then, you know to remind me that I shouldn't try to be something I'm not, that I shouldn't be there...and how I'm the reason my mom." Kyle's unfinished sentence spoke volumes about the emotional scars he carried.

"Stop Kyle...you know all that talk is from the bottle. He is a broken man. He has never been able to move on, he only knows how to lash out. I know I'm not your father and I have never tried to be, but you have made me proud. Your running is only part of the reason…Kyle."

"I know, but in his eyes, I can't seem to do anything right. I just can't break through to him. He only sees me as the reason his wife, my mom, is gone. I am the reason he lost his job and the reason he has had to struggle to carve out a living. I'm the reason he drinks." Kyles words grew soft as he completed his thoughts.

"That is a lot to carry for anyone, even a strong young man like you. So, what are your plans?" Leann asked hoping to change the subject.

Kyle thought for a few seconds then measured his reply. "I really do hope I can get my job back, and I do want to lay low. I need to figure out if I want to continue to run competitively."

"Done, you start tomorrow, opening shift 9 to 5 and one day each weekend." Jim snapped back. "Your room is just the way you left it upstairs."

Kyle paused to clear his thought. Thank you, it will be good to get back into a familiar routine. Once I get settled, I really want to go visit my mom. There's something about being close to her that settles my soul. I only wish I could have held her hand, felt her warmth and had her in my life.

Pictures of you

Chapter 4

Life once again settled into a predictable chorus of work, household chores and running. Back in town for three months Kyle found himself happy and content as he tried to figure out where his life was headed.

Most of his time was spent working at the running store. Kyle did not view his time there as work. He liked interacting with the customers and he enjoyed maintaining his link within the running community.

Most days he spent a good amount of time answering customer's questions about what it was like to run with Meb, Deena and Ryan as he diagnosed what type of a shoe was a best fit. When Kyle wasn't talking about running in Mammoth Lakes, he was recalling the Olympic trials. Truth be told he gradually warmed up to the idea that although he did not accomplish his goal, he did accomplish something few could even attempt. He finally and humbly accepted that he was one of the top marathon runners his country had to offer. Eventually, he reasoned that it was after all his first attempt and considering his age there very well may be a second opportunity. He began to grow content with the outcome, yet he still was not happy about the fact that his body failed him. Over time he realized that those miles were in the past. There was nothing he could do to change the outcome or to rerun that race. He decided it was time to move on. No longer was he going to live in the past, he wasn't going to let that one failed attempt define him. He refused to let one shortcoming ruin the rest of his life or influence any relationship.

Running and working at the store were only one dimension of Kyle's talents and personality. When not running he had a talent for taking a plain white sheet of paper and creating a still life snapshot. Perhaps a gift that rivaled his ability to run fast was his ability to capture a setting in his mind's eye and then recreate that image in life like detail. Many who saw his artwork compared the lines and shading to a high-resolution photograph. Where someone without his gift might see a simple picture, a collection of black lines, Kyle saw the meaning and placement of each weighted line related to the image he was trying to create. He saw how the weight and length of each line collectively gave birth to the complete image.

Kyle's talent was not limited to one avenue of art. Where many could draw a landscape, a portrait or a wildlife feature, Kyle could span the entire spectrum of artworks. He boasted that he could draw a Disney feature that would compare well to the staff artists at the Magic Kingdom. When not working with customers at the store, or engaged in running related conversations, scrape pieces of paper, napkins, or notebooks became his canvas. Laying around his apartment were tablets filled with the examples of his work.

When needed, Kyle would venture off to nearby Cacapon State Park or up into the Blue Ridge Mountains to escape into nature or to simply sit quietly to consider where life was taking him. He also spent many hours in the woods staring off into space, his mind thinking about his mother. Hours were spent daydreaming and wondering if his artistic talents were a gift from her. He often tried to visualize what life may have been like with her in it.

As a child when times were difficult with his father, Kyle would often venture out into the woods nearby his home to escape the onslaught of guilt his father would lay upon him. It was always something of a curiosity to him that for the number of times he ran away, for all the nights he spent away from home, his father never came looking for him. Now Cacapon was his hiding place, his place of recollection and solitude. Cacapon State Park was one of Kyle's favorite places to escape.

Just outside of Berkley Springs, Cacapon, the Shawnee Indian word for "medicine waters", is nestled near the highest peak of the eastern portion of West Virginia. The nearly 6,000-acre State Park was the perfect hiding place to disappear from the world. Kyle would sometimes run the miles upon miles of challenging trails to break up the routine of road marathon training. Other times he would venture off a trail in search of a quiet spot under a tree to simply think about life. Occasionally he would stop near one of the many small lakes inside the park and wait for a trout or a large-mouth bass to break the water's surface tension. Then there were times he simply sat quietly and listened to the subtle sounds of nature's orchestra.

Today as he sat along the trail next to a fallen moss covered oak tree, he noticed some movement off in the distance. At first, Kyle thought it might be a large squirrel scurrying along trying to find a stash of nuts. Or he reasoned it could be a raccoon out enjoying the morning sun. After studying the random movements for a bit, he came to realize that a small dog was running back and forth in a small clearing. The dog appeared to be having the time of its life randomly running back and forth with no apparent pattern. As much fun as the dog appeared to be having, Kyle wondered why this four-legged track star would be running about. He soon realized the dog, a miniature schnauzer with a light-colored coat, was chasing something being tossed about by its owner. This playful act of fetch caught Kyle's attention and made him smile. Kyle enjoyed the simple pleasures of life and although he never had a dog as a companion, because his father would never tolerate the extra expense, he always felt drawn to man's best friend.

He moved closer seeking a better vantage point to watch the events unfold and to capture the scene before him. While he repositioned himself he was careful to not to interfere or to become noticed.

In a prime location, close enough to transfer to paper the delicate details of life, yet half hidden from the action by an old picnic pavilion, Kyle sat on a bench and began to put his pencil to paper. He first captured the outline of the four-legged companion as he or she ran back and forth. His eye and talented hand laid out an image that captured the dog's joyful motions and physical characteristics. The shading perfectly breathed life into the depth and breadth of the animal's movements. To the left of the main character of his work, Kyle placed the figure of a supporting character. Off to the side stood the dog's owner, friend, companion and in this scene his or her playmate. Kyle's lines laid out the figure of a tall slender girl with long flowing hair. The backdrop of the picture was set upon a beautiful mountain range with low hanging clouds cast among rays of sunlight peeking through. As Kyle added warmth and range to the mountains a voice broke his concentration.

"Hey you!" A female's voice rang out and instantly alerted him that he may be trespassing.

"What are you doing over there, staring at us? Every time I look up you're leering our way?"

"Ah, me?" Kyle's voice half broken, half confused after being torn away from his work. "I'm drawing…a picture. Do you want to see?"

"A picture of what, may I ask? You keep looking at us. You know, my dog and I."

"I guess a picture of you…and the mountains in the background, really…the mountains and your dog playing, not so much of you." Kyle tried to piece together an answer that would defuse the situation that he could feel was getting out of hand rather quickly.

"Hey, listen I don't need a picture, I don't need any extra attention and I don't need lunch, coffee or anything else you try to offer. I don't need to be saved and I'm happy playing with my dog alone. So, go away."

"WOW, okay I was just sitting here. And you're the one walking towards me, but okay I won't offer you anything. Let's just leave each other alone. Frankly, I'm out of here."

Kyle wasn't sure but he felt like he had just been through an interrogation.

Speed Work

Chapter 5

It was bound to happen sooner or later. Although life had become comfortable with Kyle settled back into a normal routine, he knew the day would come. He knew he would one day have to answer the question. Was he up for the conflict, the struggle and the demands of competitive running? Could he harness the will, and the drive, and would he once again be tough enough to rise to the challenge?

Kyle had not run consistently since coming up short in Texas. He ran a few times with friends but he had not been out on a run that held any performance value. None of these outings, "fun runs" really, could be considered a workout. The casual miles he had logged were nothing more than attempts to keep his legs moving. His outings up to this point were simply an attempt to hold on to any measure of elite level fitness and to fight off the home-made treats that regularly poured into the shop.

He wasn't against the free food. He loved the tasty treats nearly as much as he loved running. The pleasure of a warm chocolate chip cookie was only rivaled by the joy that running provided. It was his happy place. His elite level speed over long distances was a cherished gift. The desire to run the marathon distance felt like a natural calling. Fighting off the desire to eat an entire plate of homemade goodness, that was a challenge. The cookies, banana bread, carrot cake and pumpkin loafs seemed to never end. Fighting off the large amount of calories he could consume while devouring these snacks that came extremely hard with a weak spot for any type of cookie or cake.

Today would not be about icing, nuts or glazing. Today was about getting back to work. Kyle sat on the edge of his bed and silently turned off the alarm before it could go off. Five a.m. came fast no matter what time he hit the hay the night before. Although getting up so early at times was rough, these bonus hours provided a magical time for him. There was something special about the hours before the rest of the world got moving. To Kyle, it was in these morning hours that the world was quiet, still and calm. He was never sure where he got the ability to function this early in the morning. He was never sure why he got up before sunrise but for most of his young life, and for as far back as he could remember he was always up before the crack of dawn.

This morning in the stillness of his apartment above the running store Kyle sat listening to the hum of his refrigerator. "Easy running has been fun, it's been nice to just get out with friends... but today it's time to go to work." He thought to himself. In the very next moment, his very next thought contradicted himself. "Do I really want to?"

Kyle walked across the room and pulled open the bottom draw of an old style high boy dresser. Inside lay countless pairs of black running shorts. Slowly he pulled out a pair and with a one-legged balancing routine that would have made an Olympic gymnast proud, he pulled them on. He next opened the drawer right above. This one was overstuffed with high tech moisture wicking shirts in every recognizable color. Kyle picked out a bright green shirt from one of the many local half marathons he ran. As he pulled the shirt over his head he tried to remembered how he placed at that race. He couldn't remember if he won this event or suffered a disappointing finish? He tried to recall if this was the race where he kicked into high gear to early only to run out of gas giving up the win in the final quarter of a mile. Or perhaps this was the race where he faded to a second-place finish as a more veteran and half marathon specialist overtook him in the end?

From the top drawer came a pair of socks. Kyle sat down and drank a few sips of piping hot coffee out of a solid black mug featuring the yellow Batman logo. He picked up drinking coffee during his time at Mammoth Lakes. Prior to his trip out west, he was never much of a coffee drinker. He had preferred an ice-cold can of diet Mountain Dew as his morning caffeine infusion. Hanging out with the guys in Mammoth Lakes he was introduced to the black gold that now was a staple of his morning routine. A simple guy, he resisted the call of fancy and expensive coffees, lattes, and mochas. Straight up black, dark roasted was his choice.

On the counter sat his training log. For something that held the plan for his Olympic dreams, it was really simple looking. A black covered spiral notebook. The cover was rough on the edges with a dogged ear crease in one corner. It looked a little ragged, somewhat beat-up and a bit out of place with technology. Although a child of the computer age, his generation was sandwiched between the baby boomers and the millennials. This 20-year span was known as generation X. Despite being born during this block of time, he did not identify himself with one generation. Kyle was a bit of a free spirit and lived his life in a fashion that spanned time.

Kyle preferred to track his workouts with old fashion pen and paper. After the fact, he would load the results on to a fancy excel spreadsheet with graphs, data sorting and pivot tables. In the moment, he preferred to review the workout of the day in black text on a white sheet of paper. Today, the first day of officially getting back on the horse, in his notes was written "Fitness check, Yasso 800s." Affectionately known as "Yassos" the 800-meter test would effectively gauge how fast an athlete could run the marathon by comparing their collective 800-meter times. Today the Yasso workout would not be used as a prediction tool but as a gavel held in judgment.

Normally there would be a number written after the workout statement "Yasso 800s x 6, 8 or 10", but today there was no set number jotted down. No high number, no low number, no minimum, and no maximum. Written down after "Yasso 800s" were three simple words.

"UNTIL. YOU. PUKE."

After downing a blueberry fig bar and the final sips of his dark roasted coffee, Kyle pulled on a pair of his racing flats, ran his hand through his wavy air and walked to the door. Inside he was surprised to feel a shot of nervousness take over his system. Even though today did not count toward any qualifying standard, no official time would be recorded, no victory would be achieved, today's workout might just be one of the most defining moments in his short life. The door locked behind him as he left his apartment. He slowly walked down the flight of stairs and stepped out on to the sidewalk of a town still slumbering. The air felt cool on his skin.

The dawn of a new day broke over the horizon as a random mixture of cars, buses and trucks made their way rumbling down main street en route to the interstate. Kyle felt the early rays of sunshine on his face as he took a breath and pushed off to begin his run. Today would begin with an easy three-mile run along the side streets of state route 522 or S. Washington Street. In no time at all his legs settled into the familiar pattern and his stride began to lengthen. Where most recreational runners strive to keep up a sub-nine-minute pace, Kyle's warm up would keep him moving along in the high 6-minute per mile bracket. After a few out and backs along the side streets Kyle turned left on Cacapon Road where he would face a nice long stretch where he could bring his legs up to near racing speed allowing his muscles to warm up and gain full elasticity. Kyle ran about a mile and a half along this road then turned on his heels and reran his steps back into town until he reached Meyers Road where he took a right turn towards Widmyer Elementary school. Widmyer had the closest track that he could access without much effort to get in some speed work.

On a few occasions, he would run there with a few of the local fast guys. This morning he was all alone.

The elementary track was not up to the standards of Olympic competition but this morning it provided the perfect setting for a test of his fitness level. The track represented the small town that it serviced. A rough and tumble surface that showed many years of use. The footing would not provide the tacky surfaces of some of the top-level facilities he previously trained on. Knowing that, he expected his times could be a bit slower today. The surface with all its faults would provide the ability to see where he stood.

Kyle timed out his warm up run with near perfection and arrived at the track precisely when he wanted to. His legs were ready, his heart rate was in the target zone and he felt light and fast. Kyle took a second to adjust his watch, check the laces on his shoes and grab a drink from his hand-held water bottle. Kyle paused another few seconds to take in a few deep breaths and put his water bottle down along the side of the track. Before beginning his slow jog around the track, he took one long breath into his lungs and held it for a count. As if trying to exhale any past demons he forced this cleansing breath out into the world. Kyle believed this run would tell him if he could really push himself to the limits. This test would gauge where he stood fitness wise. Most importantly, he hoped this outing would answer the question if he still had the competitive desire he once had.

At a slow jog, he worked his way around the track growing ever closer to the starting line just opposite the elementary school. As that line drew near, Kyle performed a mental inventory of his body. Physically he felt poised, and mentally he was as ready as he would ever be. The starting line was now only a few feet in front of him. Slowing to a walking pace Kyle reached down and pushed the button on the side of his watch. The GPS device on his wrist with a few near silent beeps switched over to run mode. The watch face displayed distance over elapsed time. Kyle glanced down to see the upper display of his watch. He saw, four zeros separated by a colon and two zeros on the other side. The distance display likewise was set on zero. The GPS signal had been acquired during the run over to the track and now the watch was ready to be the judge and jury on his efforts, abilities and desires.

Kyle stopped short of the starting line to take in a few deep breaths and again found the button on the side of his watch. In an instant Kyle thought he heard an imaginary gun go off. Without delay he was off. At first effort, his legs knew exactly what to do, and went right to work. Like a wildcat attacking its pray, his fast twitch muscles fired into action. His long stride grew with each series of leg turnovers until he was covering nearly six feet with each stride. All his natural rhythm and timing came right back and it took very little time for his body to get up to top speed. It then became an exercise in keeping up the tempo, maintaining the pace and holding his physical motions in line developing maximum speed with the minimal amount of energy consumption.

Motoring down the back-stretch Kyle marveled at how easy it felt. Things came back so fast, he thought for an instant that perhaps he had not lost any fitness nor speed during his nearly four-month layoff. Kyle rolled out of turn four in high gear completing one lap. He resisted the desire to look at his watch for any validation of his pace or the time it had taken him to cover that distance. He was free and running in the moment. Kyle believed he was running fast. In what seemed like not much time at all, he was racing down the backstretch again. As he leaned into the turn he concentrated on running the shortest distance around the four-hundred-meter track. Kyle's footfall was landing right outside the white line of the inside lane with near perfect placement every time. The outside of his orange flats fell just outside of that painted line time after time. It appeared to him that his feet landed the same distance from the line in rapid fire successions. In no time, he rolled out of turn four and headed for the completion of his first Yasso of the day.

As Kyle crossed the finish line he reached for the button that would stop his watch and record his time. As he slowed his gait to the point of a slow jog Kyle finally allowed his eyes to read the display on his watch. 2:42. Kyle ran his first 800-meters in two minutes and forty-two seconds. His eyes could not believe what he had seen.

"There's no way, that lap felt so much faster, I was running so easy...there is no way I've lost almost 25 seconds." Kyle angrily said to himself as he jogged out of turn two on his cool down loop. That time ate at him the rest of the way around the track. It bothered him that although he felt like he was running fast, that he felt like his speed had come back or never left that in fact, he was no longer at Olympic levels. He approached the starting line for his next 800. He was determined to prove his watch wrong.

2:38 flashed on the display of his watch as he slowed to a jog at the end of Yasso #2. "You have got to be kidding me, I nailed that one." Kyle told himself out loud as he made his way around his second cool down lap.

As Kyle approached the start of Yasso #3 he convinced himself that his form had broken down. He reasoned that his legs felt alive during both of the previous laps. Likewise, his breathing did not appear to be labored. If he had to categorize his effort, it felt like he was running at 80%. He had to be losing time with poor form. His time had to get better if he paid more attention to his form. The next opportunity came fast.

His legs fired off hard. The sole of his shoes pushed hard into the rubber compound that made up the track surface. The tension building up in his large muscle groups recoiled and pushed him forward only to repeat the action over and over again. This time the energy transfer felt different, this time his body felt in sync, this time he knew his time would be more up to the Olympic standards he had been running in Mammoth. This time he knew his watch would be displaying 2:20 or faster. The front stretch of this 800 came fast. With his head slightly tilted forward and his eyes focused on the track in front of him his legs fired off in rapid succession as Kyle concentrated on a strong finish.

This time his eyes quickly glanced at his watch faster than his fingers could find the reset button. This time the true weight of the displayed set in. This time he believed what was displayed. The jury had returned three verdicts. This time the display crushed his spirit, 2:40.

"What..." Kyle dejectedly shouted skyward. "I can't believe this. I've lost nearly 20 seconds off my pace. This is slower than before I left for Mammoth, how in the world." For the remainder of his cool-down lap, Kyle was beside himself with questions. Beside himself with anger and destructively tearing himself down with self-doubt.

It was time to run again. Where before the push off from the line was easy and fluid. This time Kyle pushed off with anger and pent-up rage. His legs reached out in front of himself, pounded into the ground and pushed off violently trying to propel himself faster and faster around the track. With emotional rage, Kyle willed his muscles to explode in violent fashion. To cover more ground faster Kyle compelled his stride to reach out further. In anger, he took deeper and deeper breaths trying to force feed oxygen laden fuel into his muscles enabling them to move at a more rapid pace.

2:46 was the unfavorable results at the end of the fourth lap.

This time Kyle jogged around the track without saying a word out loud. He hardly spoke to himself. One simple thought entered his mind in a hushed and quiet comment. "I don't have it anymore."

Again, the starting line grew near and again Kyle ran in anger. In haste, he willed his legs to answer. In desperation, he pleaded with his body to respond, to break out, to give him one fast lap to prove he was still capable. He needed to see that there was still a flame burning.

Again, his watch posted a time that Kyle was not fond of, 2:44.

Kyle's body was beginning to feel the Yasso effects. Heavy legs, tired lungs and now a heavy heart. Mentally he had already taken up residency in the pit of misery. His body from the start was unable to deliver the performance that he wanted. After five 800-meter laps his body began to fail.

Making the final turn of his sixth Yasso his legs began to feel tired. Just laps before he was able to accelerate to a strong finish, now his legs began to fail in a painful and all too familiar way. "Come on, keep fighting, don't give up." He cried out as he pushed home to finish the sixth Yasso 800. 2:55 displayed on his watch.

Like a hot knife through butter that elapsed time cut him deep. The pain was beginning to sink in not only with his self-esteem as an elite level athlete but also physically. His quads were growing tight and he could feel a stiffness develop in his calf muscles. He knew how to deal with the physical effects...he had been down that road before. Kyle was not sure how to deal with his lacking confidence. From the time he had found his gift of running his performance curve had always been on an upswing. His times had always gotten faster, the only speed bump had been that morning on the streets of Houston. Now that crack in his running foundation became exposed and he began to question if he could truly run at that level again. The growing self-doubt began to manifest itself as a small voice that called his attention to the fact that his times would barely keep him up front in any one of the local marathons.

Kyle had always believed in the power of positive thoughts. Whenever he would get beaten down as a child, when the harsh comments that his father tossed his way got to him he always fought them off with positive self-talk. At the time, he wasn't really sure what he was doing. All he knew was that it made him feel better if he followed some advice given to him from a close friend of his mother, her name was Nancy. A classmate of his mother's in high school, Kyle knew her most of his life. She was a fill-in babysitter and someone he often felt comfortable with. She would tell the young boy to always believe in himself, to never believe the hurtful words of others. This kind-hearted woman would instill in him that he could be anything he wanted to be if only he believed in himself. She often suggested that he repeat something positive to himself for every negative thing he heard. This simple lesson lived with him partially fueling his Olympic dream. Today he called on it again.

"Those times are only snapshots," he told himself in an ongoing ramble of positive messages as he jogged around the track getting ready for his seventh attack on the clock. "I'm not going to let a time define me, limit, or undermine me." Kyle began to feel more confident. "One good lap and we will have something to build on. One good effort will put this day into perspective, one fast run and the world will look a whole lot better, it's time. It is time to get to work."

The starting line stood out before him this time. Not as a line on the track where he should begin his run. Not as a point where he should begin timing his effort. The line stood out as a milestone in his life where he could choose which direction to take. A line in the sand that could become a defining moment in his life story. With a deep breath and a surge of adrenaline Kyle's thighs exploded like a mid-century cannon. With nearly the same explosive thrust his legs pushed into the track surface converting pent up energy and potential into motion. Forward motion that in seconds had him running hard and at full speed. Something was different this time. In a blink of an eye, he was coming out of turn two and facing the 1/8-mile backstretch. Flat and fast, his legs fired off like high-pressure springs pushing his body weight forward then recoiling for another round of compression, stored energy and a rapid release. Rolling into the third turn Kyle thought for sure he had found his groove. The front stretch provided another opportunity to run unbridled. Another opportunity for his feet to land fast, his muscles to compress and another chance to propel his body down a long straight section making up ground on the clock. The white line beneath his feet passed by in rapid fashion. Almost as a burr his footfall was again laser-focused on the shortest distance around the track.

Rounding into backstretch Kyle glanced down at his wrist. He had trained himself to not worry about times while in the middle of a workout, but today he had to know. In racing form, he willed himself to only pay attention to the amount of effort he was putting into his pace and not his overall time. Today in this make or break run his discipline broke. Kyle stole a glimpse of the elapsed time displayed in bold digital numbers on the face of his watch. In what he believed was his fastest lap of the day time betrayed him.

Instantly he pulled up and came to a stop. Breathing deep, sweat rolling off his forehead, with his eyes tearing up with shades of anger ever present on his face he shook his fist to the sky.

"No way, I can't believe I can be running this slow. At this pace, this lap would have taken over three rotten minutes to complete."

Kyle walked the rest of the way around the track and sat on the aluminum bleachers. Alone with his body striving to recover from the effort on the track he felt lost and without his identity. Where he thought he would find direction he was now unsure of where he should turn.

"What happened, have I really fallen that far? Have I lost whatever I had? Now what?" He sat alone and lost on the cold seats looking for answers. He remained there until his body began to shiver and his legs started to cramp up.

"I'm going home." He declared to himself and the void surrounding him.

Kyle walked the nearly three-quarters of a mile back to his home. His posture was slumped over, his gait slow, labored and dejected. The walk home may have been the longest distance he had ever covered. Arriving at his apartment, he found very little solace in the empty room littered with tokens of his running accomplishments. His damp, cold shirt and shorts grew heavy on his body. The weight of his sweat made his shirt cling to his skin.

The cold fabric sucking whatever warmth his body could generate right out of him. In the stillness, he peeled off his running clothes tossed them into the makeshift hamper and walked to his shower. The long walk home allowed him to consider many things, central was the thought that this might be the last time he attempted to run at the elite level.

After a warm shower and a sandwich, he went to bed. Not much was thought of for the rest of the day. Even his internal dialog of which he relied upon to lift him out of many dark and depressed times had been eerily quiet. In the stillness of the dark apartment, with absolute quiet surrounding him a final thought came to mind.

"I'm not sure I want this anymore."

Berkeley Springs

Chapter 6

Being part of a small-town America, the merchants up and down Main Street relied on customer service and personal relationships over discount pricing to grow a customer base and remain in business. Competing with the big box stores and online retailers, while being profitable, was a daily challenge. The small running store in the center of Berkeley Springs was known for outstanding customer service. What kept the doors open was that the store was an integral part of the community. Run Berkeley was as much of a local hang out as it was a shoe store. Runners were not the only customers who frequented the store. A parade of local hikers, outdoor adventurers, people seeking to improve their fitness, and vacationers who found themselves on the doorsteps of the Blue Ridge Mountains, stopped in to talk about the local area, pick up some gear, or try on a new pair of shoes.

Jim Holt and his bride came to this small hamlet of a town to get away from the rust belt of south-western Pennsylvania. He enjoyed teaching high school and he enjoyed seeing young adults blossom into fine members of the community. But he hated being stuck within the confines of an old steel and manufacturing town. Jim and his wife Leann longed for the outdoors. They desired the simple life where their passion for adventure would intermix with a calling to start their own business. The pair moved to Berkeley Springs to answer that calling.

- - -

The couple enjoyed two years of marriage when Kyle ran his last year of cross country for the Jeannette Jayhawks. Leann noticed instantly how invested Jim was with this young runner who clearly had a gift. Outwardly he could see that Kyle had something special that the other boys on the team did not. Masked by his athletic gifts, what Jim did not see at first was the emotional baggage this "once in a lifetime talent," as Jim referred to him, carried.

Kyle saw his coach as a positive role model for how a man should live his life. He witnessed the love his coach had for running, how he cared about life, his athletes and how he treated everyone with respect. Being a high school sports coach, unless you're in charge of the football program, usually comes as a burden filled, additional duty. Not for Jim. Kyle and the rest of the boys on the cross-country team understood from day one that "coach" loved the time he spent with his team. Their coach was a runner, loved running, and wanted the very best for his team.

It was obvious in the way Jim handled practice, drills, assignments and arranged their training runs. If the quality of his workouts did not convince the team that Jim was more than an ordinary coach, the day he laced up his shoes and went for a 5-mile run with the team closed the deal. Jim may not have won the impromptu race that broke out that day. In fact, he came in second to last, but he won the team over and most importantly he gained their respect. At the end of the day, his boys would run through a brick wall for their coach.

At first, Kyle wasn't sure why, but he felt especially connected to his coach. Over time he came to realize that Jim was the first significant male figure in his life who did not undermine his self-esteem. More so, Coach Jim, as he requested the boys on the team call him, uplifted what someone could achieve, not highlight and expose what they could not accomplish. Jim did not sugar coat it if his runners gave him and the team less than their best effort. He was not one to mince words, but he did so in a fashion that his team trusted him. His boys believed that with his guidance they could achieve much more together than alone. Whatever it was, Kyle trusted Jim. That trust got tested one late night.

Kyle's father was in a bad place. Kyle was never sure what set him off. Was it the booze? Was it something he said? Was it the lack of money or a bill that got paid late? Kyle wasn't sure but he was well aware of the fact that he was going to bear the brunt of the frustration, anger and rage.

The words stung, they hurt his feelings and left him confused and worried. Up to this point, the spiteful attacks were confined to harsh words, negative remarks and pointed accusations. Up to this point, they never left a physical mark. At first, he could only recall the pointed words.

"There's no money left. It's not my fault your mother died...I've had to live with the mess she left me, with you." Kyle's father ended another typical tirade with the worst possible ending.

"If only..." He did not finish the sentence. He did not need too, Kyle was too familiar with what would follow.

Kyle decided it was time. He knew it wasn't going to get any better. He had heard enough of the insults. He had no real plan he simply wanted out of that environment. Fed up with the hostilities Kyle made a move for the door. His only route to escape the confrontation would bring him directly into the path of the very thing he was trying to avoid. No matter what, he had to get away.

In that instant, their relationship changed forever. It may have been that he caught his father off guard. He wasn't sure. The two never spoke about it. He never asked and his father never apologized. For a reason never uncovered, in a rage of anger and with a closed fist Kyle was struck. The boy never saw it coming, he had no reason to. Kyle was only trying to leave, to get away from the ugly words being thrown at him and now he was trying to get up off the floor.

The surface was cold and hard. He wasn't sure what happened. The right side of his face hurt and there was a burning sensation near the corner of his eye. The impact not only shocked him physically but it also devastated him emotionally when he realized what had just happened.

Kyle ended up at Jim's house. He had nowhere else to turn. He had no family, no close friends and as dysfunctional as his relationship was with his father, he was the only family he had. Now on the doorstep of his coaches' home, Kyle, a shaken young man not yet out of high school, told the one person he trusted, Coach Jim, everything about his life.

From that fateful night, the rest of Kyles life path changed. The rift between his father only grew wider fueled by the unspeakable act of that night. Their relationship may have survived. The damage could have recovered if only his father had acknowledged the misstep. Instead he chose to ignore and distance himself from his son even more.

In the aftermath of his high school graduation Kyle bounced around finding temporary accommodations with Jim, some friends and the occasional cheap living arrangement. He worked at whatever jobs he could find and continued his running and studies after high school. He eventually followed Jim and Leann to West Virginia and their adventures as owners of a thriving running store.

- - -

It was a long way from Jeanette, Pennsylvania to Berkeley Springs, West Virginia and the failed time trials which threated to derail the young man's dreams.

Kyle slowly walked into the running store and made his way to the backroom to drop off his backpack and hang up his coat.

“Hey, Kyle” Jim called out from behind a display rack and a mountain of socks that had just arrived.

Coming back out-front Kyle took up a position near the counter pondering life while he looked out the store window.

“What’s up Kyle? Not even a grunt for a greeting this morning.” Jim could sense that something was up.

“Some tough times on the track yesterday, Jim.”

Oh that’s right. You said you were going to get back after it…so how bad was it? Could not have been end of the world.” Jim questioned.

“Nowhere near my goal pace…and it only got worse as the laps went by. I could not get my form together. I could not get into high gear. Well, I thought I was in high gear but the watch said otherwise. Really disappointing. Jim, I really wonder if I still have it. Maybe worse, I question if I ever really had it.” Kyle lamented.

As the former coach and his star athlete stood at the sales counter, Jim tried to get Kyle to open up about his training session. Kyle was not very forthcoming with details. The coach inside of Jim wanted to uncover what went wrong. He tried to pry out of Kyle what his split times were and how he felt running each segment. When it seemed like he was just about to make some headway the front door of the store opened and a cheerful, perky and radiating female voice called out.

“Hey, guys I need some shoes over here.”

Broken off from their conversation, the two instantly turned and looked in the direction of their customer as she made her way into the store.

Candy had only been in Berkeley Springs for a few months although with her vibrant personality, she was well known by most of the merchants. Candy walked into the store wearing a pair of white capris, a red camisole top, red flip-flops with a pair of sunglasses perched atop an overflowing mass of blonde hair tied back in a ponytail. Besides her stunning looks, and radiating smile she was well known for her grand entrances.

Without another word, she knew she had their attention. Candy was a beautiful girl, in her mid-20s, fit and trim. She recently found a love for the outdoors, enjoyed rock climbing, hiking trails, escaping into the wild and spending time with her four-legged best friend.

“You sure know how to make an entrance,” Jim commented, instantly recognizing her voice.

Kyle was next. “Oh hi.” His voice slowly faded off. “Crap it's you.”

“Oh…I see now you're the stalker from the park the other day. The guy spying on me. Drawing you said. More like watching Carly and I. Like a peeping Tom.”

Jim burst into the conversation. “Kyle a stalker, watching you, peeping Tom? Okay that's funny, but no way.”

“No that's not me, just wait, I can fix this.” Kyle let out a short claim of innocence as he made his way to the back of the store.

“Okay but don't try and run, I have the police outside, the SWAT team has the building surrounded.” Candy said as Kyle disappeared into the back room of the store.

“What? Candy, what's going on?” Jim wasn't sure how to take the last statement.

“Jim don't you worry, but I think I got your boy here a little nervous.” Candy let out in a soft laugh as she adjusted the sunglasses on the top of her head.

Walking back to the front of the store, Kyle handed his accuser a rolled-up poster-sized sheet of off-white paper. Candy looked puzzled as she unrolled it. Silently she stared her eyes were glued to the paper. A defenseless smile came across her face.

"This is wonderful..." She turned the paper towards Jim.

"It sure is. Very nice work Kyle," Jim commented.

On the oversized sheet of paper was a lifelike drawing of Candy's dog running across a field of shortcut grass chasing after a round toy thrown against a backdrop of mountains. Each feature of the ridgeline was clear, perfectly placed, balanced and shadowed in such a way that it looked as if the mountains had come to life on that simple sheet of paper. That wasn't what stole Candy's attention. Kyle had captured in perfect detail the joyful expression of happiness that her dog displayed while playing a game of fetch. With his unique ability, he captured the depth of Carly's brown eyes, the shape of her body, the lightness of her buff colored coat and the fluidness of her movements. Kyle nailed the scene in life like proportions and expressions. The drawing took Candy's breath away. She was lost for words and a tear formed in the corner of her eyes.

There was a long pause. Candy held the picture and simply stared. "Beautiful." The silence was broken. "Wow, and I thought you were some hack job just trying to hit on me. I had no idea that you hardly noticed me. I'm nothing more than a shadow of a figure, a supporting cast member to this wonderful picture of my Carly Q."

Kyle finally spoke up. "It's okay, it's what I do, I like to draw."

"It's not all he does, Kyle here" Jim paused allowing the moment to draw some tension. "He is also an Olympic hopeful for the marathon. He placed top 10 in the U.S. and for the next Olympics in 2016 he will be top 3 and I'm sure will be representing our country at the games."

"Thank you, Jim, I sure hope so, but right now I'm not feeling it." Kyle smiled at the picture and at Candy. "You can have it, my gift to you. It was my pleasure."

Candy smiled and wiped the tear from her eye. "Can I pay you something for your time, it's really beautiful. Or buy you lunch, dinner a case of beer? Something."

Kyle with a big grin on his face saw an opportunity to set the score right, "so you're asking me out?"

Friends

Chapter 7

It was easy for Kyle to fall back into his running routine. After all, running was his all-consuming passion through high school and the years leading up to his Olympic qualifying bid. This morning while he laced up his shoes and pulled an old shirt over his head he felt more like a would-be runner trying to maintain his fitness, balance his weight or fight off the encroaching years than someone trying to go after a gold medal. Today an easy run was highlighted in his training journal and he hoped this run would settle where he fit within the running community.

Slowly he made his way down the flight of stairs and arrived at the door which opened to the parking lot behind the running shop. Taking in a deep breath of crisp mountain air he hoped he might find some clarity to his future. Today Kyle planned to run 10-miles at a pace hovering around a high six minutes per mile. He wouldn't win any races today, score any medals or claim a spot on the team. This run was designed as a maintenance run, a workout to simply keep his legs churning and his lungs operating fully. This outing he anticipated would give him a chance to think, to ponder the future and provide him some answers.

"Kyle, is that you?" A voice beckoned from just over Kyle's shoulder as he stood in the parking lot. Surprised that anyone else would be moving at this hour of the morning Kyle wiped away the last remains of sleep from his eyes as he turned to see who had called him.

"JT is that you?" Kyle replied. "Hey man, what are you doing up this early on a Saturday morning? Most everyone I know around your age is still sound asleep."

JT was a regular at the running shop. A freshman in high school and a gifted runner. Kyle was someone JT looked up to. The young runner would hang out in the shop, talk about running and watch the running movies and documentaries that were constantly on the big screen T.V. behind the wall of shoes. JT was also one of the rising stars on the high school cross-country team. He was also one of Kyle's favorite customers, team members and all-around runner.

"From what you're wearing I can tell you plan to run this morning?" Kyle stated to his young protégé when he was close enough so that he did not have to raise his voice.

"Is it okay? Jim told me you were going to run easy today and I figured I could keep up with you on a slow day. He also told me what time you normally run and I just took a chance. I hope you don't mind." Said a slightly nervous JT, his words falling off in an unexpecting tone.

Kyle's face turned cold and serious. "No way…you think you can run with me? He paused for effect. "I'm kidding. Dude, you're welcome to hang with me anytime." Kyle snapped back realizing he caught the young man off guard with his attempt at humor. "Plus, this morning I could really use some company, I'm too much in my own head today. I'd love to have you run with me."

"Dang, you got me, Kyle."

The pair took off up Washington street shaking the morning rust off their legs as they moved along the sidewalk heading north. Kyle motioned for JT to follow him with a right-hand turn to cross over Washington street to Independence. They then made their way on to Fairway Street. Fairway was a nice road to run an out and back training segment on. Less traveled with some gradual inclines but nothing that would zap your legs. Kyle logged many miles on this road sometimes searching for speed, other times maintaining a targeted tempo and like today simply to add miles to his running log book.

In most sports running was a tool used to advance the ball, position the player, or to block and defend your goal. In most sports running also served as the punishment or conditioning mechanism to get the players to a level of fitness needed to participate in the game of choice. In these athletic avenues, running could be a struggle, a chore, a demanding task to simply get through, put up with or to survive. In this vein, running seemed almost unnatural. In today's modern sports you could be an athlete and not be considered a runner.

Non-runners never seem to find the fluidity of physical movement that make up the runners' gait. Their efforts appear laborious and unorganized. The arm swing and footfall are hardly graceful and often looked forced. Their leg turnover is slow, awkward and appears heavy. Physically the body seems out of position, never in rhythm and far from coordinated. Forced into an activity the body appears to be fighting with itself, taxing vital energy and oxygen it needs to keep moving forward.

Non-runners struggle not only with the physical concert of movement but also battle with their natural ability to breath. An inherent act becomes unnatural, forced and foreign. An act they take for granted when stationary becomes something which requires a great amount of effort and thought when the body becomes taxed, tired and depleted. Breathing becomes an effort where it should fit into the perfectly timed movements of their arms and legs. On this quiet morning, the natural rhythm of running was never more on display.

This morning Kyle's body fell right into the patterns he believed it was designed for. His movements were easy, natural and fluid. With an effortless gait, his legs covered ground quickly and landed without effort. His footfall was light on landing and quickly transitioned into the action that propelled him further down the road. With a slight lean, his hips and chest moved forward with a minimal amount of wasted effort or energy. The swing of his arms completed the motion while his head and eyes hardly darted off course. Absent were any sounds of labored breathing as his movements were purpose-built for covering the maxium amount of ground. Breathing came easy and perfectly timed, his expanding lungs matched the movements of his legs. During most runs, his face displayed a half smile.

JT was the first one to break the silence. "Kyle, so what's next?" he asked as the two settled into a steady and repetitive groove.

Today the smile was missing. "I don't really know JT," Kyle answered shortly. Then after a few strides, he continued. "I got back on the track this week and it did not go so well. I sometimes wonder if I'm overreaching my abilities. Do I really have it?"

Although the pace today required that JT put in a little more effort to match strides with Kyle he held onto every word.

"The Olympics is such a big dream. I wondered where I got the idea that I have that kind of talent?" Kyle continued. "Lately I've been waking up every morning and asking myself, is it worth it?" Kyle paused. "You know when I'm at the shop, talking with you guys or helping someone start running I do feel special, like I have something, as if I belong. When I came up short at the trials…that day, that failure eats at me. I put so much into that day. I gave it everything I had and when I needed that extra push. I didn't have it. I've been wondering if I ever had it."

JT wasn't ready for the context of the conversation that was playing out between them. He was not aware that his role model struggled at anything. In his eyes, Kyle was an elite athlete the model American long distance runner. He found inspiration in

Kyle, and hoped he could one day rise to Kyle's level. JT also did not realize that his hero would open up to him like that. He fought for something positive to say.

"Kyle, we all get down, sometimes," was the best statement JT could come up with. The young athlete was caught in-between being star struck and totally unprepared that someone like Kyle had self-doubt.

Kyle understood he caught the impressionable runner off guard. "Oh, I'm sorry I did not mean to be a downer, I had a bad workout and it got to me. I'm okay." Kyle tried to defuse the situation.

"I get it, Kyle really you're human just like us...well, but a lot faster. We all need a little support. I'm just a high school kid, I know but if you ever need someone, a friend...you are more than some runner to me. You're my hero and I hope my friend. You've helped me with my running. You've been to my meets, I've seen you standing along the finishing chute. I'm always here." JT finished his thought.

"Thanks, man. I'll figure this out...and I respect that. Thank you, for being a friend." Kyle said as the two made the halfway point. Kyle pulled up, JT followed and looked at his watch.

"Five miles, are we heading back now?"

"Sure thing." Kyle moved forward and unexpectedly gave his young friend a big hug. "Really JT, we are friends. You're important to me and I appreciate your offer to be there for me. I won't let you down."

"There's no way you could Kyle." JT commented as the two started the run towards home.

The conversation on the way back into town was much lighter. The youngster asked about what it was like to run with Ryan Hall and Deena Kastor. He asked questions about the workouts and if their training was any different than what Kyle had been doing. JT had an enquiring mind about everything Mammoth Lakes. Kyle tried to give him the low down on everything.

Back in town, they came to a stop at the corner of Washington and Independence. “Thanks for coming out. It was nice to run with someone and I could not have picked a better training partner.”

Berkeley Springs was beginning to come to life. The sun rose over the horizon, and the air felt a little warmer. The sounds of motion grew louder about the city center. Kyle had always enjoyed getting out before the rest of the world got moving. He believed in beating the world to the punch. The idea of having his miles in the logbook before the world got in the way always fit his lifestyle. As much as he loved to run, if he did not get the miles logged before the world tossed around its distractions he could easily fall prey to putting it off for another day. The only issue still open for discussion was in which direction was his running life taking him.

JT and Kyle walked back to the running store. They approached the big display windows and could see Jim making coffee. Kyle tapped on the window and waved as Jim turned to see who was calling for his attention. Once Jim saw Kyle, he pointed at his watch. Kyle knew that was a sign that he better hurry, get cleaned up and report to work on time. Jim hated anyone being late for their shift at the store, even Kyle.

“Alright JT, I really have to run now. Jim is a great guy but a tough boss. Thanks again.”

“Anytime Kyle,” JT said as the two departed. Kyle ducked upstairs, he had 27 minutes to shower and get changed for work.

A Lunch Date

Chapter 8

Not an early riser. She preferred to be tucked into a warm bed, nestled under an oversized comforter during the wee hours of the morning. Still, Candy marveled at the beauty of a new day breaking over a sun-filled horizon. She appreciated the radiating mixture of colors within the first rays of light which washed over the edge of a dark landscape. Her day and that of her faithful furry companion, her curvy little miniature schnauzer, normally began around mid-morning or even sometimes a bit later in the day. Candy was not one to hang out at bars or to be part of the late-night scene. A self-declared "night owl" she preferred to be safe at home after the sun went down. Where some would brag they got more done before 9 a.m., Candy often said her best work happened between 8 p.m. and 2 in the morning.

Candy and Carly enjoyed walking among the old town vibe that is town center of Berkeley Springs. She loved the brick and mortar buildings, cobblestone roadways, and the warmth of a small town all appealed to her low-key nature. The history of the town was not lost on her. So, fascinated with the historical backdrop of Berkeley Springs that she interwove the towns unique setting into her current literary works.

Candy's chosen profession was that of an independent author. Her tales were spun out of rural America, based loosely on historical fact crossing the line between non-fiction and fiction. Her faithful readers and new followers had a tough time telling if her stories were personal histories or fictional narratives set upon real-world settings. Berkeley Springs would be the location for her next book. The title that came to her mind was "Troubles in Bath."

Carly enjoyed getting out for her walks as much as Candy did. The short-legged schnauzer who was a bit overweight, curvy as Candy called her, loved to walk with the sun on her face and a cool breeze blowing through her beard. She was a unique dog, liver in color according to the American Kennel Society, she appeared more tan, almost white to the untrained eye. Carly had deep brown eyes that penetrated your soul when she looked at you. A rescue dog adopted from a professional breeder who retired her at the age of 5, for two years she had been Candy's near constant companion. She was the perfect dog and a better friend. For the most part, she was well behaved, mild mannered, and required minimal maintenance. The 14-pound ball of fur had only one "bad trait." Carly, for a reason hidden deep within her own personal story, did not like "new" people.

The pair approached town center at the corner of Fairfax and Washington street, where they stopped as local and inter-state traffic roamed by. "Hold on little girl, we don't want to become a speed bump." Carly stopped next to Candy and without a command sat on her hind legs staring into the sun, her eyes partially closed. On the south side of Fairfax stood a small branch bank; directly across the street to the north was the impressive building of the Morgan County Courthouse. To the west of the courthouse a two-story brick building which today housed a locally owned gift shop and second floor residential apartments. To the south was the Berkeley Springs State Park.

The state park, on the site of a natural spring, marked the center of the historic spa town. For over 200 years warm mineral-filled waters flowed from the nearby springs creating a gateway for those looking to partake of the healing waters. The town had a rich history prior to the first settlers of 1730. Indian tribes of lower

Canada and the early colonists came to the warm waters for natural earth-based healings. Over the years the town transformed itself from a haven catering to the upper crust of society to that of a resort community for families. Perhaps its most famous of visitor was also the person who literally put the town, then known as Bath, on the map.

George Washington, an impressionable young explorer and future commander of the U.S. revolutionary army scouted the area for the Lord of Fairfax. In 1748 Washington spent a night in the area noting the warm springs in his reports and diaries. For years Washington would return to the springs for their believed healing powers. In future years, the British government was convinced to convey the land to the Colony of Virginia. Later it was sold to public investors which included many who signed the Declaration of Independence and the Constitution including Washington himself. From that time forward, the area grew as a center of healing and relaxation.

Candy thought the city would provide the perfect landscape for a novel she was writing. The plot centered around a young girl who met the man of her dreams. The conflict would come within the social separation of the working class and the elite, the wealthy and the privileged who visited the small town. Although the two central figures of the story could overlook their social separation, their families could not. Status, wealth, political views and family history would come to a violent eruption when the two ran away to be married.

Today Candy and Carly were headed to the site of George Washington's bathtub; an historic site within the park. Candy planned to walk around the grounds and draft an outline for one of the more pivotal chapters in her book. After she had crafted the fate of the central characters she promised to take Carly out for lunch.

Being an early riser has its disadvantages. By 11:30 each day Kyle was as hungry as a bear. Jim was thankful that Kyle was such a loyal, faithful and hardworking employee and friend. He did not hesitate to leave Kyle in control of what was, in fact, his life savings and retirement plan, aka the store. With any good friendship or working relationship, albeit boss and employee, there were boundaries. Jim had learned a harsh lesson over time, to not get in the way when Kyle was hungry. Today was no exception.

Kyle and Jim were engaged in an epic struggle to hang a new display banner across the back of the store. It may have been smarter to move some of the store's inventory around to gain access to the wall. The pair thought it much more of a challenge to work around the obstacles.

If the safety of the two hadn't been in question, this morning's escapade would have rivaled the best episode of the Three Stooges. With the banner finally in place, Jim and Kyle both looked on with appreciation and marveled at their handiwork. Silently they were more surprised that either of them hadn't fallen off their makeshift and hardly OSHA approved ladder system.

Jim was the first to say it. "This would have been so much easier if we just moved the shoe display."

Kyle simply laughed partially under his breath. A smile of content accomplishment glanced across his face.

"Well I have to eat, all this work… I'm starving," Kyle remarked.

"I wasn't sure if that was your stomach or a wild yeti that had gotten into the store. Don't hurry back, remember you are closing tonight."

Kyle clutched his notebook, pulled on his high tech lightweight running jacket and headed for the door. "You know me, I won't be long…want me to pick you up anything?"

It was less than a block to the Black Cat. The Black Cat was a restaurant and coffee bar, owned by a local artisan. The quaint eating establishment specialized in four things. Locally made sandwiches that were to die for, hot coffee, cozy chairs and an atmosphere where everyone was welcome to hang out after their meal had been consumed. Kyle loved to enjoy his mid-day meal there, then sit back and watch the world go by. People watching was one of his many talents and often an inspiration for his artwork. He often remarked that people watching should be an Olympic sport. Today he was looking forward to spending some down time finishing up a few drawings.

Barely inside the threshold of the doorway a familiar voice greeted him. "Kyle...great to see you again, what has it been a day or two?" The shop owner, a middle-aged woman named Rose, had a fondness for Kyle. They talked often when he visited the restaurant. She was in her mid to late 50s Kyle wasn't sure of her age but also knew better than to ask. Rose shared with Kyle that if the world had not thrown her a bizarre twist of fate, her son would have been around Kyle's age. Rose and her husband Bill ran the eatery. Very friendly people. As easy as it was to tell that Kyle enjoyed getting out to run, Bill and Rose enjoyed tasty food. Both hard workers, strong personalities and faithful friends to many in town. When not taking orders, serving customers behind the counter or in the kitchen, they were central figures in the community.

"Good to see you too Rose. What special are you offering up today? I'm starved. Jim has been working my tail feathers off this morning."

"Today, my special is a grilled cheese sandwich with a creamy basil tomato soup from a family recipe. Trust me you want some." Rose answered as she pointed him to a simple table covered with a checkered red and white tablecloth encircled by two miss-matched chairs.

As Kyle made his way to the two-seat table he noticed a familiar face towards the back of the café. Kyle knew instantly who it was even though her face was buried behind her laptop. For better or worse he decided to move closer and say Hi.

The creaking wooden floors and the vibration from his footsteps failed to garner her attention. Candy was lost in the tapping and clicking sounds of her keyboard and the movements of her characters to notice the happenings around her. Kyle drew a few steps closer and was on the verge of saying something.

From under the table that Candy was sitting at came a notice that he should not approach much closer. Carly nestled next to her master's feet barked two times and growled in a tone that let Kyle know he came a bit to close. Candy's attention was instantly broken from the storyline of her third novel. Her eyes lifted to see what was going on around her.

"Easy Carly..." She said in a confident tone.

"Oh, it's you." Candy was the first one to break the silence. Are you stalking us again? My little girl Carly is on to you."

"No, come on I just wanted to say hi..." Kyle replied in a somewhat embarrassed tone.

"Just giving you a tough time. Jim said you're harmless. That's good enough for me, but Ms. Carly here, she doesn't like new people. You might want to keep your distance."

"I see that. Come on Carly girl...I'm harmless."

Carly responded with a low toned growl. It was obvious that she was not so happy with a stranger approaching her best friend.

Kyle walked backward to the front of the restaurant and sat on the floor.

"What are you doing?" Candy asked.

"I want to be on her level, I've never had a dog, not like me. Dogs have been a big part of my life. I've never had my own but I would spend a lot of time caring for, walking and playing with my neighbors or stray dogs growing up. Let her go..." Kyle replied in a soft tone just loud enough for Candy to hear him but not in a pitch to be threating.

Kyle sat on the floor at eye level and called for Carly. "Here girl, Carly come."

Carly came out from the table slowly, her hair on end and although she stopped growling, the tension on her face was obvious. Kyle's timing was perfect as the restaurant was near empty and those that were present, workers and customers stopped whatever they were doing to watch the dramatic scene play out in front of them. A few comments could be heard, "He's going to get bitten."

Carly continued her way toward Kyle then stopped about 3 feet in front of him and growled.

In a low comforting tone, Kyle talked to her. "Hey Carly, I'm Kyle and I want to be your friend. I really do like doggies like you and would never hurt you or anyone you love." He slowly reached out his hand with the back of his palm facing Carly. Carly took one more step forward and smelled the air. Kyle continued to talk.

"You are a very pretty girl. I'd like to be friends and I am a sucker when it comes to dog treats."

Carly ears perked up and she instantly looked his way, where before she had avoided eye contact now she looked deep into his eyes. With Kyle sitting on the floor and Carly standing firmly in front of him, the two stared at each other for an instant, then Kyle looked away. Without saying anything Kyle noticed how deep her brown eyes appeared. He had interacted with many dogs in his life but he could not remember such emotional eyes. He knew her eyes held the story of her life. It was within that story that Kyle believed was the reason she was on edge. In that moment, Carly also saw something.

A second or two after Kyle looked away, Carly stopped growling, the hair on her back settled and she moved slowly towards Kyle stopping next to his right knee and she sat down. Kyle moved his hand slowly and noticed that Carly eyes watched his every move. His hand went past the crown of her head and now her eyes were looking up at him, he assumed reading his intentions by the expressions on his face. Not wanting to threaten her, he looked off to the side and talked calmly. "Carly girl…I bet you have a story to tell." He asked. "I would love to be your friend, we could hang out, go for walks and play." Kyle lowered his hand behind her ears and stroked her fur lightly. Carly moved closer.

In the back of the room, Candy stood up and walked to the front of the restaurant where the show was and talked quietly. "I have never seen Carly warm up to someone like this. It normally takes her a few interactions, but she does come around. I'm really surprised she hasn't tried to eat you. Candy bent down and patted Carly on the head. "He's a good guy, I think…Carly." And with that one simple move, Carly moved closer to Kyle's lap, stood up, climbed up on his thighs and laid down with a thump.

"Well, now… Hey Rose, I'll take my meal down here." A collective awe filled the Black Cat restaurant. The show appeared to be over as everyone went back to their lunch routine. Except for Kyle…anytime he would stop rubbing Carly's ears she would nudge his hand with her nose requesting that he keep up his handy work.

Since Kyle was stuck in between tending to his new best friend and trying to eat his lunch, Candy sat on the floor next to him. As he took a bite out his sandwich, Candy gave him the low down on how she came about adopting Carly. She had rescued her from an in-home breeder two years prior. Candy cautioned that the word "rescued" may be too strong. Carly wasn't in any distress, the breeder humanely retired her mothers after a few litters, finding them good homes to retire to so that they could enjoy the remaining years of their lives.

Although Candy was sure Carly was well cared for and loved,

she felt her little girl still had some emotional scars from the experience. Carly was the older female in the breeder's home. Candy rationalized that her dog's behavior around meeting new people stemmed from her experiences meeting people at the breeder's home. In the eyes of a little dog, a new mother to a litter of puppies,' new people showing up meant that she would be losing one of her puppies. Candy figured that to Carly new people triggered a feeling of losing something, someone she loved. Whether that was true or not, many people scoffed at that logic, to Candy it made perfect sense. Candy was sure that Carly acted out of fear of losing her security, her home and her companion.

The pair that sat along with Carly both had their own stories, their own heartbreak and both knew something about loss.

Lost Years and Dreams

Chapter 9

Kyle would find out that Candy was a complex character. On the surface, she was a pretty girl who put very little time into trying to look the part. A bit taller than most girls, around five feet eight and although she wasn't one to hang out in a gym, she had a very attractive and athletic build. Rough and tumble from a life that tossed her a few curve balls, she could hold her own in a tough situation.

In a world fashioned by the models of Victoria's secret, Candy took her natural beauty, and went with it. She didn't have time for anything fake nor for someone who would be looking for more than she was. Thick, wavy, long blonde hair held natural highlights and short bangs tossed to the right. Her face was round and cute, her smile infectious and her green eyes with full eyebrows captured your soul. A conversation with her drew you in and made it hard to disengage when you were in her presence. Always one who projected self-confidence and strength, Candy brought a sense of calm to whatever situation she took part in, unless she decided that she wanted to stir the pot. She was fun, lively and engaging to be around. Most people were instantly drawn to her and felt at ease in her presence. Many she interacted with knew the Candy she kept on display. Behind her good looks, bright smile and self-confidence was a different person. If you could find yourself behind her guarded perimeter, behind her warmth and welcoming nature, one would see the unexposed world which she kept buried deep inside. The hidden truth was that for a few years she had lost herself.

- - -

The oldest of two children in a stereotypical American household that included a white picket fence and the black and white beagle. Candy was always trusting, easy going and the leader of the pack whether at home, on the playground or in the classroom. Friendships came easy and young love was never far off. She had her fair share of suitors chasing after her all the way through high school. Candy mostly found her male companions entertaining and fun to hang out with but nothing that would distract her from her ambitions. Not being successful was never part of the plan. She was a very smart girl, level-headed, driven from an early age and the center of the crowd of good kids. Attending college and eventually Veterinarian school was part of her master plan.

With graduation behind her, her high school roadmap was complete. With a college acceptance letter proudly displayed on the refrigerator door, the final summer before attending the College of Veterinary Medicine at North Carolina State promised to be the best one yet.

A Friday night summer concert series in the local park in late July changed everything. The afternoon sun was fading in the sky while a group of college students in a makeshift cover band played her favorite music. Candy and a few friends sat on a multi-colored blanket and soaked in the warmth of the sun among the sounds broadcasting from the stage. In between sets the conversations bounced between the highlights of their final year of high school and everyone's plans for the fall semester. Most in the group had been accepted to either an out of town big name school or the local community college. There were a few boys in the group who had planned to attend a trade school, enrolled in an apprenticeship with a local manufacturing company, or like a close friend Dennis had enlisted in the military. The future seemed open and endless to the small social circle who had been friends since elementary school. Collectively the group made it to high school graduation together.

A close friend of Candy's, showed up late. A tall, skinny girl with hair past the top of her Levi jeans, Julie and Candy had been friends since the sixth grade. Then the new kid in town, Julie and her mother moved into a small rental home after her parents' divorce. Her father lived on the edge of town, although she did not get to see him much. Candy took to the new girl and the two hit it off almost instantly. Like opposite poles on a magnet, Candy was calm and driven Julie was wild and a bit lazy. Even though personality wise they were total opposites they became, in fact, good friends.

Today accompanying Julie was an older boy named Devin, the newest in a lengthy line of boyfriends. He wasn't part of their high school class. In fact, no one was sure where he was from or how he met Julie. The stranger to the group, he tried to fit in but always hung on the outer edge of the group.

The day wore on and slowly the collection of high school grads thinned out as the skies grew dark. After the final set and two encores, Candy and Julie walked from the park through the nearby woods back to the center of town. Devin quietly followed nearby.

To this day, Candy is unsure of what happened next. At some point during the passage through the woods, she either asked for or was offered a drink. She thought it was lemonade or a yellow colored sports drink. Whatever it was, that innocent looking mixture changed her life.

She woke up the next morning near the back porch of her home. The morning sun beaming down on her clammy skin jolted her out of a drunken slumber. At first, she was scared, shocked and completely out of sorts. As she slowly gained more consciousness she realized with panic-stricken fear where she was. Fear gripped her being, a fear of anyone finding out that she had passed out in the backyard. Panic ran wild as she pieced together the realization that she spent the night or part of it asleep in the grass.

The house was quiet and still. The rooms were dimly lit as her family slept upstairs. Without arising any suspicion Candy made it to the safety of her bedroom where she closed the door undetected. On the edge of her bed she sat trying to replay the events of the night before. Struggling to remember and wishing to forget what had happened.

Her mind arranged together a patchwork of memories like a poorly edited horror movie. She had been with Julie and her boyfriend walking in the woods. It was hot, she was thirsty and Devin offered her a drink. After drinking from the Gatorade bottle her world became confused and unsteady. When she resisted Julie told her they were taking her to a party, that it was too early to go home. She trusted them. It was getting hotter. She had another drink.

At the party hours later, her world felt fuzzy, more disoriented and strangely electric. The lights were brighter, the sounds more intense and even though she felt off center she also felt free and more alive than she had ever felt before. All the pressure of school, college and doing the right thing had been lifted. Her mind appeared open and free. She remembered laughing, singing out loud and playing silly games, unlike anything she had ever experienced.

In the process of trying to uncover what happened, Candy's mind went from a place of trying to make sense of the night to a position of need. Where she was once scared and put off by the unknown, now she wanted to relive the experience. She desired to find that euphoric feeling again. Temped for the first time by a new reality, she crawled down a rabbit hole that she knew little about, had little exposure to and found she had zero control over. She craved to feel the winds of change, to be able to capture the feelings of hypersensitivities, the unencumbered rush of free thought and the release of pent-up emotions.

For five years Candy found herself falling deeper and deeper into a form of humanity she had never known. A world of suburban housing, steady meals, safety and trust had been replaced with homelessness, hunger and paranoia. She risked all that she had in her quest for the next high. She allowed herself to fall out of control. Her world shifted off its axis so fast and so far, that at times she wasn't sure who she had become. Soon she forgot about her plans and turned her back on her family, breaking ties with everyone from her past life. Her new circle of friends became those who could supply her with the means to feed her cravings. The only thing that mattered was scoring her next fix. Her only desire became the need to acquire those magic chemicals that enabled her to disappear into the abyss of her dream like state.

After a seemingly endless night of chasing a distorted reality somewhere between ecstasy and paranoia, Candy woke up on the cold damp floor of a flea-ridden motel room surround by people she did not know. Her eyes were sore, her mouth dry and her head pounded out its own discord on the state of her life. She tried to reason her way out of the environment in which she found herself. It didn't work. Full of despair she noticed the torrid smell, a mixture of smoke, stale air, spoiled food and body odor. For the first time in years, caught in a moment of self-reflection, she saw herself swallowed up by the depths of her addiction. Her confused mind raced with questions. Who was she? Where was her life going and how did she find herself here?

The awkward sounds of drunken sleep came from across the room. How did her life turn into such a state of remorse? She wondered. The chemical addiction transported her to places that at one time seemed foreign, remote and not of this world.

Sitting within her own personal ground zero, a moment of clarity and self-reflection shocked her into movement. Candy noticed she was naked wrapped only in a towel. The depths of despair grew deeper. People in various stages of undress surrounded her. Her companions were two girls and a handful of guys. She recognized no one. She could barely recognize herself. Finally, able see where her life was headed, she knew that this was not where she wanted to be. Something this morning, as she came out of another night of partying, was different this time. Something unsettled her that for years she kept silent. Candy knew it had to stop. This lifestyle had to end.

There were remains of a glass plate, some powdery material, a pipe and empty bottles scattered around the faux wood coffee table. As she looked around the room that at this moment housed the chaos of her life, Candy was at a turning point. For reasons, she could not understand, and going against the remaining attraction to the chemicals that still raced within her system she knew it was time to move. It was time to change, it was time to get out of that place. Candy's soul was telling her it was time to claim her life back. With whatever strength she had left, wrapped only in a stained white towel she walked out of that room.

With no contact with the outside world, she never learned of the passing of her parents. They died as the result of a hit and run accident. Her parents were out searching for her late into the evening. The driver was under the influence. On the police report, it would be noted that the driver had a blood alcohol level of .13. The prosecuting District Attorney categorized it as "an extreme case." Her younger brother was so upset over losing contact with her and with his parents being killed that he later committed suicide. Leaving that hotel room Candy would be successful at reclaiming her life. Although her life would be much different than the one she left behind.

Five years since her fall, she would reclaim a life that was destined to be another casualty, another body on the pile of lost souls in the world of addiction. Candy kept her time in this world hidden away, locked in a drawer that only she held the key. Few in her life ever got that close to her and even those who might venture into that private space never knew what she had lived through in detail. Even less understood the cost these experiences had on her life and her self-esteem.

Recovery comes in many forms. Candy had to deal with the chemical addictions, the physical aftereffects and more importantly the loss of her self-esteem. A form of self-counseling came in writing. Candy had always enjoyed reading in high school. She was drawn to new and strange worlds of adventure and mischief. An honor student with a fondness for English and literature. She never saw herself as an author but when her Addiction Counselor suggested she should write about “the lost years” as an attempt to fill in the gaps. Candy put the figurative pen to paper and began to write the narrative of her life. From the start, she found it was therapeutic. It helped to uncover the hidden turmoil. It helped to express her feelings. It helped to uncover the truth and to compartmentalize that she was no longer that girl.

During their counseling sessions, her counselor pieced together all her works into a patchwork of her life’s story. She believed in the rough elements of Candy’s life there was something greater, something that could help others. Her counselor believed there was an overreaching story of survival. Shocked, Candy laughed at first. She could hardly believe that anything she had experienced could help others, let alone shed any light on the world of addiction. She was caught off guard when she learned that her counselor had followed up with a publisher and they were interested in moving forward.

Her life changed when her book, her life story, sold 100,000 copies in six months. Even with all the success, above all else, Candy wanted to get back to as near normal a life as she could after her escape from the darkness of her lost years. She published the book under a pen name, Rebecca Jones.

The financial success of her first book established her as a full-time author. Candy followed up Rebecca’s story, with a fictional account based among a real-life setting. Her form of storytelling used emotions and conflict interwoven within details and storylines that blurred the boundaries between fiction and her day to day life. It was that very success that brought Candy to Berkeley Springs and to the Black Cat diner.

- - -

Candy remained on the floor alongside Kyle as he finished up his lunch with Carly now a sleeping schnauzer sprawled out on his lap. To pass the time the two made small talk about life. Mingled within the conversation were probing questions where they found out they were near the same age and had many common interests. The conversation flowed easily with no awkward pauses or interruptions. He enjoyed listening to the sound of her voice as Candy shared a thumbnail version of her life but kept the darker parts close to her vest.

As they talked, Candy mentioned that at this point in her life she was happy being alone, that she wasn't against a relationship but that she also was not looking for one. This made their impromptu lunch date easy to accept and non-threatening. Behind her words, Candy hoped Kyle would keep coming around.

All in A Day's Work

Chapter 10

After lunch, Kyle headed back to the running store. His shift would have him on duty the remainder of the day. Jim had plans to treat his wife to a fancy dinner and a locally produced show at the playhouse. For much of Kyle's life he lacked a good example of how a husband and wife should interact. Now that he was older, Kyle paid close attention whenever he was around successful relationships. He marveled at how Jim and Leann got along and wondered if this would have been how his parents would have interacted if his mother had not passed. Often when he daydreamed he got lost in a world where his parents were the model couple, laughing, joking and carrying on the way he believed a husband and a wife should. He also dreamed of the day when he would find that special someone.

To some, a day behind the counter of a retail store might be a torturous assignment. If it had been any other store Kyle may have agreed with them. Working in the running store was perfect for his personality and suited for his passion. He loved all things running. He loved the physical challenge. He cherished the opportunity to be outdoors. He enjoyed the experiences and thrived on the competition. Kyle also craved the opportunity to share his passion with others.

Jim was preparing to leave for the day and in a bit of a rush. He still needed time to get dressed and pick up a special gift for his date. As Jim was almost clear of the door, Kyle stopped him and spoke "Jim, do you know much about this Candy character, you know the girl who thought I was stalking her?"

Where Jim was once in a hurry to get out of the store, he instantly shifted into a lower gear. After stopping dead in his tracks, he walked over to Kyle standing behind the 6-foot-long display counter that separated them. Jim paused for a second and cleared his throat.

"You know Kyle, I don't. She showed up in town about six months ago. I'm told she is an author of some kind. Been told she has a few successful books. She has been in the store a few times, easy to like and although I haven't known her long it feels like we have been friends for a long time. She has the type of personality that pulls you in, you know what I mean?" Jim replied. "And you know Kyle, she is very pretty."

"I sure do. We kind of had lunch together this afternoon."

"That sounds interesting…Kyle. Be easy, it's a small town we live in."

Kyle laughed, "yea you know me, I'm slow as a turtle, I only run fast."

Jim thought about his comment for a few seconds, "That's for sure. Come to think of it other than running and your artwork, I don't think I've ever heard you talk about anything else. Well, and your family situation."

"I don't like to talk about that much…no fixing that one."

"Don't give up Kyle, you know I'm here for you. Just not right now I've got to go…I cannot stand up my wife. That would not be good for my long-term health." Jim replied tapping Kyle on the shoulder.

For a small town running store, the day had already been very busy. Kyle was in the process of fitting a new customer with his first pair of running shoes. The part of working at the running store that Kyle enjoyed the most was interacting with other runners. Most elite level athletes tend to get isolated from the everyday runner. In preparing for their next big race, the next chance to climb the professional rankings or to earn an Olympic qualifying place the elite crowd tended to stay within their small circle. Kyle fell into that trap prior to leaving for Mammoth Lakes. While he enjoyed running with the top runners in the country, he noticed that his passion for running was replaced with the pressure of running fast. Since his return to Berkeley Springs Kyle wanted to distance himself from that world. He needed a breather. He needed time to find his competitive desire again.

Kyle's customer was an older gentleman, about that same age as his father. His name was Tom. He was a retired mine worker from just north of town. After retiring early, Tom found that he stopped moving. The physical mine work was replaced with sitting on the couch watching "The Price is Right" or "Judge Judy" and his 3 p.m. march to the American Legion post. Tom soon found out he was turning into one of those old retired guys with a permanent spot at the bar and an oversized beer belly.

When Kyle asked him why today was "the day" he decided to get moving, Tom had a simple answer. "One day you look in the mirror and you realize you have to change your ways. Today is that day."

Tom was determined to gain some form of fitness that would help with his long-term health. An unplanned visit to his doctor for high blood pressure convinced him that getting old was a one-way street. The doctors' matter of fact declaration that he was in the high-speed lane kicked him in the butt. The retired mine worker had heard enough; he was going to make a change. Tom decided he wanted to do something to slow down the aging process or at least get his butt out of the express lane. Once determined to get moving, to become more active he received perhaps the most important piece of information for a new runner.

"I was told I should get a good pair of shoes." The old man laughed.

With that great but simple piece of advice, Tom stopped at the store. Tom knew little about running but assumed that if the store had running in its name it had to sell good running shoes.

"I was a bit nervous walking in here." He confessed.

Tom realized he was stepping into a world he knew very little about. He saw people running along the roads of Berkeley Springs. He even had a few relatives who ran for fun. Although he always thought it odd that they never seemed to be smiling. He enjoyed following the US track and field athletes in the Olympics and knew about this little race called the Boston Marathon, but other than that he knew very little about how to be a runner himself. To Tom running was simply a way to get out of the way of something else. Today that was going to change.

Kyle's job, and one he took very seriously, was getting this man and anyone walking into the store fitted with the right pair of shoes. Most customers new to running had no idea of what kind of shoe they needed. Never sure how serious his customers were about running when they entered the store, a few simple questions always provided Kyle some insight. A simple question, got the ball rolling. "What kind of shoe do you want?" was the fastest way to get down to business. Kyle got some laughs out of some of the responses. "White ones." "NIKE, air somethings..." Kyles favorite reply was "the ones that make you run faster." After introducing himself to Tom and gaining some background information on his customer the question again came up.

"So, Tom, do you know what kind of shoes you're looking for?"

A man of few words, he got right to the point. "I have no idea. You're the running guy, you tell me." Kyle instantly knew this was a customer he could work with.

After a few moments of taking measurements, looking at the wear patterns of Tom's old "loaf around" shoes and watching him walk in his sock covered feet, Kyle excused himself and went into the backroom. A few minutes passed when Kyle returned with a selection of shoes and began the rest of the fitting process while the two men generations apart made small talk.

After questions and statements about the weather, the upcoming football season and the current events around town. Tom sheepishly asked. "How do I start running?"

"Now that is a darn good question, Tom." Kyle piped up while tying the laces on a pair of sporty-looking blue shoes with red trim.

"I'm not sure I'm ready for these flashy shoes there Kyle."

"Don't start running, that is how you start running," Kyle answered Tom's question.

With a puzzled but confident look, Tom replied with the only thing that came to mind. "Well okay, I got that part down. In fact in the last few years I may have won a gold medal in that event." The two chuckled a bit as Kyle finished tying the laces.

"Ha, don't we all. But I mean, start walking first. Go out and walk 20 to 30 minutes at a semi brisk pace for a week or two. You have got to ease into this. If you go out and run a mile tomorrow, you'll be sore, hate running, want to punch me in the face and you'll never run again. Because I don't want to be punched, just go out and walk. Enjoy the outside, smell the air, see the birds and experience the wildlife. Feel your body moving. Get used to moving again. Get to the point that your new movements feel natural. When you begin to feel better and look forward to your walks then you can run." Kyle paused, as he finished up tying the second shoe.

"Okay so I'll just walk for a while, I get that." Tom stared at the bright blue shoes on his feet.

"Stand up, how do they feel? Then when you're ready to run, go for a short walk to warm up, maybe ten minutes then run for 30 seconds, one-minute max. Then finish up walking. Do that for a week and slowly add in more run time until you're running more than walking. Once you get to where you're running around twenty minutes, come back and see me."

"Deal." Tom walked around the shop before Kyle asked him to step on the store's treadmill and walk for a few minutes.

Tom asked. "Where should I start my walking, I don't feel comfortable on the roads to be honest. You know people are driving like crazy, talking, texting, playing games...Words with Friends, something called Farmville."

"Very good question, Tom. We don't want to get these pretty kicks messed up by some errant car running you over. Start on the elementary school track." Kyle replied.

"Oh man not sure I'm any more comfortable there."

"What...you're kidding me. Tom a strong guy like you? You think Bigfoot, the Yeti himself is going to get you." Kyle laughed. "Tell you what I'll meet you there tomorrow morning. I'll walk with you. Together we'll get you off on the right foot."

Tom got off the treadmill, sweat just starting to come to the surface of his forehead and walked to the counter. "I'll take them. How does zero nine hundred sound?" Tom asked.

"Deal," Kyle replied with a big smile. "Do I need to salute?"

The unlikely pair of workout partners met at 9 a.m. on the dot. Kyle was dressed in a black pair of shorts with a gray top, sunglasses on the top of his head and pair of bright orange shoes with black socks. Tom was wearing a pair of Khaki shorts, a faded camo tee-shirt emblazoned with "Once a Marine always a Marine" across the front and his bright new trainers and a cup of coffee.

“Tom, next time you’re out shopping, you need to stop by the store. We really have to get you some real athletic gear. Those shorts are killing me. And white socks.”

“Funny wise guy, remember I’m 30+ years older than you. My legs don’t look like that!” Tom quickly snapped back. “My legs, I’ve been told make me look like I’m riding a chicken.”

“Oh, that’s funny. Let’s get moving before you get a ticket for indecent exposure with those things.”

Tom laughed then punched Kyle squarely in the shoulder as the two walked to the track.

The pair slowly made their way around the track with Kyle letting the retired mine worker set the pace. Kyle talked about things like form, pace, breathing and arm swing. Most importantly he talked about not running. Not a single step. He made Tom promise to not run as they had agreed.

As they made their way around for the third time Tom asked a very pointed question.

“Kyle, my wife told me she heard you’re kind of good at this running thing. What is it like to really run fast?”

“Kind of good, I’m okay.” Kyle paused.

He thought about the question for a few quiet seconds. “You know Tom when I get into the zone, the rhythm, into that upper gear where I’m really running, it’s like all the world’s troubles, my troubles get peeled away. Like flames trailing off my body. I feel light, free, untied to anything and fast. When I run I don’t always feel that way. No matter what level you are running at we all struggle. There are days I just don’t feel it. Times, I can’t wait for the run to be over, to have my miles in the bank. The elite level guys just run faster as we struggle. But when I get into the sweet spot, that spot in the upper gear…man, it’s awesome.”

"Well let's see it." Tom challenged Kyle.

"What, you want me to show you what fast is..."

"Well, let's see what running is all about, it will give me something to work towards. Or are you scared this old man would beat you." Tom laughed.

"Okay, I'll run a few fast laps for you. I need to loosen up my legs anyway."

To Tom, it was instantly apparent that Kyle's form of running was different than anything he had ever witnessed before. Kyle pushed off and began a slow acceleration to bring his legs up to a pace that would allow his large muscle groups to warm up. Kyle's motions appeared nearly effortless. His shoes barely made any noise as they contacted the track surface. With each stride, Tom noticed that in between Kyle's leg turnover it looked as if he was flying. Tom noticed the amount of ground covered with each stride. He estimated it to be nearly 6 feet.

Kyle came around completing one lap as Tom continued his walk. Kyle ratcheted it up a notch as he passed Tom and rolled into the first turn. Tom was surprised at just how fast Kyle had made his lap around the track. To see athletic speed on the television was one thing but to see what must be world class speed in person was another thing. Tom got to witness what it must be like when a thoroughbred stretched out his legs.

Kyle was just about ready to pass by Tom for the second time when things felt right. Although he had not set his watch to gain insight on his pace Kyle estimated by feel that he must have been running a low 6-minute per mile pace. Now he was ready to really put on a show. Kyle went into high gear and widened his stride. Everything fell into place. His leg turnover was perfect. His footfall light and quick. Arm swing, breathing and body lean fell into perfect form. In that instant, his body went to work, all his movements were synchronized to cover the most amount of ground for the least amount of expended energy.

At some point, Tom stopped walking. Standing in the middle of the track he simply looked in awe at the show that was playing out in front of him. The term "world-class athlete" got tossed around a lot by armchair quarterbacks when talking about sports. Tom knew in that instant that he had never been this close to the real deal.

To Kyle, everything felt perfect. His body was reaching his redline and today, compared to his failed speed session a few weeks back, today it felt easy. He ran two more laps to complete four laps and slowly brought his body back to a slower speed and eventually to a walk. Tom caught up with him on the back straight away.

Kyle was slightly out of breath but not winded at all. The two walked for a bit without saying anything.

"Not bad, but when I was young." Tom let that opening remark just hang out in the breeze. "No really, that was... Wow, that was fast. So, you are kind of good at this running thing."

Kyle smiled and turned to look at Tom as the two continued to walk. "Yea not good enough. I failed to qualify for the Olympic team. I was seven places short of making the marathon team."

"Ah what? The Olympics. Is that what you just said. Rings, gold medals and all of that? I had no idea. You finished tenth is that what you're saying, Kyle.?"

"Pretty much and I'm not sure I have it in me to try again."

"Sure, you do. You're young, you're fast you must keep after it." Tom snapped back rather quickly. "Well, that is if it's your dream. Only you hold that piece of the puzzle."

Photographs and Daydreams

Chapter 11

Although with Olympic aspirations, Kyle had a simple narrative in mind for his life. He dreamed about having a functional relationship with his father. He desired a life in which he didn't feel the weight of his families' shortcomings on his back. The young man often imagined what it must feel like to be wanted, valued, to feel secure in his place in life and important to the one person who mattered the most, his father.

- - -

A young Kyle often daydreamed about his mother. When times were quiet and he was alone, he envisioned a life where the love of his mother was a comforting blanket of acceptance. For as far back as he could remember he longed for one thing in life. He wanted to be a normal boy with a normal family. He wanted to feel the touch of his mother's hand. He desired to hear her voice and he wanted to be surrounded by her love and acceptance. His young mind at times accepted his lot in life but never fully understood how he had gotten to this place. A place so much different than that of his friends and classmates at school.

Those feelings came to a head over dinner one night. He was in the fifth grade. Kyle had finished setting the make shift dinner table. Tonight's offering would be a cold leftover sandwich from the night before and some stale chips. Kyle in an innocently framed question asked his father why he didn't have a mother like all the rest of his classmates. Although he had asked before, the question was never fully addressed, or if it had been answered the reply was packaged in such a way that a young boy could not understand the gravity of the words being used. Tonight, after his first inquiry went unanswered Kyle asked a second time. This query had a bit more forcefulness behind it. The tone of his voice more direct and with an air of desperation.

"Kyle, I've told you before. I'm the only parent you have. I'm it." His father went back to his evening meal. Kyle persisted a third time.

"But dad, doesn't it take? I mean everyone at school tells me you must have a mom and a dad. I only have you. I don't understand where did my mom go? I had to have a mother, right?" The young boy began to break down.

"Kyle now stop it. I can't answer these questions. I've told you before you don't have a mother. I'm it. I'm all you have. You are all I have and that's how it's going to be. That's why I must work two jobs, keep the house up, do your clothes, cook, clean and be everything all at once. I'm it, period." His father snapped. His words rang deep with anger, despair, desperation, emptiness and hopelessness.

Kyle began to cry. He didn't understand. He wanted to have a mother like everyone else. He remembered being told she was gone, she was in a better place. He could not understand where that better place would be other than with him. His questions were met with cold harsh words, lies and anger. Yet something this time told Kyle to ask again.

"Dad, please tell me about my mom," He pleaded.

That request pushed his father over the edge. The pressure of working nearly every hour of the day when he was not tending to his son got to him. The stress of working two low paying jobs to cover the bills was too much. His own hurt and sense of loss which he kept bottled up and medicated with alcohol came rushing to the surface.

"She's dead." The words hit the room like a piece of cold steel hitting the floor.

"Kyle, she is dead. Your mother is buried, buried in the ground, she died when you were born. She died giving birth to you. She left me Kyle. SHE. IS. DEAD. Stop asking me about her," His father's voice trailed off as his face raged in anger and hurt.

Kyle sat on the edge of the vinyl chair motionless. His eyes filled with tears and his heart broke into a million pieces. He stopped talking, his eyes stained with emotions were fixated on the wall across the dimly lit room. He sat in silence, his entire world had crashed down in an uncontrolled freefall. Nothing could have prepared the young boy for the news he just received nor the fashion in which it had been delivered.

His father walked out of the room and collapsed into a torn and tattered Lazy Boy recliner. In his favorite chair, he dealt with the world as he had since her passing. He opened a bottle of beer. With an expressionless face, his eyesight focused on the wall in front of him. His forehead pounded with a combination of anger and high blood pressure. The cold beer felt good on his throat as a tear rolled down his cheek. The only noise that could be heard for the remainder of the night would be that of multiple beer bottles being opened while the empties dropped on the floor around the brown leather chair.

Kyle woke up hunched over the kitchen table. His eyes hurt. His throat was sore and he felt empty inside. The only thing he could remember from the night before was that his mother was dead, she was buried in the ground and it was his fault for being born. He slowly got up and wiped the sleep from his eyes as he walked out of the kitchen and hesitantly made his way to the living room.

His father was asleep in the chair with empty beer bottles laying scattered around the floor. The smell of stale beer was not uncommon. Kyle never got used to it and hated the way it made his father smell.

Approaching the sleeping figure Kyle felt a sense of fear he had never been exposed to before. Standing over his father the boy did not know what to do. He wanted to disappear. He choose instead to try and wake up his father. He thought maybe his dad would tell him everything would be alright. He had hope that last night was just a bad dream. He found out just the opposite.

"Dad, it's time to get to school. I think I might be late." Kyle said softly at first.

"DAD, I have to get to school or I'm going to get in trouble and you have to get to work." Kyle tried a second time to wake his father.

"D. DAD. DAD, it's late." This time it worked but Kyle wished he had remained quiet. When his dad woke up it was like a bomb of guilt went off and Kyle was the only target around to absorb the blow. Kyle wished that maybe he could have kept sleeping and joined his mother in that better place.

"What, WHAT…I'm late for work. Get your shit together Kyle lets go. It's your fault for all of this...LET'S GO"

The pair rushed out the door, without time for Kyle to wash his face, eat anything, or change his clothes. In the whirlwind, Kyle continued to get hit with guilt laden comments, hurled off haphazardly by the most significant person in his life.

Every comment pointed to the fact that in his father's opinion Kyle's birth directly related to his mother's death. To his father losing his job. To their low income and social status. To his father living alone. The entire 30-minute drive to town was a ticker tape parade of comments about how Kyle's birth was the linchpin for all the heartache and despair in his father's life.

Kyle walked into school that day no less shell-shocked than a combat soldier after 12 hours in a foxhole during the battle for Europe.

As the clock hanging in his classroom marked time, Kyle never let on to his teachers, his friends or anyone around him that his entire world had been torn apart the night before. The hurtful words continued to play on a repetitive unending loop. For the remainder of the day the young man concentrated on staying out of trouble, and accomplishing his school work done. When he had free time outside of structured studies, time to play or to dream he focused his thoughts on the mother he longed for and would never have a chance to meet.

Finally, the school day ended and he returned home to the scene of the crime. Kyle as always got home before his father and quickly finished his homework and tended to his chores. His father arrived home at the normal time and the two sat down to have dinner. Tonight, his father brought home a pepperoni pizza and a 2-liter bottle of Pepsi. Both of those were Kyle's favorites. Hardly a word had been said over dinner as the two made fast work of the meal. Strangely nothing was said about the happenings of the night before. After dinner, the pair fell back into their routine of neglect, loneliness and sorrow.

A few days later Kyle arrived home afterschool to find a collection of old pictures tossed randomly on his bed. In between the wrinkled sheets, the ill fitted pillows and one lone Teddy bear that he had for his entire life, there were seven pictures. At first, Kyle wasn't sure what to do with them. It was strange for something like this to simply appear. He stared at the foreign images captured in the prints. He wondered in amazement at the faces in the still images and questioned whom it was looking directly back at him. It was someone he had never met before. Someone he had no recall over. Then something in her smile. Something he noted in the shape of her face. Something in the glimmer of her eyes broke open the vault of mystery. With one sparkling clue, it all became clear. Kyle for the first time in his life was looking at pictures of his mother.

Kyle instantly broke down and began to cry. Through the tears and a shortness of breath, he studied every picture with steel hardened resolve. He focused on every detail, the color of her hair, the shadows of her features and the smile on her face. In six of the pictures, she stood or sat alone. All were taken outside, in the sunlight of a day which must have brought extraordinary joy. Her smile was bold and bright. Kyle's mom had medium length mousy blonde hair with short and choppy curls around her face. A pretty smile, round checks and blue eyes. She was attractive, slender, not tall but also not short and she looked lively. Kyle stared at each picture taking in all the subtle features. The seventh picture stunned the young boy.

The seventh photograph was one that captured his attention and one he would never forget. The seventh picture was the one that would change his life. This picture captured an image of his mother that the other snapshots could not. She looked completely different. Her face a bit rounded. Her eyes wider. Her smile was bolder. In this picture, his mother was a bit heavier with a round belly. His mother was pregnant.

Kyle focused on the picture where his mother held him in her womb. He had no idea how far along she was but to the young boy's eye his mother was very pregnant. She wore a great big smile, beaming highlights in her eyes and a face that told him she was overwhelmingly joyful to be expecting a child. Through that moment captured in time, Kyle felt the warmth of love and acceptance of a parent. That simple picture brought forth feelings of immense joy and unleashed a wave of emotions in the young soul. Kyle felt valued. Loved. He felt wanted. He couldn't take his eyes off the image he held in his hand. He finally knew that he had a mother, he finally saw the person who gave him life and he for once saw someone who he believed loved him. Kyle, years removed from his birth met his mother for the first time.

A sound from the front room announced that his father was home. Scared and frightened to return to a world of heartbreak and rejection Kyle hid the pictures, wiped his face, and ran off to the kitchen. He sat quietly, the small nearly worn out compressor motor in the General Electric refrigerator making the only sound. His heart beat furiously in rapid succession as he waited for his father to enter the room.

"You're home." His father said.

"Yes, sir." Kyle paused to clear his throat. "I was, ah I was waiting for you to come home before I got some food and I'll do my homework, right after," Kyle answered his father while looking down at the table. He was sure that his father could hear the overzealous pounding of his heart.

"Good, I have to go back to work for some overtime hours." Stay inside and do not get into trouble. I do not need any more heartaches from you."

His father departed as quickly as he entered the room. Kyle sat motionless at the table until he was sure that his father was gone for the night. In the now quiet and less threatening house the young boy returned to his room, closed the door and retrieved the pictures. He sat quietly for the remainder of the night looking at each one of the photos individually. The night passed slowly, as every detail in each photo was carefully examined. This was the first time in his life that he spent any time alone with his mother.

As he began to get ready for bed he did something out of the ordinary. The scene was uncommon in his home, something foreign to his upbringing. That night was the first time Kyle ever said a meaningful prayer beyond simply repeating words that some adult for unknown reasons forced him to say. He wasn't sure why but he felt moved to kneel beside his bed. He lowered his head and closed his eyes. In the stillness of the room, he collected his thoughts and arranged the only words that at that time held any meaning to him.

In a soft spoken and timid voice, he prayed.

"Dear God,

Thank you for giving me my Mom.

Tell her I love her." He paused and thought for a moment.

"And that I miss her.

Amen."

He wasn't sure how to pray or why he felt motivated to pray to a God he knew very little about. Something inside of him reached out to a force he believed would offer some hope. Kyle could not remember ever going to church. He had only witnessed other people praying when he would happen across Christian television programming on Sunday morning TV. Before drifting off to sleep, Kyle once again hid the pictures in a small box and placed that box behind his nightstand. The pictures provided a link to something more than the empty life he felt he was living. Kyle never asked his father about his mother again.

- - -

In the years that followed he tried the best he could to stay out of his father's way. There were no family outings, no birthday parties, holidays were celebrated at the bare minimum and there were no family vacations. For Kyle, life had become an exercise in trying to get through one 24-hour period so he could begin the next cycle of trying to avoid conflict once again. Time at home was spent trying to go unnoticed. While attempting to not upset his father, he spent a lot of time outdoors. He made up games, threw a football around the yard or spent time running from point A to point B. The physical activity and his time out of the house provided a release for his frustrations.

The hours he spent in school provided a small degree of normalcy. He kept up a good front while in the company of his teachers and classmates. Other than occasionally showing up in miss-matched clothes his problems at home went largely unnoticed. The faculty would universally agree that he was a good kid, a bit shy, quiet and tried his best to master his studies. In the day to day routines of school life he went mostly unnoticed. Kyle felt comfortable in that role.

For many students, physical education class, PE, or gym class was a time of adolescent torture. If you were uncomfortable with your body, dressing in short shorts and ill-fitting tee-shirts was sure to feed the monster of your insecurities. Being uncoordinated and awkward in a maturing body then being asked to assemble to be selected by team captains for a competitive game would surely erode anyone's self-esteem. Although Kyle enjoyed being active, he hated gym class.

At first, it started out as just another unpopular and tedious exercise assignments for second-period PE. After a series of new workouts that included square dancing and yoga, the PE teacher announced that the class would run a "timed" mile. Most students in the class, including Kyle, moaned and groaned in a rambunctious effort to show their displeasure. Unrelenting, the middle-aged, former Marine Corps drill instructor informed the group that the mile run would be timed and recorded. He further explained that today's run would be considered their baseline fitness level. He reinforced that at the end of the school year they would once again be timed in the mile run to measure their improved fitness level.

The retired Devil Dog also explained that each student would have another opportunity to post a better baseline time if they were unhappy with today's time and felt they could do better. In detail, he explained that the difference in time, either good or bad would be a weighted factor in their overall class grade.

That statement set off another tidal wave of displeasure from the second-period mob. The additional explanation did little to calm their cantankerous complaining. Against the backdrop of verbal chatter, the stopwatches were broken out, the student body was assembled and the class was escorted to the track. For some including Kyle, this was the first time they had been on the surface of the track. Groups of four in random order were selected for their timed run on the quarter mile oval. Kyle would run in the third group.

The first group finished with Kelly Wright a tall and athletic girl crossing the finish line first. This timed run was considered a class assignment, comparable to a standard writing assignment for an English grade. The timed run was not intended to be another sporting event designed to induce competition. When a girl won the first heat the contest was on and the battle lines were drawn. The general complaining about the "assignment" was quickly replaced with deep spirited compassion and excitement. The boys in the class instantly took this first defeat on the chin feeding an "Us vs. Them" threat to their juvenile manhood.

Kyle stood off alone. He felt the pressure building. Not a star athlete or someone who was comfortable out in front of his classmates, he began to fear his turn on the track. The second group took off with the entire gym class standing trackside rooting for their favorite runners. It was apparent to anyone remotely close to the track that this turned into a "Boys vs. Girls" confrontation with World War III proportions. Ricky Fox won the second heat by a wide margin. The battle of the sexes score was tied at one heat win for each side. The PE teacher commented that Ricky's time was the fastest up to this point at 6:57.

With the conclusion of the second race, it was Kyle's time on the track. As he made his way to the quarter-mile surface his heart began to pound uncontrollably in his chest. The palms of his hands became damp as he heard the catcalls, the rambunctious cheers and the argumentative back and forth heckling in the background.

"Girl Power." Roared one side of the battle lines.

"You better not let a girl beat you, KYLE." One of his closest friends shouted.

When called to the starting line, Kyle and the three others moved forward. He wasn't sure what to do and wasn't sure how to run a race. Instinctively with his toe resting on the white starting line he leaned forward and waited for the makeshift verbal gunshot blast that would start the match race between sexes. In that moment, everything became quiet. The only noise Kyle could hear was the pounding of his own heartbeat and the self-doubt that raged in his mind. In the quiet before the storm, he feared what would happen over the course of the four laps that laid out in front of him. He didn't want to embarrass himself in front of his classmates. More worrisome was the thought of going home to face his father and have it come up in conversations that he had lost a foot race to a girl. He didn't want another reason for his father to be disappointed in him. In that moment, Kyle wanted to merely be absorbed into the surface of the track. To hide, to disappear.

The group was caught off guard as the PE teacher yelled "GO" at the top of his lungs. Kyle lost his balance, stumbled with his foot placement and got off the starting line last. He quickly caught his balance. With his sluggish start, he would have to work hard to catch up with the three others now a few yards in front of him.

The trio consisted of Natalie Harvey, a basketball player, tall and lean. She was by far the most athletic student in his class. Jeffery Green was of average height, but strong and muscle-bound. He was fit, but no one would call him fast afoot. The grouping rounded out with Cindy Phillips, she was a pretty girl on the shorter side of the growth curve. What she lacked in height she made up for in Hollywood beauty. She was voted "Most likely to be a movie star" by her junior high classmates. Today, everyone was pretty sure this was the first time anyone had seen her run. Kyle was the wild card. He went unnoticed throughout much of the school day including gym class. Everyone knew he was a classmate but because he kept to himself so much no one truly knew anything about him.

Kyle fell behind early after his misstep on the starting line, but before the group made it out of the second turn he had caught and passed Cindy. Jeff was next in line as Kyle caught up to him in the middle of the backstretch and hung on his heel. Kyle and Jeff ran side by side rolling from turn three and into the fourth turn of this first of four laps. Kyle sized up his competitor as he leaned into the turn and began to align himself for the run down the front stretch. Out in front was Natalie Harvey who had stretched out her lead as the two boys matched strides.

Completing the first lap still hanging on Jeff's hip Kyle began to feel comfortable. His running motions began to feel natural, comfortable and synchronized. His movements fell into an easily repeatable groove. The harmonized movement was all too familiar to him. All the time he spent playing games alone, and running from place to place to avoid his father's wrath had ingrained in him the muscle memory that were the same set of skills and abilities he called on today. With running, among its repeatable and consistent groove was where he found comfort among all the chaos surrounding his home life. Today's comfort within the running action was broken when he realized Jeff was holding him up and at the front of the pack Natalie was getting away.

Normally Kyle was not a competitive person, but today something inside of him came alive when he realized that he could run with the jocks of his class. This competitive spirit got ignited within the young man when a group of boys shouted out, "Kyle you're going to get beat by a girl. A GIRL." The taunts rang out in his ears.

Going into turn one for the second time Kyle saw Natalie out in front and she was pulling away. He knew it was time to make a move if he had any hopes of not "letting a girl" beat him. Running with Jeff, Kyle had run comfortably without straining or peaking his effort. Stride after stride it was easy for him to run at this pace. On the other hand, Jeff was laboring, breathing heavy, his feet landed on the track surface with ever increasing sounds of impact.

Kyle knew he had to make his move. He had to run his race and he had to make up ground. Like a high-performance sports car shifting into a higher gear range in one solid effort he pulled away from Jeff. By the time he exited the second turn, he opened up a five-yard gap. Natalie was now about 60 yards out in front. Kyle wondered if he had time to run her down.

Had she gotten too far out in front while he kept pace with Jeff? By reputation alone, she was the better athlete. In all his school years, Kyle was never considered in the athletic group. He never took part in organized sports, participated in after-school activities and seldom played in neighborhood pickup games. Feeling a natural competitive steak for the first time, Kyle locked in on the front runner. At first, he focused on keeping her from getting any further away. The two front leaders matched strides all the way down the backstretch on their second lap. The crowd along trackside began to call out to their favorites.

"You got her Kyle…run faster."

"Natalie, he will run out of gas just wait." Said one group of girls.

"He can't run any faster." Echoed another.

The unlikely pair made their way through turn three and four for the second time. No one involved with second period PE had any idea about what they were about to witness.

In a short distance, he proved he could match strides with the obviously more athletic girl, but could he gain ground. He reasoned that he wasn't running all that hard to keep up with her. He felt if he tried a little harder, shifted up to another gear he would be able to catch her. His mind reasoned, if he could run her down would he be able to pass her? That was a question bouncing around within his mind. If he could get out in front, to lead the race could he keep her from catching up and passing him at the end. He was running what felt like a moderate pace but was it, he had no idea. Other than running to keep himself entertained and out of the house he had never run like this before.

In uncharted territory, Kyle had no idea what he was doing. He had no idea if he could run faster, if he could keep it up or if he would explode and burn out unable to walk to the finish line. The pair stayed step for step down the front stretch and into turn one and two.

Kyle focused on one thing, matching strides with Natalie. The sounds emanating from the crowd of students around the track began to pile on the pressure. Kyle was beginning to feel the effects of the rapid pace and his own lack of confidence began to mount. Entering the back straightaway for the third time it was time to see if he could win. His brain fired off a signal to his fast twitch muscle groups. It was time to go. Time to win or time to find out he wasn't good enough. In one explosive and repeating cycle, his legs pushed hard into the ground building tension and releasing it as they propelled his body forward. With each leg turnover cycle, his tempo got faster and faster. Kyle kept waiting for the pace of his leg turn over to settle out, but with each stride, it appeared his foot speed increased. Faster and faster his shoes hit the track's surface landing lighter and quicker. In a rapid crescendo, it felt like the world was being stripped away. His daily battles to avoid conflict were being released with each impact of his shoes on the track's surface. Like a comet shooting across the sky, all of Kyle's frustrations, worry and self-doubt trailed behind him in a burning contrail of fire. In that moment, nothing mattered but running faster.

By the time the pair exited turn four Kyle had caught up to Natalie and began to separate. Natalie was no longer a competitor as Kyle made his way down the front stretch for the next to last time. This would be the bell lap. As Kyle completed the third lap the PE teacher shouted out, one lap to go. The crowd along the sides of the track began to roar. This time there was no divide between girls and boys. The group of students collectively were now edging Kyle on. The individual grouping of students; the jocks, the bookworms, the socials and the dropouts were all united watching this amazingly fast mile play out in front of them.

One boy along trackside shouted out "Kyle you ...you go, boy! Bury her."

Kyle was embarrassed by the comment. He did not mean to show anyone up, he did not want to "bury" anyone. Kyle simply enjoyed running and running fast. He finally found a talent that separated himself from others. Kyle wondered if he finally found something that made him special. He was not one to be showy or show off at another student's detriment. Kyle was easy going and somewhat shy around his classmates. This sudden thrust into the spotlight made him uncomfortable.

Kyle ran alone all the way down the backstretch and into the final turn. The finish line was out in front of him as he put his head down and dug deeper than he had all day. Kyle hammered his legs into the track surface striding out as far forward as he could. His legs fired off with every ounce of energy they had reaching out further and further with each turnover. The ground below him passed in a blur. Arms pounding away at the air, his lung expanding and contracting to fuel his major muscle groups Kyle put his all into those last strides.

Kyle crossed the finish line first of his grouping. Natalie was just completing her run down the backstretch. Jeff and Cindy were more than a lap down.

The crowd around the track cheered. Some of the students came out on to the track surface to congratulate Kyle on his remarkable run. The PE teacher stood next to the finish line with a surprised look on his face staring at his stopwatch. Taping on the glass dial of the old fashion wind up watch he walked over to Kyle. Walking back slowly from a cool down run Kyle met up with the PE teacher in the middle of turn one.

"Kyle, I'm not sure what fast is for a really fast high school mile. I suggest you go talk to the track and field coach, I think you may have some real talent."

Natalie joined the crowd that had surrounded Kyle and the PE teacher. She looked over the teacher's shoulder and noted the time on the stop watch.

"Holy cow speed racer. Kyle, you have something here." She said as she walked away talking to a small group of friends. "That guy pulled away from me so fast, I had nothing. I could not keep up. He turned on the jets and just ran away from me. I had nothing for him."

An Unlikely Pair

Chapter 12

Normally she liked to start her day a little later than most. When Candy had an adventure planned she was happy being an early riser. On those occasions, she enjoyed the quiet stillness and the promise of a new day. This day held a special promise. It was a beautiful morning as the seasons began to shift from spring to summer. The rebirth of spring was still in the air and the excitement of summer was approaching fast.

Sitting in her favorite overstuffed green recliner, her view of Berkeley Springs out the large old fashion window was unobstructed. Candy loved the outdoors and she enjoyed the comfort of small-town life. When she wasn't lost in the worlds she created, she daydreamed about hiking remote and challenging trails. Often, she found herself lost among thoughts of exploring the Pacific Coast Trail, hiking the Grand Canyon or setting out on Vermont's 273-mile Long Trail. This morning over the penetrating smell of freshly roasted coffee, Candy's mind was torn between two exciting dreamlands.

She had been developing a plan to hike sections of the Appalachian Trail, affectionately known as the AT. Part of her up-coming novel would feature scenes played out along the rugged mountainous trails. Candy believed she needed firsthand experience to accurately capture the depth and scope of the trails.

She felt she needed to feel the elements of the AT to fully describe its essence and personality in words. It would be her first trip on the world-famous trail that extends from Springer Mountain in Georgia to Mount Katahdin in Maine.

This day hike had been planned for a few weeks. It was a chance for her to become part of the story, to live in the scenes she created and to feel the environment that her characters lived among. The goal of the trip was to experience the countryside, the terrain and a depth of the scenery. She wanted to experience the trail, become part of the trail culture and fully enable herself to pull from her feelings while she filled the pages with beautiful and dramatic scenes. As the day of the hike grew near, her mind was full of thoughts and actions.

Normally when she was in her writing mode Candy had the mental fortitude to focus in on that one task. This morning as she sat completely relaxed in her overstuffed chair her mind would often get torn away from the creative process. Today her mind wandered in a way she had not experienced before. Candy's attention was divided, challenged and at times fixated on something else. Alarmingly in the last few days, she had become more and more distracted from her work.

Among the storyline, maps, trail reviews, character development and packing lists were thoughts about Kyle. The encounter over lunch slowly became a featured scene in her own most personal novel. For reasons she couldn't explain, even to herself, she could not stop thinking about him. Kyle's cameo appearance slowly transformed into a feature role, one in which if she was true to herself would eventually turn into a starring role. While trying to prepare for the Appalachian trip she couldn't stop thinking about him.

Over the last few sips of her morning coffee, Candy concluded that she needed some "additional" hiking supplies. Although her trail pack had been complete for days; that every item had been carefully thought out and selected. She convinced herself that she needed a few "more items" for the hike. Inside she wasn't fooling herself, she knew there was only one reason she needed to make a trip to the running store.

The store was a bustle of activity this morning. Jim was busy tending to customers while Kyle was in the back receiving a shipment of new running shoes. Kyle found it hard to consider anything about his time at the store as "work." Where stocking shelves or tending to retail duties to some may seem boring and laborious, Kyle loved it. Although if production rates equaled pounds stocked over time, then he wasn't a very good employee. The root cause of Kyle's poor employee performance was that he simply loved running too much. With each new shoe style that made its way into inventory, Kyle would excitedly open the boxes and do a critical examination of styling and performance potential of each pair. Jim gave him a tough time about his slow work pace, but he knew it helped when it came time to help his customers.

"Hey, Jim," Kyle yelled from the back room just as Candy entered the store.

"What Kyle, the place is on fire? I'm kind of busy up here." Jim jokingly replied.

"No fire but you have got to see the new color combinations on the new line of shoes. These babies look fast right out of the box. And the fit...they are awesome!"

"Kyle you're not trying on all the shoes are you? An important customer just came in." Jim waved at Candy. "I need a little help up here, buddy." He motioned for Candy to go to the back of the store.

Candy overheard Kyle's voice from the backroom and at Jim's direction made her way towards the sound of his voice. Jim winked at her as she moved closer to where Kyle was.

Unaware of the collision course set up in front of him, Kyle quickly took off the pair of flashy neon green shoes and put his old pair of racers back on. Once the laces were tied, he quickly stood up and made his way forward. The two met up in the middle.

"Oh, Candy what are you doing here." Kyle stumbled with his reply. His heart rate climbed with excitement upon seeing her. If this would have been a training cycle his heart rate would have matched the closing laps of a speed session.

"It's so nice to see you, did you bring Carly Q with you? I've kind of missed you guys." Kyle felt a little exposed with that statement and hedged his bet. "I've missed seeing your attack dog, I mean. I am a dog person, you know a dog whisperer." He laughed recalling how he became Carly's best friend during their chance encounter over lunch.

"I wanted to stop in and say hi, and pick up a few things. Kind of missed you too and Carly hasn't stopped talking about you. But no, I left her at home. She got out on the wrong side of bed today. She was cranky, needs her beauty sleep.

The two made small talk about Carly, Candy's planned hike, Kyle's running and about the store.

Between the spontaneous chit-chat and the casual eye contact, the pair made their way around the store picking out items that Candy "needed" for her upcoming trip. Jim who was in the background was determined to keep the pair on their toes kept asking Kyle to help with the customer flow in the store. Much to Jim's dislike, his requests went pretty much unnoticed. A regular customer, Ruthie, a tall and fast runner looking to qualify for Boston was more like family. She like Jim watched the romantic drama play out. Although Ruthie gave Jim the evil eye every time he tried to interrupt the moment. It was obvious to anyone within eyeshot that there was more to this scene than selling some running gear.

Candy picked out items she needed and placed them in a small wicker basket. When Jim opened the store, he wanted a local feel, a tie to the local vibe, he wanted anything but a big box store atmosphere. In his store, instead of shopping baskets, customers could hold their items in locally made wicker baskets. It was just part of his plan to make the running store a community, not simply a retail outlet. A new pair of shoelaces, a few packs of snack bars, some lip balm and a new trucker hat were resting inside Candy's basket. Kyle didn't pay much attention to what Candy was picking out. He was solely focused on every word she said and every movement she made. So was nearly everyone else in the store.

Ruthie leaned over to Jim as he was fitting a pair of running shoes. "Jim, he hasn't taken his eyes off her the entire time. That young man is smitten."

Jim's customer added. "You noticed that too."

With her shopping done, Candy made her way to the counter and fumbled with her items as she waited for Kyle to ring up her sale.

"Is that all you need Candy?" Kyle sheepishly questioned.

"Aw...well I really didn't have a list. These items just kind of jumped out at me." Candy replied.

With that innocent comment, Jim couldn't help himself and began to laugh. Ruthie tossed a foam roller at him.

"Well okay then, that will be $32.95, cash, charge or check?"

"I have cash," she replied.

Kyle took two twenty-dollar bills from her hand. Reaching for the crisp Andrew Jacksons his hand brushed over hers. Their skin made contact. Kyle lacked any extensive dating experience and was caught off guard. He always wanted to have someone special in his life but his focus had always been on staying out of trouble, running fast and trying to figure out his place in a complicated world. Feeling the softness of her skin on his, if even for a moment, sent excitement through his veins. The connection caused him to pause for just a second. While trying to draw attention away from this encounter he began to ask her a question but stumbled when trying to formulate the words needed to convey the message.

"You are?" He stopped, took a deep breath and started his question over again. "I mean are you doing anything tonight?" Kyle looked up from the cash register and made eye contact with Candy's beautiful blue eyes. Instantly he was lost in her presence. It lasted a second maximum then his vision was diverted back to the register as he finished up making change. "I'm kind of hungry…thought we could share some pi….."

Candy interrupted.

"Oh Kyle...that sounds like a great idea, but." Candy's words hung in the air. Inside a jolt of fear went through her core. She liked Kyle. She wanted someone in her life as well. But since her self-rescue and recovery from her addictive years, she kept herself guarded and removed the dating world. Candy found it hard to trust anyone. Hard to believe people were not trying to manipulate her. She feared being hurt, used and disappointed. What she feared even more, was finding that special someone, someone like Kyle and then trying to tell them all that she had been through. All that she had done, to herself, to others and how it changed her. She feared it would be too much, that Kyle would lose interest or worse that he would no longer respect her. She feared her past life would forever haunt her and drive her future life away.

"I need to do some writing today, I mean tonight." She paused making some sounds that were inaudible to Kyle. Inside she was torn, she liked Kyle. Getting past their rocky first encounter, he seemed grounded, wholesome and not someone who would be into playing games. In the little time that they knew each other she felt something unique about him and she believed that he liked her too. At this moment, the demons from her past life used her vulnerability to come to the surface. Instantly she felt fearful, tormented by her failings and uncomfortable. Everything she had put behind her, had somehow found the light of day again. She thought she was past this point in her life, but once again fear gripped her.

"Tonight, I just can't. Maybe another day?"

The sting of rejection hit Kyle hard. With a low depressed tone, he tried to make the best of it.

"Yea, okay then...sure." He handed her change from forty dollars.

What once was a warm moment between two equally attracted people now turned into a tension-filled mess. Without further conversation, Kyle placed Candy's items in a white plastic bag. Then there was a long uncomfortable pause and he thanked her for stopping by slowly returning back to tending the shelves.

Candy tried to smile as she walked out of the store but the tension kept her from putting a happy face on the encounter. She didn't know what to say. She knew she hurt him, she knew she wanted to be with him and she knew her past life was messing up her today. She believed she very well may have been making a big mistake.

The end of the day came quickly. Kyles' brain ran in overdrive for the remainder of the day. Uncomfortable around girls he had an interest in, he questioned everything that he had done, said and the way he touched her hand. He wondered where it had gone off course. Did he misread a signal? Did he say something wrong? All the lights in the shop were off as Jim and Kyle locked the backdoor and closed the store.

"So, Kyle, did you get a date with young Ms. Candy?" Jim jokingly asked.

This caught Kyle off guard and a little embarrassed. "No, she did not seem to be interested in me." Kyle grew more despondent as he told Jim what had happened.

"You're kidding me, Kyle she was definitely into you. Anyone could tell that from a mile away. You two were in your own little world making eyes at each other like high school kids. Following each other around the store like little puppies, even to an old fart like me that was cute. It was a hoot watching you two. Poor Candy, she was just grasping for items around the store to spend more time with you. I bet I'll get some returns from this Mr. Don Juan."

Kyle was shocked. "You could tell I like her. I didn't even notice anyone else in the store."

"Well that should tell you right there and Kyle she may have said no…but her body language said she is interested. Maybe she is just a little scared, cautious and maybe awkward. Kind of like you." Jim offered up some encouragement.

"So, what should I do, what would you do?" Kyle asked.

"Go slow but I would not take that no as a dead end. Just be cool, do something to surprise her. But respect that she might be a little timid, you know a little afraid. We all have a story. She might be dealing with her own "family" issues." Jim used the air quote hand gesture to highlight that like Kyle, a lot of people have issues that they need to work through.

These words seem to fill Kyle with resolve, inspiration and motivation. He was no longer downcast and gloomy. A smile became fixed on his face, he gave Jim a big hug and rushed off telling Jim he knew just what he needed to do.

"Okay Kyle, but don't forget the go-slow part. Mainly treat her with respect."

Whether his Olympic speed helped him or not Kyle stood facing

Candy's door in a very brief amount of time after speaking with Jim. Three solid raps on the door let Candy know someone was on the other side and that this someone was pretty set on talking with her. She quickly got up from a chair at a small table that her laptop rested on. An old fashioned shaker style writing table nestled in front of a tall window overlooking the center of town was the perfect spot for someone to daydream and create. Candy's daydreams filled the pages of her books. Tonight, she was rounding out the last chapter of her latest novel.

The sound from the other side of the door broke her away from the fictitious world she had created. Now separated from the inspirational mood, Candy made her way across the room. The cold oak flooring on her bare feet quickened her pace. As she reached the door she wondered who could be on the other side. She wasn't expecting any visitors, she didn't know that many people in town to have an unannounced visitor. With some hesitation, she gazed through the peephole and reached for the old fashion brass doorknob.

Her eyes were surprised to see Kyle on the other side of the door. He was wearing the same clothes he had on at the running store. A pair of jeans, a yellow t-shirt from a race he had run, and the pair of retired racing flats. The only thing different was that Candy could tell he freshened himself up before heading her way. His curly hair had been rustled up a bit and she instantly noticed the return of his bright smile. As happy as she was to see him, anxiety also fired off rounds of panic as she opened the door.

"Kyle, I just can't...not tonight."

"Candy, I get it but you got me all wrong. I'm not here to bug you. I know you are busy, heck I'm not sure you even like me. I'm here to see Carly Q." Kyle paused.

Candy was flat-footed. She wasn't sure what to say. Her thought patterns were confused and stuck somewhere between "not sure you like me, and I want to see Carly Q." She wanted to tell him that in fact she did like him and wanted to spend more time with him but she was caught totally off guard with his request.

"Can I take her for a walk? You said she missed me and I've got nothing better to do tonight. I promise I'll have her home at a reasonable time. And yes I'll make sure to pick up after her, you have doggy bags right?" Kyle continued.

Carly heard her name and from around the corner of the living room she came running. If Kyle thought Candy was beautiful nothing prepared him for Carly. Her shiny liver-colored coat was perfectly groomed, with her small brown nose and bright eyes were leading the way. What was completely out of place was that Carly ran with one ear pointed up and the other ear flopped down. Kyle laughed and thought to himself that this dog was so cute he could just pick her up on the spot. Carly, for her reputation, let out a low growl when she saw someone at her owner's door. Kyle then worked his magic.

"Come on Carly girl, we're not going to do this all over again are we?" He paused and kneeled to get on her level. "You like me…remember? You want to go for a walk?" His soft tone broke the spell. Like a light switch on the wall moved into a new position Carly was instantly overly excited to get out of the house that she pranced on her hind legs and turned in circles as Kyle asked for her leash.

"I'm not sure how you do that," a surprised Candy commented. "She really doesn't like new people, I'm constantly trying to figure out how to keep her from eating someone, but you just walk in and you're best buddies."

"I have a gift. Okay, now you go back to work, the laptop or whatever it was that you were doing. I'll have her home safe and sound, don't worry about us."

Kyle clipped the gray leash onto Carly's pink collar and off they went. Candy closed the door, walked back to her laptop and wondered what had just happened. She thought that Kyle was cute, one of a kind for sure, she also thought that he might just be crazy. She wondered if she had made some terrible mistake hours before. She feared Kyle wasn't interested anymore. She wondered how long they would be gone. She knew she wanted to see him again. In a strange way, she was kind of jealous of her four-legged friend. Carly was getting to hang out with the one person she wanted to be with. Yet Candy by her own doing was stuck behind a 17" laptop screen.

Candy sat behind the small desk and noticed that the room was deadly still. The clock on the wall made the only sound yet she couldn't find her way back to a place where she could make progress with the words on the screen. Candy had never suffered from writers' block before. Her stories poured out of her like water from a broken dam. Her words normally flowed at a rate that their only limiting factor was her typing skills. Now she was stuck. Not a single word came forward. The creative energy was bottled up, stuck or restricted by her thoughts centered on Kyle.

She glanced at the clock and noticed that nearly two hours had passed, it was approaching 8:30 when she heard movements on the other side of the door. Candy jumped out of the chair that felt like a lonely jail cell and raced to the door. She quickly reached for and rotated the doorknob. Her heart raced as the door opened. Her breath paused. Standing in the now open-door way with nothing to hide behind she was not ready for what she saw.

Kyle approached with Carly's leash in one hand and a pizza box in the other. When his eyes caught hers, a big smile came across his face as the distance between the two drew shorter. Carly walked along his left side. Candy thought for sure she saw a smile on her doggie's face.

"Well hi there Ms. Hemmingway, I figure even a New York style writer like you gets hungry so I figured I would bring you some dinner." Kyle paused for just a second, then he remembered what Jim said about being bold. "Carly girl told me," he paused again, drawing from a source of strength and self-confidence he wasn't sure he had. "That you needed to hang out with us some...She wants to tell you the work day is done." Kyle hedged his bet some. "Okay?"

Caught off guard somewhere between wanting to fall into his arms and wanting to run away to a safe place, Candy was slow to say anything. Kyle reached her doorway and stopped as Carly made her way between the pair and tugged to enter her home. Kyle dropped her leash. Carly disappeared around the corner and could be heard drinking out of her water bowl. The two-stood face to face in the doorway for a second which felt like a lifetime before Candy finally broke the silence. The tension between them was obvious. Kyle believed, he overstepped his bounds. Candy wanting to reach out and hug him.

Candy joked to break the tension. She turned and lead Kyle into her home. "Come on in then, guess we are having pizza. I got that going for me."

Over slices of pizza and tall cold glasses of soda, they talked about their lives, their dreams and where they saw themselves in the future. For some reasons he did not understand, after all, he did not know Candy well, he felt comfortable with her enough to tell her everything about his life.

The conversation with her was so relaxed that once he began peeling back the tragic layers of his past it was easier to expose everything than to try and navigate around the bad parts. Candy, on the other hand, avoided some chapters within her personal story. Kyle could tell something was missing but he did not want to pry, he understood how hard it was to appear vulnerable. He understood some stories were hard to relive. He respected her privacy and was happy just to spend some time with her.

The night ended with the two of them standing awkwardly in the hallway exchanging a prolonged and uncomfortable goodbye. Kyle wasn't sure if he should try and kiss her, shake her hand or give her an arousing high-five. Paralyzed to act, he was sure that only one of those options was acceptable. But, which one? He knew that he "wanted" to kiss her. Scared to make the wrong move, Kyle leaned forward, extended his arm and shook her hand as he turned to leave.

"I hope we can do this again, Candy," Kyle said as he walked away.

Candy stood motionless. Her hand still out reached toward his. She felt like both a witness to the scene and the main character who was deeply engaged in the action. Candy centered in a wave of feelings she had not felt in a very long time was confused. She was also very scared.

A Morning Encounter

Chapter 13

Kyle was busy turning on the lights and getting the cash register opened as Jim tended to the coffee station. Centered in the middle of the shop, surrounded by the latest style of shoes, hydration belts, foam rollers and running books was the lifeblood of the store. The runner's coffee bar as Jim called it. Jim prided himself on customer service and gallons of free coffee. The first pot had hardly a chance to simmer when the door of the shop opened with the first customers of the day. Kyle looked up from the register and offered a greeting "Morning Ladies." The store had only been open a few minutes and the day was already off to a fast start.

A group of friends from a small town without a dedicated running shop drove over an hour one way to visit Jim's store. Run Berkeley was accustomed to visitors from both the surrounding communities and die-hard runners from the bigger cities to the south and north-west. This morning the group of running friends substituted their normal rest day pedicures and mimosas for a girl's day out. They had heard so much talk about this "special little running store" that they decided a day shopping in Berkeley Springs was in order. Walking into to Jim's establishment that morning, the group hoped the shop was worth the drive. For a small-town store, Jim built a reputation for customer service and expert care within the running community. The brick and mortar storefront was more than a retail outlet that sold running products, Run Berkley was woven into the very fabric of running.

Upon entering, Jim greeted the group and thanked them for coming to his store. He offered them some hot coffee and any help they needed. One of the ladies spoke up, she seemed to be the leader of the informal pack. "Wonderful place you have here, we have nothing like this in Mineral Wells. It's either a big box store or we must order online. I'm not sure about the rest of today's consumers but I like to touch and feel before I buy something."

Jim smiled. "Thank you, I try to keep it real here...and I hope you find our prices reasonable. I'll be honest we are more expensive, the big outlets buy cheaper than I can sell the same products, but they are not runners. I'll take care of you like family."

A few of the ladies listened in. "We get it, that's why we are here." One of the ladies who was wearing a Boston Marathon jacket in the famous blue and yellow colors spoke up. "We support the little guys. You all support us at our events and local races so here we are." Said another.

"Thank you." Jim offered refills on coffee.

The group milled around the store checking out what Jim had to offer and asked questions about the local running events. Jim let it slip, as he did every time a new customer came into the store, that Kyle, his young protégé, made a run at the Olympics. The ladies' ears perked up upon hearing this bit of local news.

"Oh really, so the young man here is fast."

Kyle blushed as he made the first sale of the day. After punching in the keys of an old fashion cash register Kyle was now trying to make heads or tails out of the directions to set up a new GPS watch. He always prided himself as a lover of modern technology but quietly he was keeping a secret. Sure, he loved all the features of the newest watches, but he had a heck of a time trying to get them set up. In truth, he believed while setting up his watch, the same style and model of the one he just sold, he accidentally hit the right combinations of buttons and it just worked. Now a new customer was standing, perched over his shoulder waiting for him to set up their newly purchased watch. Kyle's heart raced, sweat built upon his forehead and he was sure his heart rate had reached its performance limits.

“Hey Speed Racer, you got that figured out yet?” Jim asked from across the store. At this rate Garmin will have five new updates out before you get that thing going.”

Jim looked over to one of the ladies, "he loves the pressure."

Jim’s encouragement was not helping. Kyle was seconds away from offering a refund when the door to the store swung open with a commotion that drew everyone’s attention. Jim closest to the door was the first to see her and he knew something was not right. From the look on her face, Jim knew something was terribly wrong and someone was in deep trouble. Jim also knew one other important piece of information, it wasn’t him.

“Kyle, you better run, Ms. Candy is here to see you…what did you mess up on her order yesterday, Mr. GPSman?” Jim was never one to miss an opportunity to harass Kyle. Although today he second guessed himself when he saw the look in her eyes as she made her way closer to her victim.

Instantly Kyle looked up from the watch that had gotten the better of him, but it was too late. Candy had already closed the distance, he was trapped. With a blank stare, all Kyle could do was look up. Kyle saw something in Candy’s eyes that he was not ready for. He knew something was different.

Candy did not stop at the edge of the counter. Acting like she owned the place and motivated by something unseen she walked around the back of the sales counter and trapped Kyle between the cash register and the rack displaying the latest offerings of power gels. He had nowhere to go, no escape. His fight or flight instinct kicked in.

"Candy...."

Forgetting about the task at hand he dropped the watch on the counter. Engaged in a hasty confrontation he wasn't sure what to do. Kyle considered jumping over the counter he also thought about putting up his arms in some form of a defensive posture. Candy did not look happy. Her face looked focused, emotional and intent. Kyle thought that she appeared to have been crying. A deeply rooted fear that he had done something terribly wrong penetrated his being. He wanted a chance to say he was sorry, for…whatever it was that he had done. He wanted a chance to make things right.

“All night, I’ve been thinking about you. All night."

Her voice cracked and grew quiet as she spoke. "I couldn’t sleep at all. What you did, what you are doing is not right. You, getting Carly on your side, you big…" And with one move Candy's words rang silent. Candy moved toward Kyle and reached out towards him. Candy slowly drew closer and in an instant, she placed her lips on his, closed her eyes, and gave him an overpowering kiss.

Kyle didn’t move. He didn’t reach out and he didn’t kiss her back. It wasn’t that he didn’t want to. He badly wanted to meet her embrace, but he had been caught off guard. Only part of him knew what was going on. Before he could convince the other part to kiss her back she pulled away.

“Now there Kyle, that is how you say goodnight to a girl. You don’t shake her hand after having pizza, talking with her for hours and walking her dog. You. Kiss. Her.”

Jim, LeAnn and a store full of customers stood haplessly glancing back and forth at Candy and Kyle. Everyone wondered what they had just witnessed. Jim’s wife was the first one to speak up.

"Ah Kyle...what did you do?"

"I'm not really sure. But I'll never do it again or I'm in for seconds. I'm not sure what the right answer is." Kyle replied now smiling ear to ear.

"I like you, Kyle, there is something about you. If you can give me some time, take this slow…I have some things in my life that I really need to work through." And with that Candy stopped talking, her eyes teared up. A small teardrop ran down her cheek. Her face cast toward the floor.

It broke Kyle's heart to hear the tone of her voice as she spoke about needing to work through some apparent problems in her life. Kyle understood that there was something there. He knew how hard life could be, he understood how good people could have such a challenging time with life. And he understood how much love a person with an unfortunate past can give. He wondered if in Candy he wasn't seeing someone much like himself.

"Candy, I'll go as slow as you want. I'll never rush or hurt you. I'm just me. I've got no ill will, no dark plans. I just want to be with you. I'm willing to be here for you, if you're willing to have me."

"Okay, then I have to go. Carly is running wild in the house she has most likely broken into the cookie jar and is eating all of her snacks. I need to get back. Can you." She paused. "Stop by after work, please."

"Sure thing, Candy…yea, sure thing." He spoke softly as he followed her around the counter.

Candy turned, Kyle continued to follow as she moved towards the door. Kyle reached for her hand and when he felt her hand in his, he smiled. "I'll see you after work."

She continued to the door. She stopped and looked back for part of a second. Then she continued her way. Everyone in the store stared as Candy walked out of the doorway. Kyle stood there watching her walk down the sidewalk and across the street. He continued to watch her until she disappeared out of view. He then remained motionless staring out the window of the store wondering what had just happened.

Jim's excited voice broke the air. "What in the world, Kyle. What is going on here? I told you to go slow, what did you do? Wait a minute, can we bottle it up? That was some kiss right out of the blue. We can make some money on this stuff, Kyle's love potion, whatever it is."

Jim, his wife and two random customers circled around Kyle who made his way back to the sales counter. Kyle stood there quietly and began to fumble with the GPS watch. Jim took the watch out of his hand, "what did you do?"

Conversations and Heartbeats

Chapter 14

For the remainder of the day, time wore on like an underpowered freight train pulling overloaded railcars up a mountain pass. The click-clack of the steel wheels on steel rails was replaced by the perfectly timed sounds of the pendulum from the old fashion regulator clock hanging on the south wall of the store. Where normally Kyle would get lost while engulfed in conversations around running. After Candy's visit, time seemed to pass at the pace of a receding glacier. Just like the old clock seemed out of place among today's newest timepieces, Kyle's mind was someplace else.

Jim noticed right away.

"Kyle, the clock won't advance any faster with you staring at it. Why don't you take off? We can manage the store. His boss commented while helping a customer. "Sounds like you and Candy have some ground to cover."

"Are you sure Jim, I don't want my personal life interfering with the store. I care about this place. I surely don't want to leave you shorthanded."

"Kyle really, we will survive. To me it sounded like she could really use someone. I mean you, right now. I think she cares about you but is also a bit scared about the fact that she does have feelings. There is something she is not telling you. You need to make sure you are there for her. If you care about her the way I'm guessing you do, you need to get to the bottom of this to ensure it's something you can live with." Jim gave off an air of confidence as he spoke about life. Jim was someone Kyle trusted beyond measure. He was someone, maybe the only person who always had given Kyle sound advice.

"You are right Jim, I do like her. A lot. After she kissed me, it killed me to hear the hurt in her voice and in the tone she used. She has a hold on me and I need to see her. Thank you, Jim. Thank you for understanding."

Kyle quickly got his things together. Before leaving the store, Kyle walked over to Jim, the two shared a very close bond. Kyle gave Jim a big hug and headed out the door. Just as he crossed the threshold of the door, Kyle paused and stepped back in.

"Jim, thank you," Kyle said looking squarely back at Jim. "Thank you for all you have done for me, today and the past few years. You have always been there for me. I'm thankful to have you in my life."

The weight of the words Kyle spoke was not lost on Jim. He understood their meaning. More importantly, he understood from where the feelings were coming from.

Kyle's mind went into overdrive as he made his way the five blocks to Candy's apartment. He rehearsed the words he planned to use over and over as he tried to figure out the best way to say what he thought needed to be said. He wanted to be sure he told her that he didn't care about the past. That he understood things happen, that life isn't always fair and that moving forward he would always be there for her. He wanted to make sure that if she wanted him in her life, that he planned to be there for the long haul. He planned to be there for as long as she would have him. He hoped he read the signals right, he hoped Jim was correct. He hoped she could care for him the way he knew he cared for her.

He hoped she would be strong enough to trust him.

Standing at the door to Candy's apartment Kyle did his best to collect his emotions. Nothing in life had prepared him for what may happen next. Growing up, Kyle's exposure to relationships had been that they served as battlegrounds. Battles were fought while trying to survive. Confrontations raged while trying to feel valued and while trying to prove to his father that he was worthy. Now Kyle would be trying to convince Candy that he could love her, care about her and respect her no matter what past indiscretions haunted her.

Kyle stood facing the door. For a moment, he was frozen in time knowing full well what he came to do, but unsure if he could. As his hand reached out to knock on the door something stopped him. He noticed it was mostly quiet on the other side, although he thought he could hear someone crying. He paused, he felt his stomach get tighter and then he knocked on the door as he held his breath.

The noise stopped. There was a long pause. He considered knocking again when Candy opened the door. Her eyes were red and swollen. It was obvious that she had been crying. She was surprised to see him. Kyle in a soft and reserved tone said Hi. Her response was delayed, for a second Candy was unable to come up with the right words with the proper greeting.

"I didn't expect to see you for a few more hours. Are you okay...is everything okay?" She turned and invited him in.

Carly came around the corner and walked up to meet Kyle. This time Candy's four-legged companion did not bark, growl or even look aggressively at him. Kyle found this unusual. Carly walked right up to him and stood up on her hind legs with her front paws resting just above his knee. He bent down and spoke to Carly, while rubbing the soft fur behind her ears. "No barking today, girl. Are you warming up to me?" Carly's brown eyes looked directly into his eyes as if communicating with him in an unspoken language. Kyle somehow knew that Carly was telling him that her friend, owner, master...that her person needed him. Candy needed some support that a dog, even the best of four-legged companions could not provide.

Kyle spoke up. "Candy could we sit and talk?"

"I think that would be great." Candy motioned for them to sit at her small breakfast table. Carly followed the pair to the table and sat at Candy's feet.

"Let's clear the air." Kyle cleared his throat. "Candy first, I've liked you, been attracted to you from that first encounter where you threatened to kick my butt." The two laughed over his comment, that seemed to break the mood. "Every time we have crossed paths I've found you more interesting, more appealing, more on my mind. I can't explain it. It just is. When you came into the store the other day I felt something. Candy I've never felt like this before. There was something, IS something connecting us."

The nervous young man paused and collected his thoughts. He reached out and took Candy's hand. "I'm here for you. I can take whatever it is you fear to tell me. If you care about me as I care about you." He stopped and looked deep within her eyes. "I don't care about the past."

Kyle's words were cut off as Candy touched his lips with her finger. Kyle stopped talking. "My past is ugly, it's dark and it's something most people run from." She paused to gain some composure and courage. "I was a drug addict in the worst way. I grew up normal." She paused. Her eye teared up. Her voice trailed off. "I was normal, I had everything going for me. Life was perfect. It was a summer day, nothing special, a concert with people I thought were my friends. I trusted someone, I trusted them. In one night, it was all taken from me."

Candy began to cry between sentences.

"I could not stop. I gave up everything. I let go of my life and I gave myself up for the drugs. I lived and breathed for only one thing, the next high." She took a deep breath wiped her eyes and looked away. A few seconds passed that felt like lifetimes. She continued.

"I could see myself falling apart. My life, coming apart at its seams. Like leaves falling away from a tree, blowing and scattering across the ground driven by an unseen force. The worst part was, I couldn't do anything to stop it. I only cared about where the next batch of drugs were coming from. I lost touch with my family. I stole money, I hurt people who loved me." Candy stopped speaking to draw on some reserve of strength.

"I gave myself away...I did anything and everything to feed the addiction."

Kyle moved closer to comfort her. "Candy, I'm sorry. I'm so very sorry this happened to you. But it does not change how I feel."

Carly rustled around on the floor.

"Kyle, I gave myself to whomever had the supply. I didn't care who, I was used like currency to pay for my drug addiction. It was not pretty, it was real life in the ghetto and on the streets. Worse then you could ever imagine.

Until one day I woke up in a place I had no idea where or how I had gotten there. I had no idea who was around me. By some miracle, I could finally see through the fog. I could finally make out heads and tails and right from wrong. I could finally see...life and death. I could see my addiction. Somehow I got up and walked out."

Candy was nearly out of breath. Simply trying to retell this story was physically taxing, and emotionally challenging. She took a few seconds to regain her composure. Kyle sat with her, held her hand, and hung on every word.

"The next two years I spent in rehab trying to put my life back together. There were ups and many downs. I had lost my family. I wanted to be free of that life, but once free from it I hated myself. I trusted no one. I didn't even trust myself. Every day was a fight to stay on track to walk away from those dark days. The guilt. The pain. The battles to remain sober. The addiction and the memories.

Kyle listened intently. He knew part of the battle she faced. He lived the life of addiction from the other side. He lived as a causality. He could feel and understood the deep-rooted emotion from where she spoke.

"Finally, Kyle, I found myself here. I feel like finally, I've put my life back together again. I feel ready to live again. Yet I'm scared out of my mind to love someone. I'm scared to give up that control. I'm scared I'll be used again, scared to lose myself to someone else. Do you understand, can you understand?"

His eyes teared up. He moved forward closing the distance between them. "Yes, Candy I do. I get it, I understand. Life is hard, I've lived it. I can only tell you I would never hurt you. You are important to me, not something to use, to take from, or to abuse. You are someone I would want to lift up, encourage, protect, cherish and love."

The conversation stopped. Kyle paused wondering if he had gone too far. Had he said to much. Had he messed everything up. Did the weight of that word, change the tone, direction and the forward motion of their conversation?

Kyle and Candy looked at each other for a moment. The air was still, there was no noise; only two people frozen in an intense moment.

"Yes, I said love. Candy call me crazy, nuts, naive or whatever word you choose to use, but I feel something for you that I have never felt. I don't care what it takes or how long I must work at it...I will love and protect you. If only you'll…" He paused. "Candy no matter how scary it is, if you will give us a chance. I promise I'll do everything to make you happy with me and maybe it will be forever."

Candy laid her head on his chest and felt comforted for the first time in years. She had heard all that Kyle had to say. His words penetrated her soul. She understood his reasoning, understood his motivation and believed everything he had said. The scared little girl still had many thoughts running wild in her mind. She wanted to hold onto the positive.

In the stillness of their encounter, she could hear Kyle's heartbeat. The chaos of her emotions grew quiet with each reverberation of his heart. In that moment, she believed she had found the one person that could love her.

Time Flies

Chapter 15

Candy thought it would be difficult to open up, hard to be vulnerable to someone. She believed it would be beyond her to trust again. She also assumed it would be next to impossible to fall in love. What she found was that her relationship with Kyle broke down all those barriers and was anything but difficult.

The small-town atmosphere provided the perfect backdrop for their budding romance. They walked the streets together. Held hands while exploring the history within town square. Had meals together at the diner while Candy plotted out the next scene for her book. Or they sat together as Kyle captured the subtle shading of colors as the summer sun disappeared over the horizon with an old weathered barn shadowed in the foreground.

Feeling comfortable and secure in their relationship Candy finally shared the final parts of her life story with Kyle as they sat together on a rustic bench while visiting town square. Mustering the strength to uncover the darkest chapter of her life provided an emotional release. Finally, being comfortable enough with someone to tell them all she had been through was healing. For the first time, she was able to express how this period of her life made her feel about herself, and about her station in life.

She exposed the concluding chapter and last sentence of her dramatic tale of recovery, not a story from a fictional manuscript, not a closing word in some story but the closing line on a painful chapter of her life. Candy could not have penned a more fitting ending. Maybe this time she truly believed that those days were behind her

"I'm here for you." Kyle said in a low hushed tone as he sat next to her on the old wooden bench in a remote part of the park. In the background birds could be heard singing their songs, mowers were tending to the grass and cars continued to make their way along the busy thoroughfare. Through all of the days trappings, Kyle looked into Candy's eyes and smiled.

"The last few weeks have been great, I love being with you. Nothing is going to come between us. I get how hard this has been on you, to trust me, to be open and to be exposed. I value your openness and your painful truth. All I can say is that part of your life is over, gone and never coming back. It is part of you and I love all of you." Kyle paused. He searched for the right words. They did not come easy. Finally, after being unable to conjure up anything new, something special, an original thought, he finished by saying.

"I Love you. It's as simple as that."

The following day at the store had been quiet. The majority of Kyles shift passed uneventfully. Candy became a fixture in the store and a faithful partner when Kyle ran on his easy training days. Always up for a new way to push her physical limits she began to understand the draw of long distance running. Her running routine grew from a few miles a day into a training plan with more structure and vastly increased distances. Today wasn't a day to run, plot a dramatic scene or to revisit her youth. Today, in the middle of Kyle's shift she was anxious to visit him and wanted to drop off some homemade snacks. Likewise, Carly was eager to get out and about.

Jim was the first one to notice the twosome as they entered the shop. "Hey Carly, are you happy to see me." Carly tugged at her purple leash letting Candy know she wanted to be on her own. Once free the little dog ran across the store stopping with a big thud against Jim's leg.

"Well I guess that is a side benefit of you hanging out here more often Candy...Carly no longer wants to feed on me." They both laughed.

Jim broke away from dusting the shelves displaying an assortment of race distance ovals. With a break in his chores Jim tossed around a pair of old socks he tied in a knot for Carly to play with during her last visit. The game of "keep away" lasted around 15 minutes before Carly grew tired and laid down under a bench the customers used to try on shoes.

"Well I guess that is my cue. Hey, you two...I'm out of here." Jim picked up a few items off the floor, straightened a display and walked towards the front door.

"See you tomorrow Kyle, Candy, I hear you have a 20-miler coming up, remember your pacing. I assume your "coach" has prepared you well enough." Jim gave Kyle his version of the stink eye. "Candy, really you'll do well, stop by anytime...Carly dog, I want my socks back."

Carly lifted her head off the floor with one ear standing straight up the other laid flopped over. The half-asleep schnauzer cocked her head and watched as Jim disappeared out of sight. As he left the store Carly reached forward and grabbed a loose sock that was lying next to her paw. With her front teeth, she pulled the light blue sock with pink hearts close and then laid her head back on the floor falling back to sleep.

The two were alone inside the empty store. Candy pulled up an old rustic bar stool. The stool was a piece of furniture that had been passed down to each owner of the building. Completely out of place somehow this piece of old world craftsmanship survived the years. The hard maple grain patterns, the scars from years of rough handling all added to its character. Kyle often wondered what stories this old stool would tell if it could talk. Candy positioned the old stool closer to the counter near where Kyle was standing.

The shop was quiet and still when she looked into his eyes and spoke three simple yet powerful words. "I love you."

Kyle stopped and smiled.

"Okay wait…that is the first time you have said that. You love me?"

"Yea I do." She paused and reached out for his hand. "You got a problem with that?"

The moment was broken when the door to the store opened and the world intruded on their romantic escape. Candy hung out as a handful of customers came and left throughout the day. Each time she would take Carly into the backroom as not to cause a scene. While Kyle helped one of the high school's cross-country runners find the perfect training shoe Candy noticed something many failed to see. Not lost on her was the gleam in Kyle's eyes and the excitement in his voice as he talked with his customers about running.

She enjoyed hearing about his running adventures, the stories about how he started running and about the day when he figured out that he had some talent. She especially enjoyed listening to him speak about his dreams. Today she saw in him that running wasn't something he simply did. It wasn't a cloak that he put on to get in some form of physical activity or to burn a few calories. Running was an identity. Kyle was a runner.

After the paying customers exited, the shop was quiet once again. Carly was sound asleep among a basket of demo shoes. Beyond Candy's imagination, her furry faced friend was comfortable enough laying among a few pairs of shoes to fall asleep. After glancing back at her sleeping beauty Candy could only shake her head as she made her way to the front of the store while Carly snoozed in the background.

"Kyle, tell me more about your running. I've heard the cliff notes version, unpack the unabridged version. I want to know why you have such joy in your eyes when you work here, when you talk about running and when you're surrounded by other runners. Why do you love it so?"

"Oh, this will be a long story to tell."

"That's okay the store is empty." Candy replied pulling up the old rugged stool once again.

"To me running is about being free. I've told you about my Mom and how my Dad viewed that whole "situation" as he likes to refer to it. Well I wanted to run away from home so badly but knew I had no way to support myself so I just ran. I couldn't run away, so I ran, I ran into the woods, I ran down the street and I ran back home. I ran to escape the moment, even though I really ran nowhere in the end."

"I had no idea what I was doing or that running could even be a talent. I simply went outside and ran. Anytime I felt overwhelmed I would run. I ran anywhere, everywhere and I ran to no place in particular. I simply ran to be someplace away from the mess that was my life. Then one day, while in the woods I noticed it was fun running over rocks, roots and jumping over fallen trees. It was fun to run fast. At that time running was simply about getting away."

"I get that." Candy commented as she listened intently.

"I guess it was in middle school or maybe my first year of high school that I figured out I had some talent. I posted the best mile time in my gym class. Later it seemed like I could run faster than even the upper-classmen. There were a few guys who could run as fast as I could, but they did have the endurance. They could not keep up the pace for as long as I could. There was this one guy, Mike Goodwin, he was faster than I was for sure. Although anything longer than a half mile and I would reel him in. In the mile distance, 1600-meters, it was a toss-up. He would beat me most of the time but in cross country, any distance race longer than 5000-meters, 3.1 miles, I'd smoke him."

Candy noticed the fire in his eye as he talked about competitive running. She hung on every word.

Kyle continued. "In high school, I broke all the school and state records above the mile distance. I found my niche as they say yet even with all of that, my dad never came to a track or cross-country meet. He also never told me I did good or that he was proud of me. In a way, it's funny. I guess."

Candy spoke up "kind of sad Kyle, if you ask me."

"After high school, I tried to get on with a community college program but my grades were lacking and the fact that I had little ability to pay my tuition turned off most schools. Jim offered to pay for my schooling but I could not let him do that. He was already giving me a place to stay and all."

"After failing to get into a program, I ran local races and worked my way up to the marathon distance. I won a few small-town marathons, taking home some prize money and making a little bit of a name for myself...on a local level. Jim told me he thought I had the talent to attempt to qualify for the Olympic team."

"What?" Candy broke into the conversation.

"Kind of shocking. Right. I was shocked too. That is how I landed back here, in Berkley Springs." Before that I spent 6 months in California. I saved up enough money to move out there to train with some of the pros. I thought I could run with the big dogs. Not 100% at first but as we trained I closed the gap and before the qualifier I felt right at home running in the front of the pack."

Candy sat motionless, her eyes fixated on Kyle, she was hanging on every word. "WOW...really Kyle I had no idea. Jim mentioned the Olympics and that you had unique talent but it never registered with me."

"Well it's no big deal. I came up short. I'm not comparing it to what you went through. Please don't take this the wrong way. This is just running. You dealt with life and death. When I came up short, my life and my self-confidence was shattered. I put so much into my training. I sold out to the dream. I believed that this was the one thing that would add value to my life. I believed somehow my father would be proud and maybe, just maybe this would bring us closer together. When I failed to make the team, it was like I was losing control of my life. The one thing that gave me a sense of value was gone."

"Three days after the qualifier in Houston." Kyle paused to catch his breath and to gain some composure over his feelings. "Three days after finishing 10th, I finally heard from my father. He called me. First time in maybe two years, that he called me. Ever since I left home, I had been the one trying to keep us connected. I would call, I would visit and it just got to be too hard. I gave up. This is the first time he reached out to me and do you know what he had to say?"

Candy, caught off guard was puzzled with the question. "That he was proud of your effort." Inside she knew that most likely that wasn't the right answer.

"No, I wish." Kyle snorted back. He paused. "I'm sorry to snap at you like that, this gets to me."

"No harm, I understand."

"I think that's why we are perfect for each other...we are both wounded and have lived with our wounds. No, he told me he wasn't surprised I came up short and that I wasted my money, my time and my efforts."

Kyle looked away during a long pause in the conversation. His gaze appeared lost, his eyes fixed on a random spot on the ground. “My Dad, then hung up the phone.” There was a small shake of his head. “I haven’t heard from him since.” Kyle stopped talking as he continued to look down at the ground his head more slumped into his shoulders.

20-Miles

Chapter 16

As a mixture of asphalt and chipped rock passed beneath their feet the first signs of a new day broke over the horizon. The orange hue of a new day began to stir the countryside and all of the trappings of life came into motion. Two lone runners preceded the dawn of a new day. This pair had been active for nearly three hours. Side by side their collective efforts primed to complete their 19th mile. For Kyle, a staple of his training program the 20-mile long run was familiar ground. Candy was entering unchartered and very unfamiliar territory. Her lungs were on fire.

The repetitive cadence of their footfall on the loose rocks along the edge of the road combined to make up a soothing tune. To an outsider it may have been lost in translation. The long-distance runner found security and peace in the recurring drum beat of rubber soles falling on a compacted surface. To those that endured the solitude of distance running it is either torture or magical.

Never in a 100-lifetimes would she have imagined herself a long-distance runner. Meeting Kyle had changed much in her life and here she was pounding out the longest run of her lifetime.

"This was a good idea a few weeks ago, but now it sucks Kyle. This sucks!" Her labored voice snorted out between tired breaths.

"Oh, come now, you're doing great. The demanding part of the run is done. The 19-miles behind you, that was the price of admission. You can't come to the 20-mile dance party without paying the price to get in the door. The miles you put in upfront earns you the reward at the end. You're reaping the benefits of all the other miles you've worked your way through." Kyle tried hard to take her mind off the mile that was still out in front of her. "You remember how we got here right? You said you wanted this…now let's push it home."

Those words transported Candy's mind back to the conversation that started it all.

- - -

Kyle was wrestling with his decision to go back to the world of competitive racing. Deep into a new and budding relationship he viewed life differently. Where before he had no conflicting demands on his time now he found it hard to put in the miles that his desired performance level required. He found it increasingly difficult to pull himself away from spending every available moment with Candy.

She was an excellent sounding board as he considered where his running career was going. Candy understood the demands, the time, the travel and the obligations. She also wanted to spend as much time with him as she could. She knew there had to be a balance. Candy respected and valued his athletic gift. She believed that to waste such talent, to not go after something you may have been born to do…would be the loss of an ability few in the world were given.

At some point during their many conversations about life, about their dreams and his running Candy said something she never imagined saying. Simple words on their own. Complex when linked together. Un-expectedly almost without warning the words crossed her lips and put herself in a position that challenged everything she ever understood about herself.

"Kyle, I get that it's a big commitment, it surely is a lot of work. I understand you may not have it in you and if you don't want to run competitively anymore I understand and support you. But if it's because you don't want to be away from me, if I'm the one stopping you or distracting you." She paused, collected her thoughts and took a deep breath as her mind reflected. "Then Kyle I'll run with you. You know I'm already a pretty good hiker and in better than average shape. How much harder can it be to run a few miles?"

As soon as that statement left her lips, Candy knew she went too far.

"You're willing to run with me?" Kyle said with a hint of laughter.

"Really thank you Candy, that is sweet but I thought you said you couldn't see yourself running long distances. You liked life at a slower pace. An easy and comfortable distance."

Candy thought for a moment about back tracking and taking the easy way out. She had the words ready, she knew just the right way to recant her offer, but again even to her surprise, something else got communicated.

"No really Kyle, I might not be as fast but I really want to run with you. I mean the stories you tell about how running makes you feel. About the drama within the race. I want to be part of that." She paused. "I want to be a part of that with you."

- - -

The conversation seemed so long ago as she willed herself to continue past the 19-mile mark.

Kyle had positioned himself just in front with Candy running off his left hip. In this vantage point, he could maintain a pace that challenged her, but also protect her from the slight headwind they had battled for much of the day. It was also in this lead spot that Kyle could turn his head slightly to provide some words of encouragement to keep her fighting for the endurance prize.

"You got this Candy…you said you wanted to run with me. You said you wanted to know what life was like during the hard miles. Well you got it…half a mile to go and you can claim your prize. You'll be ready to run a marathon. The TWENTY-mile-long run will be done." Kyle paused as he stressed the importance of the distance. "This milestone will be a thing of the past."

Quickly Candy cut him off. "Run a marathon…SIX." She took a rapid yet shallow breath. Six. Point. Two. More miles…are you crazy? When I'm done here I'm getting a bag of Oreos cookies and a gallon of milk. I plan to OD on the white creamy filling. Run a marathon…ha! I love you but you DUDE are crazy?"

He wasn't sure what to say or how to reply to that. Kyle simply kept up the pace. He could tell Candy's legs were growing heavier with each stride. He knew just what she was going through. Although it had been years since his first 20-miler, Kyle remembered it well. He remembered how in seemingly one stride his legs went from feeling strong, powerful and light to feeling like dying branches on a tree. He remembered having to use every ounce of will power to keep up his leg turn over, to lift, propel and cycle through another series of footfalls. He remembered how his lungs burned, how they seared like hot lava with each breath.

Kyle knew in these closing moments Candy was fighting her own personal battle with the endurance demons. He knew she was deciding for herself if this was what she really wanted. She would figure out if she was willing to pay the gate keeper for entrance into the society of endurance athletes. Kyle knew he could only help her so much. Candy had to be willing to pay the price herself.

He glanced down at his GPS watch. The numbers on the face sparked both excitement and fear. 2:35:05 flashed before his eyes. For a world class marathoner, this elapsed time for a 20-mile run would not hold up. Kyle knew they were a little ahead of their target of just under 3-hours. He hoped his pacing had not made it too hard on Candy.

"Under half a mile Candy."

Those words seemed to bring Candy back from the depths of the pain-cave. Her eyes lifted off the road and broke her constant stare at the road surface passing below her feet. A tilted smile seamed to appear out of nowhere. Candy took one deep breath. On the next exhale, she pushed the throttle down. Knowing she was close to home she was now more determined to get this endurance stage show over with. With every ounce of remaining determination, strength and fight Candy pushed harder and faster for the imaginary finish line that would appear when a flashing 2 0 appeared on the small digital screen of her GPS watch.

Kyle was caught a bit off guard. For a second or maybe two Candy pulled even with and may have moved ahead of him by half a stride before he knew she was running hard to close out her day. The move instilled a great amount of pride in him, he saw someone fighting for their goals. He saw the girl he loved embrace his chosen sport and he saw a soul repairing parts of itself to become whole once again. Kyle knew how long-distance running had helped him rebuild his self-worth, his self-confidence and his place in the world. He knew this day could do more than log a first 20-miler in her training plan. Today's efforts could help Candy rebuild her spirit as well.

Candy ran hard all the way to her 20-mile finish line. Kyle kept his eyes focused on the GPS display…counting down the distance. "19.80…85…90." His voice began to crack. "99." Emotions took over. "Done!" It was all he could do to keep it together himself. At the end of a marathon, a long run, a new distance PR or at the end of a race the satisfaction of accomplishing a goal can bring on very raw emotions. Maybe because of the lack of emotions in his upbringing, Kyle found he was greatly affected by witnessing others accomplish their goals.

His eyes were filled with tears and his breathing became short and broken. Between a broad smile and broken breaths, he called out. “Twenty miles. Candy, you just ran 20-miles." Kyle took in some deep breaths of his own trying to settle down his reaction to the way she finished. He called out the time.

"2-hours and 38 minutes.”

The pair came to a gliding halt along the side of the road. Kyle reached out for her. He knew they should keep moving to keep her legs from locking up, from cramps settling in, but he also couldn’t control himself.

Kyle spun around and lifted Candy off her legs and swung her around in a small semi-circle. “You did it, girl. You did it with some zip at the end…holy cow you ran that faster than we figured you could. Dang girl I’m so proud of you.”

Candy closed her eyes. She let her whole body collapse on to him as she went limp in Kyle’s arms. Her legs screamed out in pain once they stopped moving. Everything in her body hurt. She began to cry when Kyle expressed how proud he was. It had been a long time since someone had told her that they were proud of her.

Candy was proud of herself.

“Kyle.” Candy spoke up.

“Yes…what?”

“You’re carrying me home.”

New Challenges

Chapter 17

Standing at the doorway to her apartment he could feel the extra burden of Candy's weight bearing down on him. He knew she was tired, worn out and ready to get off of her feet. The extra pressure of supporting her felt good to his touch and to his soul. It felt purposeful to have someone leaning on him, it felt good to have her body pressing on his. It was thrilling to be with her after she had reached a personal goal. To run 20-miles was no simple task no matter your fitness level. He knew well enough how hard it was to push yourself in the final stages of a long run.

Like it was yesterday, he remembered that after just a few short months of training Candy told him, she felt like she was up to the task. In hindsight, he remembered how surprised he was when she told him she wanted to join along on his slower long runs. He was taken back at how fast she took to the sport. Candy surprised even herself that within the first few months of running with him she decided that she wanted to run long distances and that she felt ready to attempt the signature training run. The backbone of marathon training, the long training run could make or break most athletes.

Now holding her in his arms he was overwhelmed with pride at the completion of her run. Kyle looked into her eyes and told her how proud he was of her. He confided that initially he was shocked when she told him that she wanted to challenge herself in such a fashion. Candy worked hard transitioning herself from being an active physically fit hiker to an endurance athlete. It surprised Kyle that although she had battled through the conclusion of her run, she managed to get in the miles with a very respectable time.

Candy stood opposite him, his arms wrapped around the small of her waist. She now fully understood what running meant to the man she had lost herself to. During those hard-fought final miles, she had been exposed to the extreme conflict that arises when you ask your body to do something foreign to its normal state. Candy found that she had been introduced to the battle between desire, determination and personal weakness. With this new perspective, she stood resting in his arms feeling like her life was at a point of transformation.

She became aware of how running could be more than a sport, running could very well be a microcosm of life. Candy now could identify with how running extreme distances could strip a person bare. In those last miles, she had come to understand how the struggle to continue could expose parts of the human makeup that most kept hidden away. She related how such a simple act of forward motion could uncover weaknesses and limits within your character that no one else saw. In extreme struggles, parts of you that you kept covered up could become visible. Those final miles bared your weakness, your insecurities and your fears. While you struggled to move forward, the world was a witness to your attempts at success or the carnage of failure.

Candy now understood how running had set Kyle free of his past. She could now comprehend how reaching the bottom and the continual struggle to climb back to the top, the force to keep moving, the drive to let no force either internal or external stop your advancement could propel you to a new and improved version of yourself. Through his struggles, Kyle came to learn and believe that nothing would define his vision of success, his sense of value or set him on a course of failure. In front of her stood a young man that through his own battles found a way to transform his life story by pushing himself to run farther, faster and beyond the boundaries others had imposed on him. She now understood how much alike they both were.

"Candy, get on inside and wash up. Rest up and get a healthy meal in you to begin the recovery process." Kyle said as he kissed her on the cheek. "Get off your feet, have Carly take care of you." With those words, he could hear Carly wrestling behind the door.

"I'm going to clean up and get to my shift in the store. I'll call later to check on you, to see how you're doing, okay?"

Candy drew him in tight, "you sure you have to go?"

"Yea, I need to plus...you kind of...stink." He laughed. "No really get some rest. Oh, and don't be surprised if some chaffing shows up in the shower."

He kissed her one last time, turned and walked down the hallway leading from her apartment.

Candy stood in the doorway and watched as he moved away.

"He's not even limping, I'm about to die and he shows no signs of wear or tear. I don't think I can make it inside my doorway." Candy thought to herself as she turned and made her way inside. Once provided a clear shot, Carly jumped up to greet Candy resting her paws on Candy's mid thighs. "Oh doggie...that hurts girl, I love you but you have got to get down." Candy patted Carly on the head and headed to her room and a hot shower.

Before stepping into the shower, she stopped and looked in the mirror. Something caught her eye. Exposed to this new world of physical pain, mental fortitude and personal determination transfixed on pushing beyond your physical limits, Candy believed the self-confidence she gained could do the same for her continued recovery. In the mirror in her bathroom Candy saw a new person. The hot water touched Candy's skin, she screamed out and Carly came running. Instantly she understood Kyle's caution about chaffed skin.

Kyle made his way to his apartment for a quick bite to eat, a shower and some fresh clothes. After a short recovery of his own he was on tap for the closing shift at the store. Scanning his cell phone while tossing a left-over bowl of soup into the microwave Kyle noticed a new voice mail on his phone. Punching in his code, 26.2run, he noted Jim had left a message that he had something to share with him when he got back from his run. It wasn't normal for Jim to call, that had Kyle wondering what was going on, what news would Jim have to share.

As the door to the store swung open, Jim was on the phone. He waved as Kyle made his way in and proceeded to the backroom before settling in for his shift. Shortly afterward, with Jim still on the phone Kyle began restocking the shoe display wall with boxes of newly arrived inventory. As he placed the last box high on an overhead shelf, he noted that Jim hung up his cell phone and was making his way over to him.

The conversation started off innocently enough with a friendly greeting, some ribbing in typical former high school coach fashion with questions about how Candy handled her long run. Since Candy and Kyle had figured out that they were more than just friends, she had become an unofficial employee/sponsored runner of the store. She certainly became one employee's favorite customer. Jim had a million questions about the run, he wanted all the details and peppered Kyle with his inquiry.

“Kyle, wait a minute I got sidetracked talking about the 20-miler. I have some.” He paused for effect. “I have some news for you. Have you decided what your fall plans are yet? Are you racing anywhere? Have you applied for New York City or any of the big races to get your legs under you for a run at Boston? I assume you wanted to make a run at Boston next year?”

Kyle paused and stared out the front window of the store. "Jim I'm not really sure what I'm doing. I still feel like I want to try for the Team. You know I still feel like I can make the Olympic team but I'm not ready to go back into the grind. I have Candy now and I enjoy my time with her."

Jim cut him off in half sentence. "Are you up to try something new, different, maybe not so time focused? Something a little out of your comfort zone to light the fire?"

"What are you talking about Jim?"

"Kyle I'm friends with the race director of the oldest ultra-marathon in the country, the JFK 50. The committee has had a tough time filling the race with fast runners this year. They asked if I knew anyone who would be interested in running."

Jim coughed to clear his throat and took a long drink of coffee.

"I told him about you. Of course, the Race Director followed the trials and knew where you placed. I explained that you were taking some time off from competitive racing but that you were in great shape. He asked if you would be interested in running the race."

"JFK 50…as in 50-miles Jim?"

"Yes, it is a 50-mile race. I'm not assuming you would race it…you know to win. I figured it would be good to run something different for the experience. To find out if there are other avenues to explore in running. The ultra-marathon community is growing. There are a lot of good runners coming up in the ranks. It could be a place to make a name for yourself or at least gain some experience and find out if that type of racing is for you. The race committee is providing a free entry and hotel accommodations for the weekend. Could be fun. What do you think?"

Kyle walked around the store, he stopped to put some odds and ends back to their rightful places.

"50-miles." He commented while nervously restocking the bin of sports geared snack food.

"Do you think I could handle the extra miles, Jim?"

"You would have to run slower, pace yourself more…learn how to run trails but I don't see why not. You would have to realize you're most likely not going to win this race or even place very high but the experience would be worth it."

"You don't think I could win? Jim really, no confidence?"

"Kyle, I wouldn't put anything past you. I believe in you. I know one day you will be standing on the top podium if not of the Olympics for sure you'll be standing on the top rung of one of the world marathon majors. You have the talent. You have the drive…if you have the will, I believe you can do anything."

"I have a little over 3 months to go from top 10 marathoner to ultra-marathon runner. What could go wrong?"

Kyle milled around the store the rest of the afternoon considering the new venue provided by Jim and his connections with the JFK race. Kyle knew very little about trail running and less about the ultra-marathon community. He had crossed paths with a few marathoners who also ran ultra-distances but Kyle had never given it much thought. His running life was focused on the marathon and on qualifying for a place on the Olympic team. With that dream on hold for a few years, it was exciting to know there were other doors opening.

In between customers, Kyle pulled up some information about the race on his phone. The amount of information available was daunting, in as much as the same way he felt about the distance. Kyle settled in on the official website and found an article written by a gentleman named Mike Spinnler

"The JFK 50 Mile was first held in the spring of 1963. It was one of numerous such 50-mile events held around the country as part

of President John F. Kennedy's push to bring the country back to physical fitness.

When Kennedy was assassinated in November of 1963, most of these events were never held again. The one in Washington County, MD changed its name from the JFK 50 Mile Challenge to the JFK 50 Mile Memorial in 1964. The JFK 50 in Washington County, MD is the only original JFK 50 Mile Challenge event to be held every year.

Although open to the public, the JFK 50 Mile is in spirit a military race. It always has been and always will be. In 1963, the initial inspiration behind the event came from then President John F. Kennedy challenging his military officers to meet the requirements that Teddy Roosevelt had set for his own military officers at the dawn of the 20th Century. That Roosevelt requirement was for all military officers to be able to cover 50 miles on foot in 20 hours to maintain their commissions. When word got out about the "Kennedy Challenge", non-commissioned military personnel also wanted to take the test themselves as did certain robust members of the civilian population."

The more Kyle read up on the race, it's history and the unique course, 15-miles of running and climbing on the Application Trail, a little over 26-miles on a relatively flat canal towpath followed by 8-miles of rolling country roads. The more he learned about the race, the more eager he grew to toss his name into the entry list and give President Kennedy's 50-mile challenge a go himself.

"Jim," Kyle spoke up while Jim tended to a customer.

"I'll give it a try. There is so much about the race that appeals to me. Outside of the distance, it wouldn't even be a question on if I would want an opportunity to run in such a prestigious event. The JFK sounds like the Boston Marathon of the ultra-running world. I would be crazy to pass up an opportunity like this."

Jim looked up from his customer and smiled. "I kind of figured you would be up to something new, some new type of distance, new stage to test yourself. I told them you were a go. Hope you're not upset with me." Jim laughed silently to himself.

"Not at all, thank you for the vote of confidence, really, I mean it, thank you, Jim. You'll have to help me with a few training runs and some advice on race strategies. I have no idea how to run this type of race. We are in this together, Jim."

"Sure thing buddy, you know you can count on me."

"I know." Kyle replied. "You have always been there for me. Thank you." He paused. His facial expression changed and the mood grew somber as a heavy blanket seemed to fall over the shop.

"I need to go see my father. I haven't spoken to him since the qualifier." He paused again. "Do you need me next weekend?"

"No Kyle, go handle what you need to first, you know that is what's really important."

"Jim, really…Thank you."

Jim knew Kyle was not thanking him for the race entry, for the time off or the coaching service offered him. Jim heard the tone of Kyle's voice. He read between the lines and knew the hidden meaning. Jim knew from what depths of gratitude that simple Thank you had grown.

A Phone Call Back in Time

Chapter 18

A solemn mood hung heavy in the air. Kyle nervously entered the numbers on the touchscreen of his latest iPhone. Within seconds it made a connection with a landline 165-miles to the north-west. With his cellphone pressed against his ear, he wished it would have taken longer. The extra time may have given him more time to prepare. He needed more time to fully organize his thoughts to have a meaningful conversation with someone he barely knew. The phone stopped ringing. He took a deep breath.

"Ah…" His voice trembled as he paused to bide himself even a fraction of a second. "Hello. Dad, are you there…?" The line was silent. "Dad, it's Kyle, I wanted to see how you are doing. It's been so long, since we, you know since we last talked. The line stayed silent. Can you hear me, Dad?"

The connection between the two was good. Technology could not be blamed for the long pause or the unspoken word. Kyle heard his father breathing on the other end of the call.

"Dad, I just wanted...to talk… To maybe come see you? Soon?"

Kyle stopped talking. The silence of the connection translated volumes in unspoken words. Finally, his father's voice cut through the void.

"What would we talk about Kyle. What do we have to discuss?" His father scoffed.

The conversation felt uncomfortable, forced and unnatural. An extended olive branch was met with dialogue lacking any warmth or acceptance. Two worlds that should have come together easily spun in counterrotating directions. Moving along different paths, the pair moved along unfamiliar and opposing realities. Lives that should have spun together, that should have rotated along the same axis seemed to always be in direct opposition to each other.

In most cases no harm should have come from the result of two forces not being in perfect alignment. Much of the world goes about its daily routine without interacting. But for a father and son, misalignment in their relationship left one half of the pairing displaced and out of rhythm with the natural innerworkings of life.

Kyle never fully accepted not being a part of his father's life. He understood the situation that resulted in his father's remoteness. He understood the withdrawn life his father had chosen to live, but he never fully accepted it. Kyle always wanted to work out their differences. He believed by some miracle that time would heal, that time would transform his father's heart. Kyle always wanted to be a part of his father's life. He, unfortunately, never seemed able to make a connection. This misalignment hurt and haunted him.

On the surface Kyle understood all the issues that came between the two. He lived with the pain of being the child without a mother. He understood that when he was born his father lost everything he valued in the world. Kyle understood the feelings of emptiness that came with not being able to be with the one you loved. He appreciated the loneliness his father must have lived with. Kyle lived with the same burden but from a different view point. The young man respected the extra burden placed on an already strained man. Kyle also knew he was this man's son and could never fully accept that his father, his own flesh and blood, did not want more to do with him.

Kyle had hope for a better reception. If anything, the lifelong trail of rejection continued.

A harsh tone came across the line. "I guess we could talk about the Olympics...guess you won't be going there. What a waste of money and time."

The impact of those words burned. Like an unrelenting flow of molten lava pushing to the sea those words dissolved everything in their path. The scorn of like worded sentences uttered at him his entire life left a path of burnt ruins littered in Kyles soul.

"I tried Dad, I really tried hard. I thought you might be proud that I could get even that far. 10th overall in the UNITED STATES. Dad." A fit of anger began to boil to the top. Kyle tried to hold it all together. "But Dad, I didn't call to get into it with you about my running. I really wanted to see how you're doing, maybe I could come to visit?"

"I'm fine." A course voice snapped back. "Don't you worry about me...Boy. I'm able to take care of myself. I'm fine, alone as always and able to take care of number one."

"But Dad," Kyle attempted to interrupt.

"I'm all I have. I'll be okay. Don't worry yourself about me. Keep on running." There was a pause. "From whatever it is you are running from."

"Dad, I do worry. I have always worried about you. I get it...life has been hard. But I want to try and be part of your life, our life. Dad...we are all WE have..." Kyle stopped and collected his thoughts. "I'm not running from anything or anyone...I've been running to you, after you, my whole life."

No, you're wrong Kyle. All I had, all I loved has been gone, since..." His father stopped talking but Kyle knew the all too familiar ending to that sentence. He had heard it so many times before. It may have been said in different ways, but it always came back to the fact that the day he was born was the day that his father's wife was taken away from him.

"Dad, I'm off next weekend." He rubbed his forehead with his right hand trying to release some of the stress building up inside. Kyle could feel a headache coming on. After he collected his breath the conversation continued. "Saturday, Dad can I come to visit. Can I come see you? I would like you to meet someone. Can I come?"

The line drew quiet. There was a long pause. Then he heard a faint sound just barely able to be picked up by the microphone in the old-style handset on the wall mounted phone. It was an all too familiar sound to Kyle. He knew instantly the sound of a beer bottle being opened and the sound of his father taking a drink.

Kyle looked at his watch and noted the time. He could almost smell the stale aroma of beer over the phone line. Kyle grew up with that ever-present odor in the air. If his house did not smell like cigarettes and body odor, it smelt like stale beer. Beer spilled on the floor, on his clothes or the smell of an all-night drunk on his father's skin. Kyle knew the smell all too well and he hated it.

"Dad, I'm coming up to visit next weekend, Saturday morning…let's go out to eat. Breakfast, we can spend some time catching up. Okay?"

Kyle once again was trying to garner his father's attention. Again, desperate to gain his father's approval, hungry to have any interaction with the man he loved so dearly.

"Please Dad, breakfast, just a few hours. I want you to meet someone…please. She is important to me. You are important to me."

Kyle wasn't sure what to expect.

"Sure, Nine O'clock at the truck stop on the turnpike exit. You know the one."

"Yea I know the place...the same place we would go every year for Christmas dinner. I kind of miss it. Thank you."

"Nine." The connection went quiet.

He placed his iPhone down on the counter and attempted to release the frustration with a deep cleansing breath. It did not work, from the moment the line went silent the room seemed to close in on him.

The apartment grew dark and cold. Kyle sat back in a chair and closed his eyes. At 24 years of age, in a town where he had built a life of his own, the short phone call transported him back in time. In his apartment, instantly he felt like a 12-year-old boy. He regressed to the viewpoint of a little boy who couldn't understand why his father disliked him so much. On the surface, he understood the death of his mother surely sent his father's life unraveling. He also was his father's son…and he only wanted to be loved by him.

Behind his closed eyes all Kyle could hear was the repetitive sounds of a clock hung on the wall. His apartment was normally a bright and cheerful place. Two large windows faced the western sky filling the room with a warm setting sun. Kyle kept the place tidy and well decorated with posters of western landscape and framed prints from some of the races he had participated in. In one corner, he had arranged a wall of medals and awards. Resting next to a few bronze trophies was a picture of his mother. Kyle placed it there when he returned from Mammoth Lakes. This photo in a simple brass frame surround by little hearts went with him everywhere he went.

He could feel darkness surround him. He could sense the overwhelming void overtake his thoughts. Why was he rejected by the only parent he had? Kyle could feel a dark blanket of confusion, hurt, anger and pity attempt to pull him into a destructive spiral. This downward struggle was common for Kyle as he grew up. He battled this depressive state often.

Depression, anger and rejection were commons words in Kyle's vocabulary growing up.

Kyle always held onto the belief that things could change. Hope, acceptance, warmth and love were words that Kyle held close, forever hopeful that they might become a part of his life. He believed people could change, he had to believe that and he always believed his father would change.

A Difficult Encounter

Chapter 19

The work week progressed like the last days of school before summer break, like the day before Christmas or the last two-tenths of a mile of the marathon. The weight of anticipation hung over him like a heavy blanket of anticipation. His mind was cluttered with a nervous mixture of worry and deep-seated concern. At times, the hope of finally connecting with his father provided promise, at other times the weight of past rejection caused him to regret making the call in the first place. As the meeting with his father drew closer, the burden of the unknown weighed on him heavy like chains draped over his shoulders. The only time Kyle wasn't worried about how the visit would go was when he was helping customers, while out on a run or when he was spending time with Candy.

His time with Candy over the last few weeks had been some of the best moments of his life. The pair spent nearly all their free time together. The two were so frequently together that the town folks began to take notice. Lunch at local diners, walking with Carly dog or engaged in deep conversations while sitting on a park bench became routine. The young couple were nearly inseparable occasionally escaping the small-town scene for long weekends venturing into the surrounding mountains on extended camping trips.

The sun was high in the cloudless sky with a slight breeze in the air. It was a perfect day to have lunch in the park. While sitting on a park bench eating pizza, drinking soda and watching Carly sniff out lizards along an old moss-covered brick wall, Kyle tried to further describe his complicated and damaged relationship with his father. He explained that although the pair had spent nearly 18 years together, it was never a nurturing relationship. With emotion stained words he painted a picture of how it felt to grow up feeling like an obligation, a duty and perhaps a sentence his father had to serve.

He tried to communicate how growing up without his mother had affected him, as a child, a student and as a young man trying to find himself. Kyle exposed the darker side of the story, the complete and unabridged tale. Yet tangled within the webs of rejection and resentment he spun a defense for his father's actions. He tried to explain what life must have been like for his dad. The best he could he tried to paint a picture of love, conflict and separation in his father's life. Kyle attempted to relieve some of the blame from his dad's shoulders. He wanted her to understand the other side of the story. Perhaps as a result of conditioning or unresolved guilt his defense for his father went so far as to try and convince Candy it was his fault.

"Kyle stop…" Candy interrupted him.

"I'm sorry all this happened within your family. I'm sorry you never got to know or experience your mother's love." Her voice tailed off growing quiet and emotional. "Honey, I'm so very sorry that her death is what may have caused all of this strife. No one is to blame for that. Not you and not your father. It was a terrible happening, one that may never be explained. Why? The why we may never understand." Candy took a deep breath.

"I'm an outsider here, but I believe I can understand both sides. First off, he…no one should have ever treated you like a burden. He was the adult. Sure, I get that it may have been hard for him, your dad, but he needed to be there for you. We can't change that and I admire that you're still willing and wanting to reconnect. I'm not sure I would be so willing to do the same thing if the roles were reversed."

Candy reached out and hugged Kyle, continuing to speak as she drew him in nearer.

"Kyle I'll do whatever I can to help you, support you and to be here for you. It would be easy for me to take sides but if by some chance you are able to reconnect I promise I won't judge or look down on your father. I promise I'll give him the benefit of a doubt. He is your father and I love you. I'll help in any way I can, I'll listen, support or I'll just remain quiet. I won't turn my back on either of you. Although I won't let you feel like it was your fault. That just isn't true."

Kyle's eyes were to the point of releasing a tear down his cheek. "Thank you, Candy. I feel tomorrow may just be different."

In an instant, the tension in the air was broken. Unfazed by the emotional conversation that surrounded her, Carly's keen eye sight spotted a lizard that had scurried under the bench. Determined to catch the slippery creature she dove after it in hot pursuit Kyle could only watch and laugh as the pizza box and one slice of pepperoni pizza went flying.

To make the more than two-hour drive to Jeanette, Pennsylvania, Kyle wanted to get an early start. From experience and his disciplined upbringing, he knew showing up late would only compound matters. He pulled his Jeep into the near vacant parking lot next to Candy's apartment. The first glimpse of sunshine began to break over the horizon as he sat and gazed out of the windshield. In that moment, he wondered if those amber hues of light could be the foreshadowing promise of a new day, a new beginning, maybe the start of an improved relationship with his father. Nothing would make him happier than if at the end of this day he had his father more engaged in his life. It may have been a long shot but somehow in this opportunity he felt like he knew the right words to say. This time his father would see that he needed his son. This encounter would be the time that softened the hardness in his father's heart. Kyle believed that maybe this was the moment in which it would all work out. First, he had to get to the sleepy little town in Westmoreland county.

Kyle sent a short text, "Good morning Sunshine, I'm here."

A reply quickly returned. "Be right down." A smiley face emoji with pink puckered lips was attached and caused Kyle to laugh out loud to himself. This broke Kyle's thoughts, which for the better part of the night had been squarely focused on seeing his father. When her name popped up on his phone it broke him away from the rising pressure of the day. His thoughts turned to a comfortable place, a place and a setting in which he could envision his future. A future that included Candy full time.

Until crossing her path he had never had a relationship with such depth. Kyle knew he loved her and that she was the one for him. She impacted parts of his life that were unknown to even him. Growing up, Kyle had a tough time looking past the moment and the turmoil he found himself caught up in. He had a tough time thinking about the future. His dreams, plans and attention were focused on surviving the day and avoiding conflict with his father. Kyle's daily routines were centered on simply being told that he was the reason for everything that went wrong in his father's life.

Candy seemingly opened the chapter to the rest of his life. With her he could dream. He could see a future and he could feel an emotional force within him that was capable of giving himself fully to another. Finally, a relationship was about more than turmoil, guilt, shame and avoidance. Candy was everything he had ever wanted and more than he could have ever imagined. In the present moment during the dawn of a new day, sitting in the solitude of his Jeep Kyle could finally see more.

Kyle snapped back into the present when he noticed a silhouette bouncing across the parking lot and move in his direction.

Recognizing the outline of her face he waved and watched as she walked across the empty lot. As the distance closed he could feel his heart race, a smile grace his face and his emotions over run wild with…hope. Candy carried a small travel bag in one hand and something oddly shaped in the other. Before he could exit the truck to greet her she had already approached the passenger's side door, opened it and slid across the seat.

"Good Morning, you." A vibrant smile beamed back at him.

"Morning, cutie, how are you? Are you sure you're ready for this? I'm hopeful this will be the time but I also know my father and this could get cold and depressing." Kyle countered her spirited morning greeting.

Candy continued to slide across the seat, nestled up against him while she kissed him on the check. "I figured we needed some traveling snacks. And yes, I'm ready for anything…I'm here. That's all you need Kyle. Everything is going to be okay. Carly is still sleeping, Jim is going to look after her so we are ready to roll. Oh, and I made brownies!"

This made Kyle smile. Candy's simple comment about sticking with him no matter what confirmed in Kyle's mind that she was the one.

The drive north-west was easy. The conversation was unbroken and flowed with ease as the two were pulled together by a deep emotional, spiritual and romantic attraction. Kyle navigated his way along the Turnpike without much thought or without the use of a map. His Jeep rolled into the parking lot of the greasy spoon diner before the gravity of the situation fully settled on his shoulders.

"Time flies when you have fun, enjoyable and relaxing conversations," Candy commented.

"You know it and now I wish I had a few more hours to get ready for this."

"Everything will be fine, have an open mind and a big smile. You know that I'm on your side no matter what."

"Yes, and thank you."

The two held hands as they walked through the parking lot dodging the random 18-wheeler and a few school tour buses. Without incident they made it into the restaurant. Once inside the doorway the all too familiar aroma of fried eggs, slightly burnt coffee and toast filled his senses. Instantly he was transported back to a Christmas Eve dinner with his father. The combo had plenty of meals there. He often thought of the staff as extended family members. After all, he saw them during most holidays. One meal in particular always stood out.

- - -

Kyle remember most meals at this restaurant being cold, lonely and depressing. One occasion was an anomaly. It was one of the very few childhood memories he wanted to cling to forever.

Sitting opposite of him at a board wooden farm house style table his father ordered his regular holiday meal, fried liver, mashed potatoes and yellow corn. Kyle never grew fond of liver and could not stand to look at the way his father mixed the corn and potatoes together let alone imagine trying to eat that concoction. He had a grilled cheese and crinkle cut French fries. This was his favorite meal, one he remained fond of even as an adult. Nothing out of the ordinary happened during dinner. Their dinner was served without much fanfare or conversation as was the norm. Kyle kept quiet, ate his dinner, making sure not to spill anything or make any "eating" noises while he chewed his food. His father told him many times he ate like an animal, so to avoid any scorn, the young boy worked very hard to be as quiet as possible.

Out of the blue, his father asked him how his day had gone.

Kyle was shocked, surprised and beyond wonder. Was this a test. Would he get in trouble if he tried to answer the question and made any unacceptable noise? The small boy wondered what was the proper reply. Should he tell his father that everything was okay, that he was fine, that school was a place he enjoyed going? Or should he tell his father the truth? That he was lonely, sad and hated going to school. Should he confide in his father that he felt lost, alone and heartbroken? How he hated going to school because nearly every day he was questioned and even on occasion bullied about not having a mom. Should he come clean and convey to his dad how depressed he felt that his own father wanted very little to do with him? Should he become even more vulnerable?

Kyle raised his head, stopped eating and swallowed the remaining bites of food he had in his mouth.

"Dad, I'm okay. Thank you for taking me out to eat. I enjoy being with you." In a timid voice, the young boy replied and asked.

How was your day, Dad?

Kyle's father broke from his meal, looked his son in the eye and smiled.

Years later Kyle recalled that that may have been the first time he remembered his father smiling. It was also the last time he felt a connection with his dad.

- - -

A voice from behind his back ended the internal replay of what may have been one of his favorite childhood memories.

"Kyle, did you get a table or are we going to eat here in the doorway?" His father snapped at the nearest waitress, "we will take a booth. This one right here is fine."

Kyle followed his father over to a booth near a row of windows across from the quick service bar. Candy held Kyle's hand following him closely. She could feel his grip tighten as they walked closer to the booth. As they arrived at the booth along the windows and before sitting down Kyle broke the natural flow of sitting down to introduce Candy to his father.

"Dad, this is Candy."

"Hello." Kyle's father reached out gently to shake Candy's hand. Quickly his attention was broken, now focused on a passing waitress. "Miss, coffee please."

The threesome sat down. Candy and Kyle on one side of the booth, his father sat centered on the other side.

"I think we sat in this same booth years ago. I wonder if the grilled cheese is still good as I remember." In an honest and awkward attempt, Kyle tried to make some small talk.

Candy laughed. His father did not look up from the menu and mumbled about how things haven't changed yet everything cost more.

"Dad, I wanted you to meet Candy. She means the world to me. We have been seeing each other for a few months now, we see each other nearly every day and we...we get along so well and have so much in common. At times its like we are the same person." Kyle took a deep breath. "I love her Dad."

Candy was a bit surprised with Kyle's opening line. Not the declaration that he loved her, she had been told many times in private, around the running store and among their friends. This time she was taken aback by the conviction in Kyle's' voice. It surprised her that he would lead off this reunion of sort with such an announcement. Candy held firmly to Kyle's hand.

To a passing waitress "Miss, coffee please," his father motioned.

"Dad, I wanted to see you. You know to maybe... You know maybe be a bigger part in each other's lives. So much time has been wasted and I'm sorry if it's my fault. I can't fix any of that but I do want to be part of your life."

"Time..." Kyle's father interrupted and then paused. "Funny thing about time, they say it heals old wounds but for some, it only makes them deeper." Taking a drink of the coffee that finally arrived at the table. "I'll have the liver, fried onions and mashed potatoes and corn." He told the waitress.

After Candy ordered a blueberry waffle and some coffee Kyle broke from tradition and ordered a plain three egg omelet with bacon, fried potatoes and white toast.

After their order was placed the prophecy about time continued. "Another thing about time you can't get it back. Like the time on the marathon clock, huh Kyle...if the guy in front of you runs 20 seconds faster...you can't get that time back. 20 seconds is that about what you needed to qualify?"

If the attack on his heartstrings wasn't enough the punch to his athlete ego took the wind out of his sails.

Candy could not believe the coldness of the exchange she was witnessing. Every fiber in her body wanted to slash out, she wanted to say something. She desired to come to Kyle's defense, but she knew very well that any reply would only add fuel to the fire. She only hoped Kyle could find the right words, the right tone to counter the harsh welcoming in a way that could build a bridge.

Kyle stared expressionless across the dinner. His face pale and solemn. Lost for words he turned his gaze out the window. His heart raced, his mind ran wild and his soul was ripped in two.

"Dad, we have got to let go. Of the past, we have got to move on. Dad, I love you... YOU are all I have, my family. We need each other, we can't, I CAN'T CHANGE anything about the past. Trust me if I could bring my mother back I would. I more than anyone on this planet wish she was here with us right now and with you. I would do anything to have her in our world. I would do anything…DAD"

Kyle remained strong, remained focus on moving forward but Candy could see the pain in his eyes. She wasn't sure how he held it all together. As emotional as his reply had been, she could tell the words were well rehearsed and well thought out.

"Dad. I'm truly sorry."

"Kyle, nothing you could do could ever bring her back. The world, some super natural force chose you and left me alone. For years I've been alone and today I remain alone. She was all I had. She made me happy."

I never made you happy, Dad. Not at all?"

"Kyle, I haven't been happy in years. I've adjusted to what the world gave me. I've accepted my role, I've accepted the fate and I've come to be comfortable living this way. I don't see it changing."

And as quickly as the encounter came together it ended.

"Let's go." Kyle looked over at her with his eyes nearly bursting with rage and tears. "Please Candy, let's go."

She did not need to hear his request a third time. Candy quickly slide her way across the vinyl covered bench onto her feet and stood next to Kyle as he made his way out of the booth.

Kyle's father barley looked up from the table while he silently took a drink from his coffee.

"Dad, I'm sorry you feel this way. I really thought we could find a way. But it's clear to me now there's nothing I can do. I'm so sorry Dad. I can't live with this anger, rejection and this hatred. I love you and always will. If your ever ready to move past this to move forward, I'll always be here. Goodbye."

On his way to the exit he stopped to slide two twenties to the operator of the cash register positioned near the door.

"I have the bill for that booth right there…whatever is left keep it for yourself."

The middle-aged lady who wore the traditional waitress's white smock, a thin smile and obviously unnatural amber colored hair in a bun with black stylish eyeglasses thanked him.

"Okay. Honey…is everything alright?"

Kyle nodded as he made his way thru the door. Candy was half a step behind and determined to keep up.

The walk across the parking lot seemingly took forever. Kyle reached the Jeep first, unlocked the door, climbed in and came to rest behind the wheel. He pulled the door shut with more than enough force to activate the locking mechanism. His hands went to his face as Candy made her way around the other side, opened the door and joined him.

Kyle's head fell limp, his shoulder slumped. Candy unsure of what to say, she knew no words could convey how she felt and how much her heart hurt for him. Candy reached out to comfort him.

"I'm so sorry Kyle. He had no reason to say any of that. You were not the cause of him losing his wife. You were not the reason your mom died. You were a child just wanting to be born. Wanting to come into this world. None of this is your fault." Candy paused and chose her next words carefully.

"I can't imagine your mother blaming you."

He lifted his eyes and stared out the front windshield of the Jeep. "I've often wondered about that. Would my mother hate me knowing she died giving me life?

The Past and The Future Collide

Chapter 20

The rhythm of life seemed to return to Kyle's world in Berkeley Springs. His days began like clockwork. Either he had the opening shift at the running store or there where miles to log getting ready for the JFK 50.

The encounter with his father got filed away with so many other failed attempts to bridge the gap between the two. This time it felt different when he returned home. This time the harsh encounter left him more deeply scarred. This confrontation felt more personal leaving him feeling more resolved to finally move on. Kyle had been holding out hope for years, but he finally accepted that his desire to connect was not enough motivation to bring the two together. Resigned to allow time to heal, if possible, the conflict in his father's heart. Kyle also finally accepted that it might never happen. This encounter left him with the realization that the world does not always grant your wishes.

As he finished up the remaining miles of the mornings long run, the summer sun began to peak out from behind the horizon its warmth spilled out onto the roadway. Kyle glanced down at his watch. His closing mile clicked off at just over a 7:30 pace. Over the summer his training became refocused to account for the extra 24 miles he would cover in the fall. To build up his endurance, long run distances were extended while dialing back his per mile pace. Secretly he wanted to not only complete the 50-mile challenge but to also run a respectable race time. His first venture into the ultrarunning world would be a learning experience. Kyle knew it would be foolish to think he could go out there and race with the elites at their specialized distances. Motivated to make a respectable debut he did not want to be known as the elite marathoner who laid an egg at his first attempt at the ultra-distances. The pressure to perform was only matched by the freedom that this new racing venue provided.

At 31 miles Kyle pushed the big button on his GPS watch to stop the timing function. "Not a bad day's work," He mumbled to himself as he slowed down and walked a bit making his way back to the store. His stare fixated on the concrete in front of him, his legs still a bit unstable as he gingerly walked over the uneven surfaces of the sidewalk. His sweat covered skin began to feel cool as it clashed with the warm rays of sunshine on his checks. A familiar figure stood standing at the entrance of the store.

"Candy, what are you doing up so early? You normally sleep in?" Kyle called out from across the street.

"Waiting on you silly." In an excited tone, she replied.

Kyle had grown fond of the sound of her voice. He had also gotten attached to Carly who he noticed was sitting patiently at Candy's feet. Although still feeling the effects of his run, a smile instantly came to his face.

"Waiting on me...what did I forget? Did we have a date?" Kyle wondered silently if he had forgotten something? Did they have plans that somehow, he had forgotten about? Did he make a promise he failed to keep? Fear crept in as he approached the storefront.

"Mmmm, I'm not sure if I should give you a kiss, seeing I'm pretty smelly and." Kyle drew out his thoughts seemingly trying to figure out what the catchphrase may be. He continued. "I get the feeling I may be in trouble for forgetting something."

She had him right where she wanted him. “I don’t mind...but Carly here thinks you stink!” She laughed. “Forgetting something? What do you think you may have forgotten?”

Those words put the young man into an instant backpedal.

“I’m not really sure...maybe nothing? Maybe something important?”

“Well I wouldn’t be standing here if you.......” Candy paused a second to let her victim tousle with what was coming next.

“Ha, I got you! You haven’t forgotten anything. I got up this morning and asked Carly girl if she wanted to have breakfast with our favorite guy. She wagged her tail and here we are, timed it perfectly. I have some breakfast sandwiches right here, if you would like to have one with us before you open up the store. And I have a dry shirt for you to put on.”

After a deep breath. “Carly, were you in on this?” Kyle asked as his heart rate finally stabilized.

Carly looked up with those penetrating brown eyes that would melt even the most hardened soul.

“Yea I’m asking you, Carly...practical joker you, were you in on this? Ha...you guys had me. I’m in, I’m hungry for sure. I'll warn you both, my revenge is coming so you both better be on the lookout is all I have to say.”

Kyle, Candy and Carly dog sat down on an old cedar bench in front of the store. Candy opened a tan wicker basket, pulled out a blue and white checkered towel which she laid out on the open section of the bench between the two. Next, she proceeded to lay out all the fixings for a simple but elegant breakfast including a bowl of treats for their furry companion.

In between bites of food and cold orange juice, Candy asked a simple but probing question.

"Kyle." she paused and measured her words carefully.

"Are you okay? I mean with the way things ended the other day with your dad? I'm an outsider, I only understand to the extent of the few things you have shared with me. But there seemed like there was so much bitterness. Are you okay?"

Kyle kind of figured the questions were coming. It was a question he had answered in some form or fashion for most of his young life. He was either making up excuses or trying to explain why he didn't have his mother in his life. Why his father never showed up for the parent-teacher conferences. Why he was absent from Cub Scouts, sports, other school functions or pretty much everything. Most of the time it didn't bother Kyle to make up excuses for his father. He had grown used to his father standing him up. What he began to hate the most was the times when he had to explain why his father smelled like booze. It seemed like Kyle told this story repeatedly. It was just another part of the unfinished script that was storyline of his life.

Over time for better or worse he grew immune to it. From his point of view, it was normal. To everyone else it was shocking.

Kyle quietly told her he was fine. He paused and looked Candy in the eyes, smiled and said "It's part of my life that may never have a happy ending. It's part of life that has made me who I am and its part of my life that may never be complete. It is simply what it is."

Kyle then smiled and leaned in and placed a kiss on Candy's check.

"Although, it's not who I am. I'm not bitter, I'm not sad…I'm not pining away on the past. I've grown up looking for the littlest of things in my life to be happy about. I've decided to live, I've decided to finish what I can and always work on the things in my life which are not complete. I've decided to love…you."

A small tear welled up in Candy's eye. "Kyle that's what I like about you...you always show me how much you care about the little things in life. And about me"

"Candy...you are far from a little thing in my life. I LOVE you..."

In near perfect timing, Carly looked back at Kyle, both ears poised for attention, her head cocked a few degrees off center.

"Yes, Carly...I love you too." The spunky little pup went back to eating her treats.

The two finished the impromptu breakfast and sat outside the store as the rest of Berkeley Springs came to life. The sun felt good on his skin as he stared into Candy's eyes. The moment was picture perfect, a young couple enjoying a quiet moment alone, the day waking new and the world around them in peace and quiet. For a moment, they had it all. They were together with a day full of endless promise.

Jim came around the corner of the storefront and stopped abruptly, "Can't trust the hired help to open the store on time." In a dry sense of humor that was Jim to the core, he couldn't resist the chance to get in a jab.

"Oh, I see you two Love Birds...breakfast, did you save me any?"

"Well, maybe but you'll have to fight Carly for it," Kyle replied.

"Candy, thank you so much. I better get to work. See you later after my run this afternoon?"

"You're going out again?"

"Yea JT is coming over I'm running a double today. He wanted to go with me. The kid has talent I feel good investing in him, heck he keeps me on my toes."

"Okay, there old man...have fun and call me later. Love you!"

Jim replied, "Love you too." He winked and slapped Kyle on the back.

"Good to see you two together Kyle…she is a keeper."

The day in the store passed by rather quickly. A few customers came in, purchased new shoes or other apparel and Jim harassed Kyle about opening late and about not saving him any breakfast. Jim was sure to point out, for at least the 100th time, that if Kyle let it happen again that he could be looking for new work or he would win employee of the month.

"Jim. I'm not sure if I've ever told you but you are…" Kyle paused, "important to me."

"Yea but not enough for breakfast." The father figure had to get in a jab. "Kyle, I know. And same here."

JT showed up right at 5. Kyle would be getting off work and with a quick change back into running gear he would be ready to take the junior high cross-country runner out on a quick tour of one of his secret local trails.

"Kyle thanks a lot for running with me. It's fun getting in some miles with you. Most kids on the team run to keep in shape for some other sport. But like you…I run because well, I enjoy running."

"Yes, we are a weird bunch."

The pair ran out of town to a makeshift trail that bordered some of the local farm fields. It was far from a manicured trail but it was navigable enough that Kyle found it a fun and challenging course to run. Knowing that he would be spending a fair amount of the JFK 50 running on the Appalachian Trail, Kyle was looking for every opportunity to get in some off-road miles. A run with JT would provide an excellent opportunity to get in some trail time.

This trail, for the most part, was flat with only a short section that would gain some respectable elevation while looping around an out cropping of rocks, trees and boulders. While training for his first ultra, Kyle enjoyed the opportunity to feel the rocks, roots and dirt beneath his feet. He wanted to share this run with JT to help connect him deeper with the sport.

Two miles in both runners were beginning to pick up the pace. Kyle liked to challenge the youngster to see how long he could keep up a faster tempo. JT liked being pushed. He noticed how it had improved his speed over the last few months. With the cross-country season gearing up JT was looking for any edge he could get to improve his standings on the team.

"Come on JT, run more relaxed, let your legs do what they were designed to do...run. Smile some, you'll run faster if you're happy."

JT snapped back in between breaths. "Okay. Smile. Run faster and be happy. I got it I think."

Kyle pulled up next to JT turned his head toward the young runner. "Keep up with me....and smile."

In the length of one stride, Kyle put some distance between the two, urging JT to match his pace. "Come on don't let me drop you, open up your stride."

JT closed the gap some and Kyle held the tempo on spot as the two ran down a flat section of the trail, coming up on a tricky rooted filled turn that would point them back into town. Kyle kept up the motivational chatter as JT stuck on his hip. Kyle knew the young boy had something. He was unsure if he had the speed to make it onto the national level, but he was certain JT could get a college scholarship with just a little bit of work. Kyle enjoyed investing in him and wanted to help JT be the best he could be.

"When we hit these rocks just make light contact, don't let your foot land very hard, easy on and easy off the rocks. Quick steps. Light steps don't commit all of your weight..." Kyle was zeroed in on his young apprentices' form, wanting to find and correct any flawed motions that could shave a few seconds.

Kyle was the first to enter the rocky section. With movements that appeared almost automatically programmed, Kyle's stride adjusted quickly to landing and rebounding off the jagged edges of the rocky surface. His feet landed softly and departed the surface as quickly as he made contact almost without thinking. Kyle shifted into a stride and leg turnover pace that danced off the top of the rocks.

“JT follow suit, don’t land too hard, stay limber, light and...”

His left shoe landed off-center on the sloped face of a large rock. The rubber sole began to slip and lose traction. Sliding further off its balance point, the effect threw off the timing of a whole series of movements. His right foot landed on the trailing edge of another rock just in front of him. At too low a point of contact, the toe of his shoe stuck into the small crevice between adjoining rocks instantly stopping its forward motion. With forward momentum broken, Kyle found himself in a rapid descent towards the ground.

Kyle was sent tumbling out of control to the ground below and in front of him. Along nearly any other trail this would have resulted in a cloud of dust and a bruised spirit. At that moment he was rapidly approaching a pile of jagged rocks, each sticking out above the surface of the trail at threatening angles. Kyle had often thought while successfully running this section that a crash here would leave a mark, if not much worse.

The fact that his shoe was firmly wedged between two rocks unable to self-release caused a violent action toward the ground. Out of survival instinct, he reached forward with his hands attempting to brace himself for impact. His palms made contact first. Pain shot through his arms. A small section of white bone ripped through the skin of his left forearm. Next, his right knee made an impact on the rounded top of a broad rock. His hip followed as it impacted another sharp rock, ripping open the black fabric of his shorts and tearing lose a flap of skin. His eyes wide open as he saw the next point of contact. In horror, he saw a large flat rock leaning towards him, and directly in his path. Kyle closed his eyes.

JT heard the unmistakable sound of shoes slipping and sliding off a rock. The unchoreographed movements caught his attention. The unforgettable sound of flesh and bone impacting the ground sent fear though his being. In full stride, JT dared not take his eyes off the course in front of him for fear of falling himself. Out of the corner of his eye, he saw Kyle laying humped over a rock his friends legs were in awkward positions. JT put on the brakes and came to a near dead stop on top of a rock facing in the opposing direction. The rapid deacceleration caused his shoes to slip on the rocks surface. It took quick thinking and rapid-fire actions to keep from falling himself. Once in control, he spun around to see Kyle laying sprawled out among the distorted shapes around him.

JT moved toward the body which laid motionless in front of him. Cautious and worried, he measured every foot placement to ensure he did not join Kyle in the twisted mess of rocks. Gasping for his breath, JT tried to collect himself, he tried to gather his thoughts.

"Kyle are you okay? Kyle, that looks bad are you alright."

JT moved closer and bent down to get a better inspection of the scene. Emotions of fear and panic began to overcome him.

"What do I do? I've got to get help…I need some help." He feverously cried out to himself.

Standing over the motionless body, the scared young man looked for any signs of movement. As he waited for any sound from Kyle he noticed how disfigured his body looked among the rocky surface. There was blood on a rock underneath his legs. Kyle's foot was trapped in gap among the rocks and was bent at an angle that seemed unnatural. Frozen in time JT waited for his friend to move, to reply, he waited for Kyle to do anything. Seconds stretched out forever without a sign. Moments passed without movement. JT feared the worse yet cautiously hung on to hope.

"Oh My God Kyle. Kyle, say something. Move, do anything."

He moved even closer. Carefully JT put his hand on Kyles back over what would be the back of his rib cage on his left side. JT could feel the warmth of Kyle's body, he had hope. His hand rested there motionless for a few seconds. JT moved it to the other side. He noticed the wetness of the running shirt Kyle was wearing yet felt no movement of his friend's body.

"Kyle, say something… Move."

There was no reply to JT's request.

The young boy noticed that Kyle's chest was still.

JT's heart hung on its very next beat.

He knew, sadly that his friend was gone.

All That He Longed For...

Chapter 21

A closed sign with the words "special event" hung on the front door. It was still early in the morning. On a normal Saturday Jim would be opening the store, yet on this crisp morning the room was full. Friends, former customers, local merchants and members of the local running clubs sat on cold and uncomfortably hard white plastic folding chairs aligned in a semi-circle pattern in the center of Run Berkeley. Along the back-wall JT stood next to Tom and his wife. The young man looked pale and lost.

With a stoic expression, Jim stood in front of the crowd leaning up against the main sales counter. Most of the gathered sat quietly. A few in attendance spoke with hushed tones and carefully selected words. When they spoke, they talked about how they met Kyle or they shared instances where he had been helpful and motivating along their running journey. It was in the store, perhaps behind the counter that many who visited today first met Kyle. Everyone commented that it wasn't just his helpfulness in making the purchase. A common trait to everyone was that each felt he became invested in them as a person and a runner, not simply a customer.

Quietly and keeping to herself, Candy sat alone. On the old wooden stool tucked next to the end of the counter along the wall of shoes she silently stared at a stained spot on the hardwood floors next to where Carly was sitting. With all the white chairs filled it was standing room only yet the flow of people continued. Solemn and depressed, Candy would occasionally watch as a new person entered the store. Her eyes would follow them for a moment then she would return to her own quiet world of mourning. Anyone who witnessed the scene would have instantly been clued in to the fact that these two were most affected by the accident.

Jim looked around the room. He smiled at some who made eye contact with him. Others he simply nodded. A few approached and offered words of encouragement and strength. The room grew quiet from time to time and on one such occasion, Jim decided to speak.

Walking toward the center of the arranged chairs, in some available open space in front of the counter, Jim cleared his throat. His wife stood next to him. In any other situation, she would have looked stunning in a black dress, her long hair combed to a flip off her left side and in heels. Leann never wore heels but today she dressed the traditional part of someone in mourning.

"Thank you all so much for taking of your time to come out today. Kyle, I know would have been extremely thankful that all of you thought enough about him, to remember him on this day."

Jim paused as his voice began to stumble. Leann reached toward him and held his hand.

Candy looked in Jim's direction paying attention to every word he said but she could not make eye contact. Instead, she stared off to his side. The pain she was feeling was beginning to multiply to the point she found it hard to breathe. Carly sensing something was wrong with her companion rustled about and stood on her hind legs placing her head in Candy's lap. This broke the spell. Candy felt the air return to her lungs and reached down to comfort her little girl.

Jim continued with some of the most painful and thought-provoking words he had ever spoken.

“Kyle was full of life. He cared about each one of you, not simply as customers but as runners and friends. You were his family. He thought the world of each one of you.”

Jim scanned the room and noticed Tom, JT and the group of older ladies who would end each Saturday morning’s walking session with a stop in his store to tease Kyle about if they were only a few years younger.

“In each one of you, Kyle saw potential. I first met Kyle when he was just a young, raw high school athlete. I saw a young man who had a gift and one who was battling life. Since then, I saw a life just starting to find its direction. Kyle’s life was not typical. He overcame much to get to the point where he was. There was much about him many of us never knew. Kyle had talent, drive, energy and love. Almost on his own; he found his gift within the running community and dam near made the Olympic team. Coming up short I know firsthand that it hurt him deeply. I don’t think he ever gave himself credit for the talent he had.” Jim stopped to collect himself. Leann leaned him and whispered in his ear.

“10th in the USA. The boy worked his butt off. Kyle took what he was given and rose to the 10th fastest marathoner in our country. With that success, he never forgot to give back. He touched many of you. Leann and I grew fond of Kyle while he stayed with us. Without a family of our own, he fit right in and we are so thankful that God sent him to us, that our paths crossed for even a brief time. Kyle was as near to a son as I..." Jim paused, "As we will ever have.”

Jim stood quietly looking off into the crowd. Some looked away hiding their own emotions, some watched as he tried to collect himself. The room was full of expressions, some sad and a few measured smiles.

Leann seeing that her husband could not continue spoke up.

"Jim and I thank you all so much. You know Kyle wasn't very formal, he was very easy going and just took life as it came. We, honestly…with the quickness that this all came about we weren't sure how to honor him. We are not his biological family, but we were his family. We thought we would simply join with the people he touched here in Berkeley Springs and remember him. Would anyone like to say anything?"

The room was quiet for a few long seconds which felt like hours. JT moved forward.

"Kyle was my brother…in a way. I don't have any sisters or brothers and I always wanted someone who I could relate to, talk to and enjoy something in common with. Kyle was that brother figure to me. He always had time to talk to me about running and about my life. We didn't talk much about his life outside of running but he was always interested in me. In my life. I'm so sorry he fell on that run…with…me." JT held it together until the very end. In tears, he walked towards Jim and Leann and gave them both a long hug. He then walked over to Candy.

She stood up and hugged JT. "He always spoke highly of you and thought the world of you. I'm sure if he had to have his life cut short, if he had to leave us he would have wanted to go doing something he loved. He loved running and he enjoyed running with you."

JT captured his emotions for a second, "Thank you Candy…I'm so sorry for your loss."

He walked to the back of the room where his parents were waiting to comfort him. Tom stood next to them, a man who had seen a lot in all his years, was visibly shaken and in tears.

Jim regained enough composure to speak to those gathered again.

"Thank you, JT. Would anyone else like to say a few words, I'm sure Kyle wouldn't mind a few stories."

Tom walked forward, wiping his eyes and searching for his breath. In the center of the room he told the assembled group about the time he challenged Kyle to show him what world class speed looked like. “Boy that young man was fast.” He paused to laugh some. "With my old-man ego intact, I thought yea if I get into shape I might be able to hang with him. NOPE. Godspeed Kyle.” The retired miner walked back to his seat. His head hung low and a sober expression fell on his face.

A handful of visitors and friends related different experiences they had had with Kyle. A few told funny stories. All spoke about how they developed a personal relationship with him.

Jim sensing a break in the flow addressed the crowd again.

“Thank you all for sharing. I know Kyle would be touched.”

A voice drew Jim’s attention. It was the owner of the local sandwich shop that Kyle loved to frequent.

“Jim and Leann, I hope this is not wrong, not bad timing, but where is Kyle now? I mean if we wanted to go visit him to say our goodbyes where would that be?”

“Rose, I don’t think there’s anything wrong with asking that…”

As Jim began to reply Candy stood and spoke.

“Thank you, Jim and Rose, Kyle loved your restaurant. Your BLT’s without the T was his favorite go-to sandwich. If you remember your place was the first place Kyle and I had first date of sorts.” Candy referred to the start of their relationship.

“Everyone here today, Thank you. I loved Kyle. It very evident to me that you all cared deeply about him. His life was full of challenges, yet he never let it get him down. His entire life he longed for a family. Today, we all get to witness just how big his family had become. Kyle has been buried alongside his mother in Brush Creek Cemetery in Irwin, Pa. A small town outside of

Pittsburgh." Candy paused.

"After his passing, we contacted his only living relative, his father. The two had a difficult relationship. Over the years Kyle tried to make amends. He desperately wanted a relationship with his father, but it just never worked out. It was only right to reach out to him. Jim, his father and I thought it best for Kyle to buried there. His father had the plot and I know Kyle would have wanted to be next to his mother." Candy wiped a tear away from her cheek. She was strong, she stuck to the facts, her voice only getting rattled a few times.

"His mother passed in child birth, Kyle for this whole life only wanted to be with her and now he is."

Rose spoke up again in tears. "I had no idea, thank you, Jim, and thank you, Candy. We all feel your loss. I thought it important for people to know, there are a lot of us that had grown very fond of him. I'm sure many will pay him a visit from time to time."

"It was very thoughtful, Rose." Jim smiled.

The New Normal

Chapter 22

The quick turnover, the rebound, the push off and the ground passing below your feet on a sun-drenched morning are the elements that make a long-distance runner come alive. On this morning for a moment her life felt in sync once again. The feelings of pain, grief and mourning were forgotten if ever so briefly in the flow of movement. Grief became lost in the quest for speed displaced for a moment as lungs struggled to fill with air.

Candy put her head down and pushed through the final mile of her tempo workout. Twenty miles this morning flew by faster than ever before for the girl who months ago never dreamed of running with a purpose other than to shed a few pounds or to spend more time with her guy. Over the last four weeks, Candy felt an intense desire to run, to train and to work to become a better runner. It made her feel closer to the person she now believed she had been all along. It also made her feel much closer to Kyle.

The mid-morning sunshine radiated from behind as Candy made her way down the long asphalt roadway. Pushing herself faster than she ever thought possible, the beams of sunshine pressed hard on her back. Her singlet exposed skin absorbed the warmth of each ray of light. Nearly three hours ago she left her apartment on a chilly fall morning fighting off the urge to put on a long sleeve t-shirt. With the temperature of the day climbing rapidly and the radiating effects of the sun, she was happy to be in a lightweight outfit.

A barely audible beep combined with a vibration on her wrist made her aware that she had less than a mile remaining. With an extra jolt of energy and determination, Candy forced her legs to reach out further, extending her stride length. The weight of her stride moved forward on to her toes with her heels kicking higher in the turnover. Knowing that her morning run was coming to an end she leaned into her reserves. Her arms pushed against the wind in repeating cycles helping to catapult her body forward. Her chest swelled as a mixture of nitrogen and oxygen filled her lungs fueling the blood vessels of her large muscle groups which would propel her home. Candy instinctively knew she was running at nearly full potential and had maximized her effort the preceding 19-miles. With the hay in the proverbial barn she was not going to let her efforts go to waste with an unofficial 20-mile PR within reach.

"Drive girl, drive forward. Finish this run hard" Candy cheered herself on.

"You did not get up early, you did not come out in the cold hours of the morning to give back any time. Run!" Candy dug in deep. Her eyes focused on the ground in front of her. Her mind was fixed on a repeating internal dialog of positive self-talk. The outside world disappeared. Nothing could penetrate the small isolated bubble that she ran in. Seconds felt like an entirety as she pushed herself hard to continue to run at top speed. Her chest cavity swelled, her breathing turned forceful and rapid. Soon it would be all over. She only had to hang on. Without notice her legs felt heavy, her muscle began to feel ridged and not responsive. Her leg action began to slow.

"Not today sunshine," Candy called herself out. In a fit of self-produced rage, she beckoned on all of her reserves to feed the red-hot machine inside of her.

With a final push Candy reached for another gear, picked up the pace and gave up everything she had in her. Her lungs pushing on the boundaries of how far they could expand were about to explode. Her heart pounded repeatedly like a worn-out bass drum reverberating within her chest. Her face flush, her eyes glued on the road and her heart locked in a heated battle to achieve one small victory. In one final, concentrated effort she forced her legs to make an ever so rapid contact with the ground and then in a near instant rebound and push forward again. This pattern was repeated without fail, without missing a beat and without a skip in the cycle.

A vibration on her arm and let her know she reached her goal and the personal achievement war was over.

Jim called out as Candy walked into the store. “How did it go this morning?”

“What? Oh, I’m sorry still a little short of sugar and oxygen to the brain. Great.” 30 minutes removed she was still trying to play catch up with her breathing. “Really great Jim, 2:45 for 20.”

“WOW…that’s fast,” JT replied from behind the counter. The young and dependable cross-country star had worked himself into an inventory stocking mess when he decided to sort all the socks by color and size. Jim knew he was taking on a big retail challenge but just like when Kyle wanted to display all the gel packs by flavor. Jim let him learn his lesson the hard way.

Jim hired JT part-time to help fill in the gaps after Kyles passing. It provided the young man with some extra spending money, kept him focused on his running and it gave Jim someone to talk to when the store was slow. It also helped everyone, especially Jim a great deal with the loss of Kyle.

“Jim, I picked up your mail. I hope you don’t mind.”

Jim again looked up from helping a customer. “As long as you didn’t pocket my winning letter from Publishers Clearing House, yea then I'm good. Thank you."

Candy walked over to the counter and made small talk with JT.

With Candy's help, it didn't take long for JT to return the sock display back to something that resembled a retail display.

After completing the gait analyses for a new customer, Jim scanned through the mail looking for the winnings from Publishers House. He paused at a white business size envelope.

"Candy." Jim beckoned.

"Yea Jim, what's up, you look flushed.

He handed her the oversized envelope and motioned for her to open it. Her eyes scanned the address line. It read:

Kyle Richards
c/o Run Berkeley
754 Main Street
Berkeley Springs, WV 25411

Candy lost her breath her eyes instantly teared up. The room grew cold and quiet. She stared at the address line as a wave of emotions came crashing into her soul. It hurt to see Kyle's name written out on the envelope. As much as she knew he was gone to see something of this world still bearing his name, still carrying a piece of his information was too much.

Emotions and feelings became bare. She felt uneasy and unsure of what to do next.

"Jim do you think it's okay to open it? Can I open it?" She asked.

"Please do…"

In the oversized envelope were two documents. Candy first pulled out a letter, finding it odd that it was addressed to Jim. She looked up.

"It's addressed to you." Candy stared at him waiting for a response.

"Please read it out loud." He replied his voice shaken.

Dear Jim,

It was with great sadness that we learned of Kyle's passing.

We know no words can comfort you, his family and his many friends at this time. We at the JFK 50 wanted to offer you and his family our thoughts and prayers. We hope that you find comfort in the good times and shelter in the tough times to come.

We understand in the scale of things, our race and running pale in comparison to losing a loved one. We understand that Kyle was a wonderful person, kind spirit and an asset to your family and customers. We also understand that he was a young and bright member of our community. The members of JFK 50 looked forward to his running of the 2013 Edition of the race and we're sure that he would have made a successful transition into the ultra-running community.

We are so sorry that he will not be able to run with us and wanted you to have his elite bib with the number 26 in memory of Kyle.

Kindness regards,

The JFK board of directors.

Her hand reached inside the envelope and removed the race bid with number 26 boldly embossed on the front along with the well known JFK50 name, race date and a few corporate logos. She held it facing Jim and others who were present in the store. By this time Jim's customers had collected together and listened while Candy read the letter. JT stood off to the side, his eyes stained red and tears rolling down his checks.

Once everyone had a chance to look it over Candy turned the bib towards her so that she could get a good look at it. The room was quiet. With much more intensity and feeling than during her early morning run, her heartbeat raced within her chest. Candy's eyes grew moist. Her mind lost in a fog of hurt, pride, memories and unchecked feelings of love and loss. Candy took a deep breath.

"Unfinished business."

"What, what did you say Candy?" Jim asked.

So much of Kyle's life was unfinished business and I know that haunted him. He hated it with his father, his running, his goals…and I'm sure he hated leaving all of us with unfinished business." She paused, collected her feelings, dried the tears from her eyes and collected her thoughts. After a few seconds passed, she knew what she had to do.

"This race is not going to be another example, I'm going to run it." She stopped gained her composure and finished the statement she knew she had to make. "With your permission, Jim I want to run the race for Kyle. I would like to wear his number and finish this race for him. For you and Leann. For you JT and for all of us."

JFK 50 – Getting to the Start

Chapter 23

In Hagerstown, Maryland the alarm went off in a darkened hotel room. Out of a restless slumber she wiped the sleep from her eyes, brushed her hair back off her face and stared at the ceiling. Taking a deep breath while gaining some form of clarity, she spoke a few simple but impactful words to an empty room.

"Kyle, you got me into this…please be with me today." A small trace of a tear rolled down her cheek as she fought to remain in control of her emotions.

Alone in the room her conversation continued with a presence she longed for. "I'm scared of this race. This is longer than I have ever run before. I'm scared of living without you. At one point, I thought I would live alone for the rest of my life, but after meeting you…I'm not sure I can live without you. Kyle. I love you."

The cell phone on the bedside table erupted and shocked her back into the mornings routine. Her hand slid across the nightstand searching for the phone. She attempted to silence the obnoxious ring tone and knocked her watch and an empty food wrapper onto the floor.

"Yea, yea I hear you." Candy called out, a little louder than she had planned, while she desperately tried to silence her phone. Finally, with a right swipe across the touchscreen, she put an end to the relentless noise that she was sure could be heard across the hallway if not the entire hotel.

"Hello." She answered the call.

"Are you up…it's me, Jim."

"Yea and who else would be calling me. I'm up."

Jim and JT had crashed together in a room down the hall. They considered sharing one room but decided their runner needed the rest as much as she needed some privacy.

"Give me 30 minutes and I'll be ready to go. And thanks for supporting me on this adventure. Today is so much more than a race. Make sure you thank JT as well. I'm going to need you guys today." She swung herself around on the bed her feet landed on the floor.

These final moments of quiet time would be spent having breakfast, getting dressed and putting her game face on. Before going to bed, she had laid out her running kit on the extra bed in her room. With everything in its proper place, she double and triple checked every detail ensuring all her needed items were present and accounted for. Her favorite trail shoes were set at the bottom of the bed, purple uppers with black and white lowers accented with reflective trim. These were the shoes Kyle fitted her with when she first declared she wanted to try running trails with him. Black toe socks and a pair of black shorts greeted a red, white and blue girls v-neck running shirt. She selected the patriotic top to honor Kyle's attempt to join the US Olympic marathon team. A pair of silver arm sleeves laid out next to her shirt, a GPS watch laying on top of the left arm sleeve. A hand-held water bottle on the opposite side and resting near it was a pair of trail shoe gaiters with rainbow colored butterflies. Near the head of the imaginary figure was a pair of ear covers and a fleece cap.

She did one last inventory of everything laid out before her. With a bite of oatmeal, she walked through a mental checklist of everything that was going to happen today. This was her first race of any distance greater than a 10k and the longest distance she had ever run. Her longest run prior to this race was a 50k just three weeks before. Physically Candy felt ready to go, mentally she figured the race and the conditions around why she was running it would be a challenge for her.

As her eyes scanned her outfit one last time, she moved back to the microwave to get another bowl of oatmeal.

The calmness of the room was broken when she noticed something was out of place. Something was missing. Some part of her kit was not ready. “Oh wait a minute” she commented to herself.

Back to the nightstand she rushed to locate the four safety pins that were sitting by the base of the lamp and collected Kyle’s number from out of her travel folder. With the racing bib held in her now shaking hands, she stared at the number 26 for a few seconds and closed her eyes. At the right time she opened her eyes, placed her lips on the bold number 26 just above his name. After a small yet vastly emotional kiss she neatly pinned the number to the front left side of her black shorts.

Finishing the second bowl of oatmeal and a bottle of her favorite premade strawberry banana breakfast drink, it was time to get dressed.

Nearly ready to go she fitted her shoe gaiter to her right shoe by ensuring the clip engaged the first loop of her shoestrings. There was a knock at the door.

“Candy it’s JT are you ready?” An excited voice on the other side of the door rang out.

As Candy walked towards the door, she paid particular attention to how her shoes felt on her feet. Turning the doorknob, she noted that everything seemed just right as she pulled the door open to see Kyles young protégée standing in front of her beaming with a bright smile on his face.

"Morning Candy. How did you sleep, you ready for this?"

Still feeling some of the effects of a jittery nights sleep, she noted how much energy the young man had and thought for a moment "Maybe he should be the one running."

She motioned with her eyes and slight movement of her head that he should come in. Just as the door began to shut Jim appeared.

"Morning…the Berkeley bus to Boonsboro is leaving."

"Cute Jim, real cute." Candy smiled at him. "Alright, alright. How's the weather out there? I'm a little scared to look."

"Not bad. Maybe a little cool, but the day is going to be dry and mild. For the most part."

"That is good news," JT commented.

"I have a coat you can wear right up to the start. One of us will grab it from you, or if you wish you can run with it some and we will pick it up wherever you drop it." Jim tried to answer as many questions upfront so as to keep Candy from burning up energy worrying about the unknown.

"Thank you. I'm ready. Let's go, before I change my mind. JT you have all of the aid station stuff, snacks, clothes, shoes…you know everything? A new pair of legs?"

The plan for the day was that even though the race provided 14 fully manned aid stations, Jim and JT would be at locations along the course that crew members had access to. He tried to assure her that they would be there to provide a favorite snack and some encouraging words along the way.

"I got everything Candy. Don't you worry, we got your back." JT smiled.

"Okay make sure this little one does not get lost." Candy pointed over at Carly who was curled up in a fuzzy little ball next to an extra pillow on the bed, still either half asleep or intentionally ignoring all of them.

JT promised he would look after Carly. "No worries there, we will take loving care of your little four-footed friend. Come on Carly Q, rise and shine."

Carly looked up, shook her head and in one fluid motion jumped up and off the bed. Not to be left behind the curvy little schnauzer stood within inches of the door, her nose almost touching.

Jim drove to Boonsboro High School, about 30 minutes outside of Hagerstown. The pre-race meeting would start at 5:50 am and since the trio choose not to go to the race expo Candy wanted to catch the full briefing. The drive was quiet, uneventful and dark. Candy sat in the back seat wrapped up in a fleece blanket with Carly collected on her lap. The still sleepy schnauzer fell soundly asleep while her companion's mind worked overtime thinking about the days' challenges in front of her.

Many thought the JFK 50-miler to be three different races all rolled into one. Many looked at it as a runner's version of a Triathlon. The Nation's Oldest Ultramarathon challenges competitors over three distinct and widely varied terrain. The first segment being roughly 15-miles of single-track trails on the Appalachian Trail. A single-track trail is a mountainous technically challenging trail about the width that which a single runner or biker can navigated. Sandwiched in the middle was 26.3-miles of flat bridle trails running on the Chesapeake & Ohio Canal Towpath. Bridle trails are flat trails sections large enough for a four-wheeled vehicle to pass. Finally, the finishing segment takes runners along 8+ miles of rolling country two lane roads into the town of Williamsport.

Jim pulled the car up as close as possible to the front door of the school. Even with his propensity to always be early, there was already a mass of people formed at the entrance. Candy and JT jumped out of the car. Candy paused a minute to give Carly one last kiss on the top of her head and a rub behind her ears.

“See you in 50-miles girl. Be good for the guys.”

Candy and JT moved towards the entrance as Jim drove off to park the car. The morning air was cool it felt refreshing on the exposed skin of her face. It heightened her senses, but she did not feel cold. Walking the final feet to the entrance the blanket stayed wrapped around her arms and mid-section as she walked into the high school.

Passing thru the double glass doors into the foyer area instantly she felt out of her element. The crowd that had gathered, looked like a collection of seasoned ultramarathon veterans. She wondered if everyone that looked at her knew this would be her first 50-mile race. Colonies of butterflies seemed to instantly take up residence in her stomach. Groups of runners and support crew stood along the hallways greeting each other and talking about past events. Candy’s eyes darted from one person to the next.

She looked back at JT a nervous smile on her face. Her voice a bit timid. “I feel a bit out of my league here.”

“Never mind about that, you’ve run as much as anyone this summer. Kyle told me you’re fast and he thought you could do anything you wanted to. Trust in him.” JT paused. “Even though he is not here, trust him.”

“You are right JT, low and slow…I’ll simply run low and slow. 13-hour cut off. I got this.”

With a 13-hour cut off she calculated that averaging a fourteen-minute mile would be enough. She grew more confident that even with the extra miles ahead of her that she could handle the day. Candy had an undisclosed goal. Base on nothing more than wanting to have a finishing time in the single digits, she aimed to finish before the official timing clock could pass 9:59:59. Her private goal was a sub 10-hour finish.

The mood drastically changed when the pair made their way into the gymnasium. Candy stood in the entrance and looked around the wide-open room. The highly polished hardwood floors caught her attention. There were partially opened aluminum and plastic bleachers with blue seats on the right side. Some people sat on them while others milled around standing along the walls. Hung high on the wall opposite the bleachers were a collection of proudly displayed banners from various state athletic championships. Candy noted the ones for Track and Field and Cross Country.

They walked further into the gym taking in all the excitement while eavesdropping on the multiple conversations going on around them. For no other reason than it provided a convenient landing spot, they claimed some real estate along the front wall near a doorway on the opposite side of the gym. They settled in among three other runners sharing the same area along the front wall.

It may have been the nervous energy but Candy was the first to strike up a conversation.

"Hi, my name is Candy, I am from Berkeley Springs, West Virginia where are you all from. Is this your first JFK?"

A young man in late 30's sitting closest to Candy spoke up. "Hi, I'm Joshua from Las Vegas. I run a destination type race every year and this year its JFK. I appreciate the military connection and history of this race. Figured it was a natural. A bunch of friends have run this race so I figured I better check it off my list."

"It's nice to meet you," she greeted him. "What do you do in Vegas? Seems like a great town to visit, not sure I'd want to live there."

"I own a running store called Red Rock Running Company. It's really a great community. Away from the strip it's much like any other town and there are wonderful trails to run." Josh sitting on the floor was leaning into a stretch and tying his shoes continued, "how about you, your first?"

"Yes, it sure is." Candy replied without offering much else.

"How about you guys" JT motioned towards the younger pair.

"Not our first, I'm Woody, I ran it last year for the first time and Kimberly here, she is the veteran of the bunch. She has run the race five times."

"WOW...five times, sorry but you don't look like you have been running that long."

Kimberly answered back with a slight chuckle, "Yea I hear that a lot, but I'm a little older than you would think. I started young."

Candy posed a question. "In what time do you all plan to finish, this is my first ultra and honestly I'm not sure what to expect? I have a crazy goal in mind, but I'm really not sure how I'll hold up."

"I plan to run around a nine-hour finish pace, give or take a few minutes here or there. It really depends on how I survive the AT." Josh replied. "First ultra all together? You picked a tough one."

"Yeah, leave it to me." The nervous first timer laughed to hide her concern.

"Can I ask you something? Why is it that Berkeley Springs rings a bell?" Josh breaking from routine race talk posed the question.

Not that Candy wanted to avoid this type of question but she was still uneasy telling people about her running story without becoming overly emotional. She did her best.

"It might be because of Kyle Richards. He was an elite level marathoner who passed away a few months back. It was a running accident." She stopped short of offering much more.

"Oh, yea that's it. I remember now. I read something about the accident. He was out running, right? I saw mention of it in Runner's World or it was on a blog or podcast I think." Josh nervously stopped talking.

"Yes, it made a lot of news locally and in the running community."

"Did you know him?" Woody asked.

JT stepped in. "We did." He cut the answer short trying to protect Candy and himself.

"No, it's okay JT, thank you but it's okay. Yes, we did. I was." She stopped short to correct herself. I am, his girlfriend and my pal here was his best friend."

Josh cautiously said he was sorry for their loss.

"I'm really sorry," Woody replied.

"Really it's okay you had no ill will." Candy continued. "I'm here today. To run and to finish this race for him. He had planned to make the jump from marathons to ultras and had been training for this race. So much of his life was incomplete, I did not want this race to go unfinished as well, so here I am running the JFK 50. Running it for..." Candy paused short of completing the sentence. She looked down at the floor. "And I'm wearing his number."

She motioned at the bib pinned to her shorts.

Kimberly stepped in. "That is awesome and so nice of you. We won't bug you anymore and won't say anything. I respect what you're doing. You deserve to have this day to accomplish what you set out to do without extra pressure from anyone."

"Thank you so much. But please sit here with us."

The public-address speakers that hung along the cinder block blue and white walls came to life with a crackle and "Test, 1...2..3." The Race Director (RD), who was standing on a small stage opposite the half-opened bleachers, thanked everyone for attending the 51st annual running of the JFK 50 Mile Ultramarathon. Candy was glued to every word of the announcements. She was transfixed on everything going on around her. Her mind focused on taking in all the excitement. The RD mentioned the race history, the legendary course and the strict cutoff times. This helped her focus on the logistics of the race rather than think about the situation which brought her there.

In what seemed like a short amount of time the gathered crowd began to stand and collect up their belongings. Once on her feet and moving Candy adjusted her gear, wrapped the blanket over her shoulders once again and asked JT to help guide her out of the gym. Before departing, the group took a moment to wish each other well.

The mass of bodies began to file towards the side door of the gym and out into the darkness of a crisp fall morning. In the fuss, Candy remembered the 10-minute walk to the starting line in the center of Boonsboro. This is where they would reconnect with Jim.

“Keep an eye out for Jim,” Candy asked JT. “He said he would see us on the way to the starting line.”

“I'm sure he will be here. Keep your eyes open too. You know Jim, he just pops up out of nowhere. At that moment, a comforting and welcomed sound rang out from behind.”

A dog's bark could be heard just a few feet away. It wasn't just any old dog.

“Carly where are you, girl.” Candy looked around.

Another slightly louder bark rang out, then Candy felt the familiar weight of two paws settling on her legs.

“Awe girl so happy to see you and where's Mister Jim?”

Let's keep walking, Candy." Jim echoed from behind.

Candy bent down quickly picked up her little fur ball and wrapped her up inside the blanket as they walked toward the start.

"How are you doing? Anything you need? Do you have all your drinks, and snacks? Did you go to the bathroom?"

"I'm good, Jim well except that last part." She replied.

The trio made their way to the center of town just as the National Anthem began to play. In the collection of runners, Candy stood tall and listened to each note as Carly buried her cold wet nose under Candy's chin.

As the National Anthem came to an end, Jim quickly ushered everyone to get ready.

"Candy, they start this race quickly, give me Carly. JT, you get ready to grab that blanket. Your job for the first few miles is to find your zone, start slow, walk when you need to, drink before you're thirsty and snack all day. You got this and when it gets tough." he paused his words stuck in his throat. "Remember, Kyle believed in you. He loved you and so do we."

"Thank you. Guys really thank you so much. We are Kyle's family. I'm running today but we, together, are doing this for him. It means so much to me." Candy put her head down and reached out to touch both Jim and JT and said a short silent prayer. Everything for a moment was calm and quiet. She thought about Kyle, his kind nature, his easy-going personality, she thought about his challenges in life and the dark roads she had traveled. For a moment, she thought about the future and what could have been and about the future after this race and the promises still to come. She knew that even after finishing this race, that life would never be the same.

Before the starters gun went off Candy gazed into the early morning sky. "Kyle… I love and miss you so very, very much."

JFK 50 – A New Experience with New Friends

Chapter 24

The chilly morning air surrounded her as she stood among a group of like-minded people. Each runner came to this place from various walks of life, from different callings and for assorted reasons. Candy felt very much alone in the world since Kyle's passing but today she felt a connection to those standing around her. Even with the comfort of the crowd and amidst the distractions of the race she was very aware that 50 challenging and lonely miles laid out in front of her. She was also aware that perhaps she may face the rest of her life alone.

In a rush of emotions, it all became too real and too much to contain. Her eyes filled with tears and her breathing quicken to the point of being alarmed. In a wave of embarrassment, she quickly pulled her hands out of her gloves to wipe the tears away in an attempt to hide those emotions. A combination of loss and the unknown expectations of the future collided in that very time and place. At that moment, the challenge of the day and her life moving forward almost became insurmountable.

A piercing sound caught everyone standing around her flat-footed. The sound from the starter's gun reverberated off the century old buildings that paralleled both sides of the main road out of Boonsboro. A collection of two-story brick and frame construction, some storefronts, some residential buildings each with its own unique personality. Today in the early morning hours many of the stores were packed with race supporters. Crews and family members peered out of open windows with some standing on elevated balconies in an attempt to catch a glimpse of their favorite runner during the start of the iconic race.

At the front of the pack, the elite athletes were quickly underway and moving at a fast pace. Near the middle of the field everyone seemed lost in the excitement of the official start of the race. The sound of the starter's gun snapped Candy back into the present reality that the longest run of her life laid out in front of her. She wiped the last remaining tears from her eyes, regained control of her breathing and began a long slow inhale which filled her lungs to maximum capacity. Her rib cage strained, the hydration vest she was wearing drew tight. She paused, closed her eyes, and then slowly exhaled.

As the last sounds of the starter's gun echoed off the surrounding buildings a handful of runners and their support crew cheered, friends high-fived and others hugged random strangers. Candy looked around and tried to make sense of the moment. She tried to take in all the excitement, she tried to breathe in all the energy and the flavor of the race.

Once the initial excitement passed, the realization that the race had started caused JT and Jim to quickly dash out of the street. Out of harm's way, they reached the side of the road clear of the oncoming runners who began to move towards their 50-mile goal. Candy took a few small steps forward then paused as the field began the typical accordion styled gyrations of a mass start. This slow start provided the perfect opportunity for one last check of her gear. She adjusted some things, tightened others and re-introduced herself to the location of everything she may need over the next 10+ hours. As she looked down and secured a loose strap on her running vest a familiar voice caught her attention.

"GPS, remember to start your watch. It doesn't count if it's not on Strava."

This simple phase put a smile on her face and yet it made for a heavy heart. Kyle loved to tease JT that if his runs weren't posted online where Kyle could review his work that they didn't count. It was JT who reminded her of the need to start her watch. Her heart reminded her of her one true love.

Slowly the middle of the pack came up to speed, enabling Candy to finally settle into a steady and a fluid running motion. As she made her way out of town she noted the random collection of architecture along both shoulders of the road. The route led her past a sandwich shop, a small bakery & café and what she believed to be a shop which offered locally made chocolate, Crawford's Confectionary. "I'll be back to get some chocolate when this race is over," Candy muttered under her breath as her feet and legs continued down the road.

It was calming to finally set off on the mission she planned, thought about and had become dedicated to completing. Comfort was found in the simple rhythm of a repeating stride, the alternating footfall and the rebound of motion. With each leg turnover, the center of Boonsboro passed further behind. The revolutionary storefronts of city center turned into colonial style homes with rectangular paneled doors, steeply pitched gambrel roofs and flared eaves with large sprawling porches.

Candy worked her way to the right side of the Old National Pike road, Alt40 as it's called on most maps of the day. The first quarter of a mile disappeared quickly and without much thought. If anything, her mind was more focused on finding a comfortable position within the group around her. At this point she wanted to find her target pace and to concentrate on the plan Jim had worked out for her. It was still early in the day, but Candy knew that any pacing misstep, any deviation from the plan might go unnoticed early on, but could manifest itself into a crushing defeat later on.

It was early in the day and she felt great. Her body and all its interconnected parts came up to speed without any resistance and most importantly without any surprises. The excitement of the day was playing tricks on her mind, the early morning sun on her face, the easy stride and the pent-up energy made her forget about the challenge in front of her. For one fleeting moment, her smile beamed bright and she thought maybe this ultrarunning thing would be easier than she imagined.

The group she felt comfortable tagging along with ran easily out of Boonsboro as the morning sun began to rise over the horizon. The crisp morning air had a bit of a bite to it but with raising body temperatures she was glad she did not overdress. A few runners around her were dropping jackets, hats, gloves and makeshift windbreaks made from trash bags along the side of the road. Her mind wondered if Jim, JT and Carly made it back to the car okay.

The plan for the day would be based on a run/fast hike interval routine. Jim had gone to great lengths instructing Candy on the benefits of an interval approach. He sold her on how a run/fast hike program would save her legs for the latter stages of the race. He grounded her on the concept that if you burned out your legs early, you would have nothing left to mount a fight at the end. She bought into the program, committed herself to being a good soldier and would execute the plan to the best of her abilities. She was reminded that most importantly she should listen to her legs. “The first 15-miles of the JFK course opens up with a mixture of climbing and descending over paved roads and long sections of trails” Jim instructed her to listen to her quads.

"Hike when you begin to feel taxed. Mix in enough running to keep yourself honest, but understand you will not be able to run all of the up-hills." Jim wanted Candy to run a smart race, a race that would spell victory against the clock and more importantly closure for her heart. For her part, she did not want to do anything that might jeopardize her chance to finish up this little bit of business for Kyle.

A side benefit to the interval race tactic was that it provided opportunities to interact with other runners around her. During the early miles leading out of town, she met other JFK first-timers, a few returning veterans and an older Korean woman named Caroline.

Caroline was a slightly built woman with a conservative yet steady gait and an inspiring smile. The pair teamed up during the long climb that led to the Old South Mountain Inn and the branch of the run that led towards the trails. Candy had considered walking some but when she caught up with Caroline she was drawn to engage in a conversation. In little less than 3-minutes, Candy discovered that the women, in her mid 60s, was a veteran of many ultramarathons and was working on her 10th JFK race. Candy conversely explained that this was her first and asked the veteran if she had any secrets to help her finish.

"Honey, protect your legs early. The early miles, the easy miles can spell defeat in the final stages. You are young, much younger than me. Believe, yes believe you can do this and most importantly stay ahead of me."

They both laughed and shared a touching moment on the course. Candy reached out and touched the back of one of Caroline's hands. She noticed her skin was soft, it reminded her of her Grandmother's hand and a connection she had so many years ago. "Thank you so much for sharing a little bit of your day with me. I'll do that, I'll try and stay ahead of you, but you'll forever be in my heart."

Putting her head down and getting back to business Candy pressed on to the landmark sign that would signal the turn from the roads of Boonsboro to the Appalachian Trail (AT.) The climb out of town was more challenging than expected. Even with a conservative approach her legs were already beginning to feel the effects of climb out of town. Seemingly running uphill for the entire race her legs and spirit began to waiver as the overall challenge came into focus.

Questioning the challenge in front of her "Man, this hill goes on forever." In between baited breaths, Candy half spoke out loud and half mumbled her words as she ran. "I don't remember this hill section on the map, they must have snuck this in on me in the fine print."

Glancing at her GPS watch at just over 30-minutes into the race, Candy realized that although she felt like she was overcoming a major hurdle, better than 47-miles laid out in front of her. Her legs were already growing tired and the AT section had yet to rear its ugly head. Reaching the end of the incline out of town she was becoming aware of the nearly 1,100 feet of elevation gain.

The alternating run/hike interval provided single-mindedness to her efforts and after a few cycles, she settled into a better place. More focused and determined she knew she would face a few low points in her day. With each interval, the distance she needed to cover was slowly reduced with every step. Off to the east, the sun rose quickly and replaced the chilly morning air. On the outset Candy quietly questioned starting the race slightly on the cold side, as the temperatures slowly rose she was very happy with the running kit she selected.

Old South Mountain Inn situated at roughly 2.5 miles into the race would mark where the fun would really begin. Candy knew the upcoming trail section would be some of the most challenging and unforgiving surfaces she had ever run over. From the very beginning of the race, the fear of the AT haunted her. Even while engaged in conversations with other runners, the hazards of the trails crept into her thoughts. She tried to avoid it when tempted to ask fellow runners of their impression of this legendary section. Candy in turn bit her tongue and changed the subject. Now she faced her fears at point blank range.

JFK 50 – The Appalachian Trail

Chapter 25

Crossing over what looked to be a broken-down stone wall, Candy got her first look at the legendary Appalachian Trail (AT) and like a reluctant visitor, she wasn't sure she liked what she saw. Boulders as old as time in every shape and size imaginable laid askew on the crushed gravel and stone trail. The landscape seemed foreign and remote like something out of the vintage movie clips of settlers bushwhacking trails of the old West. As Candy's eyes scanned the new terrain, she knew instantly that the AT would live up to all its advanced billing.

The group of runners in front of her instantly broke from their running pace and stacked up like a traffic jam along the interstate. This group now resembled a slow-moving conga line more so than a competitive field of runners in the middle of a 50-mile ultramarathon. At once Candy knew exactly what Jim meant when he spoke about losing time early on in the race, "if you get stuck behind an extremely slow-moving group on the AT...you'll lose more time than you could ever make up." On one hand, she was glad for a forced opportunity to walk, to rest some, but the snail's pace quickly grew old. Candy felt pent up and frustrated as she knew the clock on E. Sunset Ave in Williamsport continued at its ever-steady pace.

The trail zigged and zagged around trees, loose rocks and moss-covered boulders the size of small cars. Fallen logs and partially exposed rocks in the middle of the trail instantly gained her full attention. It became apparent that keeping your eyes on the task in front of you was going to be key to surviving the day. What Candy enjoyed so much about being outside while participating in her former love of hiking or with her newfound romance with running, was the ever-changing scenery around her. Not one to be forced into a gym setting moving heavy plates around a drab colored, stuffy, mirror saturated room. Her soul enjoyed the freedom of being outdoors. She craved the call to explore what running offered. Unfortunately, the trails today were not the setting to allow your eyes to wander or to allow them the opportunity to soak in the beauty that surrounded you. Today required you to keep your mind on the task of remaining upright.

The trail was alive with the changing textures of fall. The field of runners were surrounded by a rainbow of colors. The sun-drenched morning sky cast a near perfect blue hue spread out across the horizon. The last remains of summer's green palette was seen in the fields of tall grass bordering both sides of the trail that cut through the earthy tones on the mountains. Along the age-old stone path multiple shades of gray, brown and black passed beneath her feet. Intermixed with the natural palette passed a wave of humanity wearing multicolored running kits which provided a contrasting kaleidoscope of color. Today the AT provided beauty, tranquility and a backdrop to many different storylines. The trail was also cloaked in danger.

The front of her left shoe caught the leading edge of a weather and broken rock that was hidden by a fresh layer of rust-colored leaves. Even with a sound impact the obstacle imbedded in the trail would not give an inch. The hazardous fixture had not moved for perhaps a hundred years and today it caused Candy to miss a step. The collision was painful and dramatic. Instantly a stabbing jolt of agony nearly caused her to fall onto the trail's surface. Her big toe took the brunt of the collision and was now telling her in no uncertain terms that it was unhappy with her choice of landing locations. She instantly became aware of how much worse it could have been if the ridgeline off in the distance had summoned more of her attention. Luckily the hidden hazard did not hold on to its unexpecting victim for long.

As fast as her left big toe made its impact it was released to find an alternative landing spot. In the hasty collision, her stride, balance and range of motion had been thrown off slightly. Safely back into a fluid running motion, the excruciating pain in her left foot let it be known that the meeting between shoe, toe and the rock had been anything but minor. Her foot ached. The pain caused a limp on the following footfall and now a burning sensation in the front of her foot caused instant concern. With all the miles leading up to this day she had avoided anything even coming close to a blister or the more common signature black toenails of a seasoned endurance runner. Now Candy was sure she would lose at least one toenail at the end of the race if not sooner. She hoped it was not broken.

“Wow, that looked like it hurt. A lot.” A voice became audible from over her shoulder.

Caught up in the moment of her own personal distress, she had forgotten that a fellow runner had been right on her heels.

He continued, “I thought for sure you were going down. I was trying to figure out if I was going to catch you or simply watch and pick up the wreckage afterward.” A lean and fit looking male runner let Candy know he had witnessed the whole thing.

"Thanks, I guess." Candy commented in between breaths. Her attention directed more intently on the placement of her feet.

“Please don’t take that the wrong way I would have liked to have caught you if you would have fallen, but I was certain that an out of balance act would have had both of us collapsed in a ball. I’m glad you saved it.”

“Me too.” Candy ran herself out of the awkward limp but her big toe burned like nothing she had ever experienced before. “Yeah, that one hurt.”

"It's going to leave a mark for sure." The male voice continued.

The two now ran side by side as the AT broke open to an asphalt trail. The course would follow this improved section until rejoining the more rugged terrain about two miles in front of them.

The athletic looking young man with a bright and wide smile, short cropped hair, brown eyes and tan skin introduced himself. “I’m Eric, sure glad you didn’t bite it back there. Are you okay, I noticed you picked up a limp.”

“I think so, it appears I have a little hitch in my giddy-up.” Candy paused while considering if her statement was true or false. “You’re in the military?”

“Hitch in your giddy-up, well that is a first, but yes I am, how did you guess?”

With a slight chuckle Candy called out the most obvious. “Well with that big U.S. star on the front of your shirt and the words, U.S. Military Endurance Sports, kind of figured.”

Matching her laugh. “16 years Air Force, I’m an Ammo Technician, stationed in Hampton, Virginia. I almost forgot I was wearing one of our team shirts, it seems like forever since I got dressed this morning.”

The two made random small talk as their legs got used to the steady footing once again. An out of place beeping sound caught both of their attentions.

“Time to run,” Eric commented. Instinctively Candy followed suit as he explained he was following a 9/1 pacing plan on any portion of the trail that was flat, or even close to flat and for the full length of the relatively flat towpath. “This might be the only section on this portion of the trail I can really run steady, I understand this section does a good bit of climbing. I'll keep it up as long as I can, but don't want to burn out.

"Sounds like a plan close to what I'm running, I'll stick with you as long as I can but I'm going to listen to my legs early on." Candy explained.

The mood on the asphalt trail was much different than the feeling of danger that hung-over intro to the AT. On the more technical trail sections most runners kept to themselves staying focused on their footing. Back on the improved surface once again conversations filled the air, laughter could be heard and the field went about advancing their day on many different paces. A spectator could easily pick out the runners who were frustrated by being caught behind the slower moving groups. Once on firm footing that did not require focused attention, the faster runners broken off trying to move forward within the overall pack. These faster runners were determined to get going while the getting was good.

Eric's nine-minute per mile interval timer went off calling out the end to the run portion of his run/walk period. "Wow, that nine-minute block went fast, in a minute we go again."

"Sure thing, that wasn't so bad. I'll try to hang with you for another segment or two, or three or until my legs fall off."

For the remainder of the section separating the two portions of the AT Candy stuck with her new-found partner. She positioned herself off of his right shoulder matching every move. The two worked in concert making time while separating themselves from the logjam of runners that was sure to come once the race rejoined the more technical and challenging trail sections.

JFK 50 – Running to Weverton

Chapter 26

Rejoining the trail at near its highest point, this section of the Appalachian Trail (AT) is very rocky, at times narrow and offers some challenging foot placements as it rambles along the ridgeline of South Mountain.

A blanket of fallen leaves covered the ground in a patchwork of earth tones. The trail was bordered with a mixture of young saplings and old growth timbers. The field of runners was now more spread out after some of the faster participants made a concentrated effort to move towards the front of the pack during the previous asphalt section. Candy shadowed every step Eric made as he moved over the collection of miss-shaped rocks, broken tree limbs and other random pieces of natural debris.

"I'm glad to see you're still hanging with me," He called out over his shoulder.

"Me too, thankfully my quads haven't exploded and are still holding up." She replied between ongoing efforts to fill her lungs with fresh oxygen.

"Stick with me for as long as you can, it will help make up some of the time we lost in that logjam on the first section. If I go too fast, if you need me to slow down some or anything just let me know. I won't run you into the ground. It's nice to have someone to run with, you know hang out with."

This gesture reminded Candy so much of Kyle. As a world-class marathoner; his training time was valuable, yet he always sought out opportunities to give back to the community. Kyle enjoyed running with JT. He believed it was important to invest in the youth of the sport. He valued the new runner as much as he was driven to help those who were struggling with their weight or health. Candy suspected that Eric had a kind and gentle soul.

Deeper into the AT section the trail demanded all of your attention. Outside of providing a steady pace, following her new guide relieved some of the pressure of having to navigate the trails on her own. On this section foot placement could not be taken for granted. The surface was littered with rocks of every shape, size and configuration. The runner who wanted to avoid a nasty fall had to be on constant watch seeking out the best place to land their next step. In this environment, you could not allow your feet to get lazy. A sluggish step, a lift-off that did not exit cleanly or an unbalanced landing provided the perfect setting for disaster. A foot that got caught up on a root of a fallen tree or the sharp edge of an ancient stone could spell the end of the line for someone who was not mindful. Candy had barely escaped disaster earlier, now she was happy to follow in the footsteps of someone who could help her survive the most challenging terrain of the day and the most technical trails she had ever run over.

Lost in the steady cadence of movement was that the sun had steadily risen over the horizon. Its powerful rays of light beamed intensely. On any other day, the sunrise at this picturesque location would have been worth a few minutes along the trail to admire and to soak in the moment. Today the pair had to remain focused and disciplined to avoid another incident. The early morning start coupled with having her stare fixated on the trail surface in front of her caused her eyes to be sensitive to light. Taking just one second to admire the new day would expose her to the most present hazard, the very sharp and jagged surfaces she was rapidly moving across.

With all her attention focused on the trail surface time became almost irrelevant. While entrenched in training for this event her focus was fixated on maintaining a certain pace, speed or cadence. Now her mind was fixated on technique. Candy's attention was divided between keeping up with her new friend and searching out safe landing locations along the trail surface. The path today was besieged with an array of landmines including: rocks, fallen tree limbs, stumps, rotten logs and an assortment of leaves that provided camouflage for more unseen hazards.

The newly minted team never missed a beat. At times, she thought following her new wingman may have pushed her pace faster than she would have liked. Although not part of her original plan she was now determined to stay with the young Air Force member for the remainder of the AT. Allowing someone else to blaze the trail relieved a lot of mental pressure. Following someone with more experience provided a level of comfort and security. Turning over the responsibility of navigating over dangerous terrain allowed the miles to pass without worrying about the danger that lurked with a misplaced step.

Although the trail narrowed in sections there were opportunities to move past slower moving runners. The twosome quickly found that where the trail rounded a tree or skirted to the side of a boulder it opened enough to allow a dutiful runner to duck to the inside or outside of the turn and gain a few positions in the race. Running with a partner, Candy was eager to take advantage of these faster routes. She was sure she would not have been brave enough to seek them out on her own. Following her personal trail guide, she felt confident bounding from one rock to another.

Foot placement was key. The athlete here was not focused on time or pacing as much as they were fixated on landing their next stride. The next landing spot needed to be solid, firm and one that would not shift, move or give way under the incoming transfer of weight and momentum. A runner needed a solid foundation to capture the energy and provide a solid base. Candy could think of few things more unnerving then landing a stride only to feel the rock shift, give way or slide out from underneath her center of gravity.

Eric and Candy were moving nicely thru the pack. In no time the two had worked their way past five or six groups. Her legs were doing a good deal of work, her lungs were running wide open but with so many distractions around her and with so much of her focus on the next stride she hardly seemed to notice how far they had progressed. Out of the blue, an unfamiliar voice rang out, it's source was two maybe three runners in front of her.

"Woooooooo"

Out of nowhere the trail backed up with runners each dodging one another then coming to a complete stop. Eric yelled out to slow down. "Hold up, the trail is blocked…" He came to an abrupt stop along a ridge of rocks and large stones covered in a thin blanket of moss.

Candy did her best to stop; her feet gave way as her footing nearly slide out from underneath her. To avoid running into Eric she placed her hand on his back to help maintain the separation between the two. She took a course slightly to the outside.

In shock and out of breath she tried to explain. "Sorry, didn't mean to push you, my momentum kept me moving forward, the rocks were too slippery to stop quickly like that."

"No harm, I get it."

"What's going on," Candy asked?

"I have no idea. Eric stood up on one of the larger rocks straining to look ahead to gain some insight or clues to what was going on ahead of them. "Strange that the trail must have gotten completely blocked for the whole group of us to come to a standstill."

Candy and Eric were now part of a string of runners each one wondering why the race had come to a standstill. Two men in front of them began to wander off the trail searching for an alternative route. Slowly a trickle of rumors and fabricated stories began to make their way through the traffic jam of athletes who stood flat-footed in the trail.

An older man with an unruly beard right in front of Eric turned his head slightly and spoke. "Someone took a pretty mean crash is the word. They said it's rough."

"Oh no," Eric replied.

Candy's face looked fallen but she said nothing about the news that was making the rounds.

Within a minute or two the group began to move forward, at first at barely the pace of a slow walk, then their forward progress was that of a slow trot. The frustration among the group could be felt. Lucky for the few with short-fuses, within a brief time they were back up to a slow jog. Eric and Candy, part of the larger collective began navigating themselves over and around some of the large stone foundations. Again, the group came to a rapid stop. Again, frustrations mounted and the mood began to take a turn.

Moving in the wrong direction to the race flow, in what would be one of the narrower sections of the trail were two First Responders carrying a stretcher. Laying on top of the litter was a middle-aged man who appeared to be in his late 40s. He had dark wavy hair, with a fit medium build and tall. His running outfit consisted of a pair of black shorts and a blue singlet with the logo of a local running club emblazoned across his chest. It was obvious he was not a JFK rookie. By his appearance, they assumed he had a few years of experience under his belt. Today experience did not help. Lying prone on the stretcher, his face was covered in sweat and trail grime, his forearms a mixture of blood, mud and torn skin. The trail did not care if you had run this race successfully for ten years or one, an untimed move, one unseen hazard, one lapse in judgment and the trail was going to unleash its wrath on you.

As the field stretcher made its way passed, Candy could see the other obvious signs of distress. Recognizable to all was the outline of a misshapen leg covered by a thin white covering. Easy to see was the look of absolute pain and the heavy weight of concern very clear on the man's face. His eyes closed, and his left hand furrowing his brow. The surrounding group where seconds ago they stood wallowing in their own frustration were now trying to provide moral support to one of their own.

"You'll be okay." One fellow JFK vet offered up.

A few more joined in.

"Recover fast and come back next year."

"Hang in there."

The signs of distress on the injured runner's face grew wider and more apparent as the medics carried him around and over the rocks.

Under her breath, Candy whispered, "I'm glad you're alive."

Once the medics moved past the field was underway again. The entire group walked slowly at first, but once into a small clearing the tragic scene was filed as another trail mishap and the pace picked up as the congestion cleared. Slow to get up to full speed Eric could feel his companion fall behind as he began to ramble over a rock and around a tree stump. Instinctively he decided to slow up to see what was going on with his new friend.

"Are you okay?"

At that moment Candy stopped took a few steps off the trail and sat down on a rather large and flat rock. Concerned he turned and followed her.

"Yea, I'm okay, you go on without me. That scene shook me up a little, I've never seen a crash like that up close and personal. I guess it took some wind out of my sails."

"No kidding, I get it, that looked pretty bad. But don't worry you're not going to take a tumble like that, we will move slow and steady. I'll make sure you are okay."

"It's not me. Really you go on."

"What, what's scaring you then?"

"I had a friend who crashed really bad on a trail, he was out running with a friend of ours and he took a really bad fall. I just wasn't ready to see something like that."

"Oh, I get it, made it a little too real."

"Yea, for sure"

"We will be okay, he'll be okay let's just keep moving it will keep your mind off everything. You know like they say, you need to get right back on the horse who threw you."

Eric's words penetrated deep into Candy soul, she needed to get back on the trail. She stared at her shoes nestled in some leaves around a patch of small rocks. Her chest expanded with a long deep inhale followed by a full cleansing breath.

"You are right, I have some unfinished work to do. I can't sit here, that won't bring him back."

Eric heard the last part of her comment loud and clear. He paused, and for a moment considered asking her to explain. His mind wrestled with the words "won't bring him back." But as the words, his questions were about to flow from his lips he thought better and decided to remain quiet.

The next few miles were peaceful in a weird but calm way. Candy followed Eric move for move, her eyes locked on to the ground in front of her only breaking long enough to survey Eric's choice of footings. The trail had her full attention. Outside of following his lead she allowed nothing to penetrate her bubble of concentration. The duo wrestled their way around tree branches and multiple rock formations. At one point, Eric had to duck under a fallen tree trunk only partially cleared from the trail.

The trail was eerily quiet with only the slight sounds of their shoes contacting the ground and the action of their lungs providing the oxygen needed to feed the large muscle groups powering their legs. Over a slight crest on the trail, the tranquility of the day was broken. A collection of random and unidentifiable noises penetrated the cover of the forest environment.

She heard it first. “What is that noise? It sounds like a party, a crowd of some sort, it’s much too early for the finish line.”

“No, it’s the break in the trail at Gathland’s gap, I think that’s what it is called. It’s a small clearing between the two portions of the AT. It’s also the first real downhill section. Stay mindful of your foot placements. We will be moving a bit faster.” Eric’s voice turned to the cautious side.

Breaking into the clearing, they passed an old split rail fence where a collection of young girls stood alongside. The group of eight were dressed in green and white athletic sweats emblazoned with the logo of a local community college. The girls cheered so loudly, and coming from the solitude of the forest, that their collective voices for a moment hurt Candy’s ears. When it became apparent to the impromptu cheerleaders that a girl was approaching them, the group sounded off in an even louder tone.

“You go girl…” Yelled one of them, who appeared to be the ring leader.

Another standing just a few feet away but on the other side of the fence yelled out “Girl power…you look awesome!”

The sound from the chorus of cheers was almost deafening as Candy passed in front of them.

Candy tried to high-five each member of the girl power pack as she smiled, thanked them for their support, and made her way into the clearing.

The aid station was well stocked and manned by energetic volunteers. Each member of the aid station team was prepared to assist each of today's racers to get to the end of the AT and the finish line.

"Grab something quick Candy, we need to keep moving. Seconds here equal minutes on the trail." Eric reminded her.

"I'll be right with you." Candy sucked down a cold cup of Coca-Cola from a Dixie cup and wondered internally if she had ever tasted anything so refreshing. Outside of refueling her body, the brief period off the trail allowed her mental focus to shift from surviving the next foot placement to worrying about what snack would best settle in her stomach.

As good as it felt to get a quick bite to eat the girl-power supporters did more to get Candy re-motivated than any salty snack or energy-laden power bar. Thankful for the support she was eager to get on with the race.

Mile 10

It was a simple jaunt across a small parking lot to rejoin the AT, but just like the proverbial line in the sand, it was also an announcement that you had to turn your concentration levels back to high. As the pair made their way to the connecting trailhead, they both realized that this was the last level ground they would see for the next five miles. Just a few steps off the black asphalt the trail began a long climb back up to the South Mountain ridgeline. A simple brown wooden sign with yellow lettering re-introduced them to the Appalachian Trail. The sign also beckoned that the trail was suitable for "foot traffic only." Candy thought that was funny, "Like someone is going to ride their bike or motorcycle over this stuff. Mountain goat maybe. Who would want to take anything else on these trails?" She asked out loud but to no one in-particular.

Here the trails seemed wider but also more challenging. The fallen leaves were thicker providing a deeper blanket of foliage which provided more disguise and concealment for any hazards which lurked in front of them. This instantly heightened Candy's sense of awareness as she progressed higher in elevation approaching the apex of the ridgeline.

Her legs began to feel heavy and for the first time she felt a bit tired. To herself, she wondered if the faster pace was beginning to affect her.

Just as she had earlier in the day, Candy paralleled every one of Eric's movements. Although glued to his every move, she ran off his hip about eighteen inches. In the distance that separated the two she felt like she could react to anything that might pop up along the trail. If Eric took a tumble she did not want to add to the chaos. She did not want to follow so closely that she could cause an issue or become part of it. If something along the trail caused him to slow down, she wanted enough room to adjust her speed. If he needed to change tactics or if a footing issue popped up, she did not want to be the tailgater who did not have enough time to avoid the collision. More than anything she wanted to make sure she was not hampering his race. As each mile clicked off it became more and more apparent that this new-found duo was working well together.

The trails here seemed to be subjected to more exposed rocks. Compared to the preceding miles, this section was more challenging and required a lighter more nimbler approach. Where the previous sections were littered with independent rocks of all shapes and sizes, here the collection appeared made up of larger more expansive rocks. The random arrangement compounded with varying lengths and heights of the rocks threw off the runners' stride length. The result was a choppier, more unpredictable gait with more start and stop adjustments to their pace and cadence. To make matters worse, another more compounding hazard got added into the fray.

Eric and Candy noticed they were passing more runners who were walking. Walking or power hiking as Jim called it was part of running an ultra or any race with elevation and technical trails. Here the duet caught more runners from behind then they had earlier in the day.

The very nature of foot race, even at the noncompetitive levels, is to catch and pass as many runners as you can. On the surface this should appear as a positive, but it's also a challenge. On an already difficult and congested trail catching a slower runner forces you to adjust your running style as you seek an opportunity to get around them. Unlike road running where a faster runner can simply pull around someone running slower. On technical trails like the JFK, a faster runner had to bide their time, had to seek an opportunity where the trail conditions and their own abilities to accelerate lined up so that they could make the move forward. Advancing towards the front became as much a game of survival as was running the race. A wrong timed move, waiting too long or pushing the issue too soon could cost you valuable time on the clock or even worse.

Candy and Eric caught up to a trio of male runners mid-way to the rapid decent known as "Weverton cliffs." Earlier in the day, this group had made short work of getting around Candy on the roads leading out of Boonsboro. They had dropped her so convincingly at that early point in the day that she was sure she would never see them again aside from possibly at the finishing line.

In a weird twist of fate that is common in long distances races where the hare tends to be caught by the more determined and consistent runner Candy recognized the group right away. A tall thin blonde-haired guy running in a pair of uniquely short Union Jack shorts and an old tattered t-shirt. With his shaggy blonde hair, wire rim glasses, thin mustache and pale skin, he looked like a leftover from a 1960s rock concert. His sidekick was a guy with a more muscular build, slightly shorter, and tightly cut hair. This chap wore more traditional running apparel and may have gone completely unnoticed except for his truly British greeting of "Tally-Ho." The straggler to the group seemed out of place, shorter, stockier, with a bit of a belly he looked truly uncomfortable. His running kit consisted of long basketball length shorts, a heavy gray sweatshirt, a New York Yankee baseball cap and a short choppy gait which called attention to his efforts. On this day, he was keeping up with his more physically fit friends but his breathing was labored, his footfall heavy and his gait was awkward. Roughly 13 miles into the day the threesome had slowed considerably and seemed out of place.

"Follow me when I go." Eric cautioned Candy turning his head slightly to ensure she heard him.

Eric was stuck behind this group for long enough. The narrow trails, the uncomfortable pacing and the fact the group had not yielded to an obviously faster moving group had Eric at wits ends. He was tired of running behind these guys and wanted a change of scenery.

"Left, we are going around you on the left."

"It's not clear." replied the slower of the three runners just in front of Eric.

"Can you slide to the side?" Eric questioned.

"You'll have to get around us on your own, nowhere for us to go mate." A thick New York accent replied.

Eric grew more frustrated, he wasn't asking them to concede the win, he simply wanted them to slow up or slide to the side so a pass by an obviously faster group could be made easier, less risky and safer. If this was for a podium finish, he understood that no favors would be given but from "middle of the pack runners" he expected more give and take.

The trail maneuvered around a group of mature trees to the left then weaved between four trees offset to one another on the right and around another group of three thin but taller trees just five feet in front of the others on the opposite side. Breaking from this small collection of timbers the trail widened. Eric figured it was now or never. If he didn't make a move he wouldn't get past them until after Weverton Cliffs and the entrance to the Chesapeake & Ohio (C&O) Canal Towpath another 4 plus miles down the trail.

With a mixture of anticipation, frustration and motivation fueled some by anger, the pressure to get around this group mounted. Sizing up just the right time, he made his move.

"Let's go."

Candy noticed Eric's thighs twitch and his powerful legs fire off. Leaving the small collection of trees which hugged the sides of the trail between two out cropping of rocks, the path opened up yielding a flat and unobstructed section. The pent-up energy propelled him around the two runners directly in front of him and within a stride of the third. Candy followed quickly behind and easily passed the first two. Success was just one runner and a few yards in front of them. The leader of the group, the lanky guy with the Union Jack shorts, was blocking up the trail. Seeing no clear route, Eric looked around him for just a moment to judge if a pass could be made. In an instant, something went wrong.

Candy was the first to see it. A misjudged landing location. Eric's foot fell off center sliding to the side of a rock. This unexpected movement caused his center of gravity to be thrown out of balance and off course. His body followed the unpredictable nature of the unbalanced load. Without stable footing and with his weight out of alignment his body creamed from one side of the trail to another. Disaster seemed apparent. All Candy could think about was the man she had seen on the stretcher and the fatal images JT had relayed to her about Kyle's accident.

Candy's heart skipped a beat.

Instinctively Eric reached out. His right forearm caught the trunk of a tree off his right side. In a flash of panicked leaden mental recall, something told him to grab a hold of the tree. He squeezed his bicep tight locking the tree in the crux of his arm. This sudden impact restrained his forward motion, allowed his body to catch up with itself and although causing him to spin around the tree kept him upright. The resistance of the tree as an anchor point provided an opportunity to gain his balance.

Without crashing to the ground Eric completed the pass and fell back in line. Through it all, Candy was wide-eyed and still right behind him.

"Holy second chances Batman…that was awesome. You so almost bit it."

"Let's not talk about that. I think I saw my life flash before my eyes. And it wasn't very long."

Okay, Batman, I'll keep it to myself. For now, ha."

Mile 15

Once on the ridgeline of South Mountain, the JFK course maintains a steady elevation with only slight changes in the overall altitude. Mostly the trail twists and turns among tree and rock formations more than it changes altitude. That is until the Weverton Cliffs. At approximately 14.5 miles into the race, the course drops over 1,000 feet in a series of steep "switchbacks." Thousands of runners and many more hikers over the years have carved the alternating trails deep into the natural terrain but even that does not make this section any less treacherous.

To survive the AT and the Weverton Cliffs demands near total concentration. Candy was beginning to feel the tiresome effects of the near constant mental strain. Approaching Weverton she felt drained, wore out and ready for a break. It was not her legs, lungs or body that had become over taxed. It was her mind. The near constant threat of falling, the 100% focus that the trail required, the near disaster of her own close call, seeing Eric almost crash and the haunting reality of the runner being carried off the course weighed on her. Lost in all the mental white noise was the fact that the trail was unbelievably quiet, except for their own labored breathing coupled with the sound of their shoes on the carpet of dirt, rocks, leaves, stones, tree branches and crushed gravel.

It caught Candy nearly by surprise. It shocked her back into the world of the living. Inconspicuous and soft at first but with each footfall it gained a life of its own. Faint voices could be heard off in the distance. Their barely audible sound slowly turned into a sharp calling, a beckoning to run faster, a charge to find the source of the sound just over the horizon.

Candy recognized its familiar quality. In an excited tone, she called out. "Eric is that, is that Weverton? Are we nearing the end of the trails…I believe I hear people cheering."

Himself lost in the repetitive motion of trail running hadn't noticed the still distant sounds. Taking his eyes off the trail he turned his attention to the faint calling muffled somewhat by the naked branches of the trees. "I believe so. Hot dawg, I'll be happy to get off this trail, I've had enough!" His eyes went directly back to the trail surface.

The subdued sounds grew with intensity, now unmistakable, growing more recognizable and coming closer. Eric and Candy both knew that with each proceeding footfall the end of the first chapter of their JFK story was drawing to a close.

Out of nowhere stood a middle-aged man with gray hair, weathered and wrinkled skin, and a great big smile. He was a volunteer dressed in blue-jeans, well insulated hunting boots, black gloves, a tan Carhart jacket and a yellow reflective vest. Candy was first to see him.

"Eric just off the trail, in front of us, look.

Waving for the runners to take a sharp right-hand turn was the man in the vest. Breaking his big smile, he warned everyone turning in front of him to take the switchbacks slow and steady.

"If things go wrong here, they go wrong fast and it's going to leave a mark. Keep your eyes on the trail, the towpath will be there waiting for you."

Years of experience had taught this volunteer that many runners try to sneak a peek at the upcoming section of the race before successfully finishing the AT. It was well ingrained in his memories that it would only take a second of distraction to end someone's race on the Weverton Cliffs.

Carved out of a stone ledge on the end of South Mountain, the switchbacks are outlined by yellow caution tape. It's unclear if this barrier is in place to better define the route, keep people from cutting the course or as the last obstacle to keep an out of control victim from plummeting to their demise. The trail here is narrow, rugged, rocky, full of roots and treacherous. Runners are faced with a surface which depending on the conditions, can provide unpredictable footing. In one instance, they would be traversing jagged stone the next running over unsteady, pulverized and slippery rocks leading them to a hairpin turn cut out of an ancient boulder partially protruding from the rock wall in front of them.

Today the course was wide open with no one in front of them to slow their progress. Their pace picked up as they moved over the steep descent. Although not experienced in running on such technical terrain Candy hung on Eric's every move. The pair darted around each hairpin turn then navigated the rugged terrain for approximately 50 yards turning back in the opposite direction to complete another downhill leg. Over the series of threatening rocks, the twosome kept a steady rate making relatively short work of the Weverton Cliff. The switchbacks would be the final challenge to the AT portion of the race.

When all was said and done, Candy enjoyed the up-tempo

nature of running the nearly 1,000-foot change in elevation. She enjoyed the rapid nature of the challenge. Here, although still focused on her footing she enjoyed the light, upbeat tempo, the quick movements and the rapid action of the run to the bottom of the trail.

Her reward at the end of the cliffs would be some welcome visitors. This would be the first time she would be able to see Jim, JT and Carly since her rapid departure in Boonsboro.

The noise now felt like the roar of a Super Bowl crowd. A sense of relief overcame the pair as the Appalachian Trail was behind them, with their final steps off the Weverton Cliffs. It was with relief that they ran across a small section of road lined on both sides by crews, well-wishers, spectators and former runners of the race. Members of a local running club outfitted in their blue hoodies with gold lettering directed traffic. Everyone, whether a stranger or an intimate friend wanted each runner to successfully finish the race there by accomplishing a bucket list item or fulfilling a personal mission.

The emotion of running through this gauntlet of support was overwhelming. Still glued to Eric's hip, Candy matched his pace as the two ran between the crowds of people held in check by yellow barricade tape supported on wooden sticks anchored in orange traffic cones. This temporary lane marked the route of travel from the AT to the next section of the race, the C&O Towpath.

"Thanks Eric...thank you so much for the help. Do you have crew here, or family? It won't take long I would like you to meet my team."

Eric slowed down enough to run side by side with Candy. "No, no crew I'm running solo. No one is here for me."

"Please say hi to my guys and my dog. Her name is Carly Q. That girl there is more than a dog. She is my family, my best friend and all I really have now. Except..." There was a slight break in Candy's thoughts. "It would be nice for you to meet them."

"Sounds good. I would like that but I plan to be in and out fast…okay?"

Jim and JT were waiting with a makeshift aid station set up just for Candy. They both caught a glimpse of her running along the short section of the blacktop road.

"What can we get you Candy?" Jim called out when she was about 10 yards away.

"A drink and a sandwich, Jim. This is Eric, we met on the trail he helped me run the AT. Without him it would have taken so much longer." She wiped the sweat and trail grime from her forehead.

Eric walked up to the table and reached out to shake Jim's hand.

"Howdy, Eric" Jim reached out his hand first. "What can we get you….?"

"Same, drink and anything to eat, something light."

"PBJ is all we have. How's that?"

"Perfect."

From behind the table, Carly barked.

"Hey Carly Q." Eric spoke as he grabbed his sandwich, a cup of Diet Dew and said his goodbyes.

Carly's head half turned, one ear stood up straight the other looped half over.

JT handed Candy a wet towel and another cup of Dew. Candy wiped her face and began adjusting her vest.

"Thank you all so much…take care of her. She is awesome." Eric paused and raised his voice an octave or two. "Candy."

Candy lifted her head from fidgeting with her vest, wiped her face one more time and turned toward Eric.

The two locked eyes.

"You finish this thing…for whomever you're running for. You. Finish. This."

Candy's eyes felt heavy. Without a word being audible she mouthed all that Eric needed.

"Thank you."

It took a few extra minutes for Candy to get herself back in running shape. As she consumed the PBJ and drank the remains of diet soda, Jim peppered her with questions.

"How's it going? Are you keeping a good pace? How are your legs? Have you fallen?"

JT stood behind the pair ready to digest all the details of the previous 15 miles. Candy did not say much. She was too busy trying to stuff the entire PBJ into her mouth as she struggled to breathe and revitalize her lungs.

Great, yea, fine, almost but I'm okay." Was all that Candy could communicate. Jim was happy and satisfied with her reply. Among the short and compact answers, he heard all he needed to hear to get an informative read on how the race was going.

The most telling sign of the day so far was that Candy did not have that beaten down look on her face like Jim had seen on a few runners already. In endurance tests like this, Jim knew he could see the condition of the athletes' spirit by the expression they wore on their face when no one was watching. When he spied her prior to her reaching their aid station, her face showed her true emotions and the amount of effort this race was costing her. In that moment, before Candy saw her team before she could put on a fake expression, Jim saw that her eyes were bright and alive. He saw that she wore a smile and interacted with spectators along the course. Jim also saw life, he saw fight and he saw a measure of joy. Instantly he knew that the race was not too big, the challenge not too daunting and the day not too long for her. Candy was running her race; the race was not running her.

As reassuring as the moment had been he was also aware that it would be a long day. 35-miles of challenges, both physical and mental still laid out in front of her.

JFK 50 – The Towpath

Chapter 27

Departing the Weverton crew zone, Candy left the blacktop surface for a small dirt and grass trail that ducked behind a row of porta-johns and into a small cove of trees. This short section would make a left-hand turn traveling under the overpass of State route 340 before dropping a few feet where it deposited her onto the Chesapeake & Ohio (C&O) Canal Towpath.

Here the character of the race changed. Where the Appalachian Trail (AT) section was hazardous, threatening and demanded your constant attention. The contrasting C&O Towpath provided a very forgiving surface that was easy to run on. Over the previous miles your mind hinged on a constant state of alert. The next 28-miles could lull an unexpecting runner into an attention robbing slumber.

The AT challenged you nearly every step of the way, the Towpath was straightforward, often tedious and so repetitive that an unexpecting runner could unknowingly settle into a slower more comfortable pace. The welcomed feelings of running relaxed after the fast-paced action and physical pounding of the AT may seem in the moment like "the medicine the doctor ordered," but in hind sight it often resulted in a waste of precious time. This more tranquil section may have cost more competitors a JFK finish than the more arduous trails. With their guard lowered, it was easy to slow to the point of falling behind the cut off times. With their focus lost one could lose so much spunk and vigor that they found it easy to quit, to give up or to simply call it a day.

"Finally, I'm on some flat and level ground." Candy spoke out loud as she logged her first mile on the C&O.

As she was getting ready to set out on the meatiest part of her day, she felt confident that nothing could go wrong. This was the kind of long-distance running she had cut her teeth on with Kyle.

The morning sun was now in full effect. With her attention constantly focused on her footing along the AT she had hardly noticed the rise in temperature. The path along the Potomac River was soaked in sunshine and dusted with a light breeze.

From its construction in the 19th and early 20th century the C&O Canal, with its 184.5 miles of pathways began as passage way for commodities. Operating for nearly 100 years the canal aided the flow of coal, lumber and agricultural products along the Potomac River headed to market. It has seen the rise of a nation, the wars between a divided land and improvements in transportation that have made it obsolete. Today the Towpath endures as a National Parkway, linking modern communities with historical, natural and recreational treasures. Since the late 1960s runners from around the world have traveled to the C&O Towpath to test their endurance will and might.

The wide-open pathway stretched out in front of her like an endless ribbon of earth tones. It's surface of crushed gravel is level and unthreatening. Taking advantage, Candy was ready for a steady diet of interval running. Before long, her wristwatch beeped signaling another mile of the race had been completed. With her attention drawn to the sights surrounding her, the alarm went nearly unnoticed. The four repetitive beeps finally broke through, startled at first, she glanced at her watch. For the first time all morning, she felt comfortable enough to take her eyes off the surface in front of her. To her surprise the 17th mile marker registered on the digital faceplate of her watch at just over 10-minutes per mile.

With steady and predictable footing underneath, she felt comfortable enough to perform some simple calculations. Simple math in general terms sounds easy enough but for an endurance athlete in the middle of a race simply trying to perform those functions while on the move could spell disaster. "Not a bad mile indeed, I just have to keep this up for a marathon. Plus." She paused as the gravity of that statement fully sunk in. "At the end of this marathon, after running up South Mountain, I'll have 8 more miles to the finish. What was I thinking?"

Candy was trying to stay upbeat. She was attempting to reassure herself that she was in a good position mentally and physically. As positive as her words may have sounded to someone on the outside, as self-assured as her own internal dialogue may have proclaimed, for the first time she noted how very far she had yet to go.

"33-miles... Wow I have further to go than I've ever run before. This all seemed like a good idea a month ago. Girl, were you nuts?"

A few of Jim's inspirational words came back to her at exactly the right moment as quickly some temporary insecurities were pushed aside.

"Run each mile on its own. This is not a 50-mile race for anyone but the two or three upfront who can legitimately win this thing. What you're taking part in is an event made up of fifty 1-mile runs. 1-mile. One. Mile. You can do anything for one mile." Candy remembered him saying to her very convincingly

On the AT, individual runners tended to keep to themselves while focused on traveling over the trails without incident. The Towpath with its easy footing offered more opportunity to take in the scenery. It also offered additional opportunities to communicate with the runners around you.

The easy to navigate surface also allowed faster runners who held themselves back or who may have gotten stuck behind slower moving traffic to break free and run unencumbered. The more predictable surface of the C&O provided the first time a runner could get in tune with how the day was progressing physically. For some the effects of the pounding that the AT delivered began to come forward. For others, the absence of pain meant they had survived the previous 15.5 miles unscathed.

Her world shifted in the course of a single stride. Like an unwelcomed guest, Candy noticed her thighs felt stiff, awkward and heavy. On her next step, her right leg buckled slightly as it landed flat footed on the surface in front of her. On the next turn over, her left leg felt nonresponsive and weak. Overall her quads felt hollow, lifeless and flat. Her gait was now completely foreign, out of whack and unreliable.

Concerned she thought to herself. "My legs, feel like I've done 10,000 squats with a 400-pound bar. Thankfully nothing really hurts, they just feel dead. Flat. My legs feel worn out."

The toll of the AT was beginning to catch up with her. Under the spell of the technical trails, her mind blocked out the physical effort she was putting forth. The constant focus on proper footing camouflaged the amount of energy it took to run over those tricky and often technical surfaces.

With the 20-mile aid station just in front of her, Candy decided to deviate from her interval routine and take an early walk break. She reasoned that her legs simply needed a little downtime. Time spent here would surely pay dividends when her large muscle group was able to rebound.

Her first line of defense was a positive internal dialogue. "Some fuel and a cold drink will fix anything, I'll walk my way into the aid station, grab something to eat and walk out allowing my stomach to settle, then we will be good as new. Then just 30-miles to go."

Making her way into the aid station the upbeat nature of the volunteer staff helped reassure her that a bad spell was not the end of her day. She remembered all the advice Jim had given her. She would experience highs and lows and that both would not last long. During all of his conversations leading up to this day, he keyed on one simple fact. That if you simply stuck with it, if you continued to move forward that you could work yourself out of any tough situation. Jim reminded her constantly that forward motion was the key to the day, that if you could continue to advance, you would make it to the end.

The volunteers were a godsend. One particularly energetic older lady seemed to attach herself to Candy about 10-feet out from the aid station.

"Is there anything I can get you, sweetie? Fill your water bottle, get you a sandwich, some cookies or maybe a candy bar anything?"

"Oh yes could you fill my bottle, dump out the old stuff put in some new, please. I'm about tired of that flavor."

"Sure, thing honey how about a bite to eat?"

Before Candy could say anything, the volunteer called out loud, Joyce, get this young lady a sandwich and a candy bar, a Reese cup, yea that's it."

"Thank you so much, you guys are the best."

In seconds, the helpful lady had Candy's bottle full and back in her hand as the pair walked out of the aid station. Candy stuffed the makeshift PB and J into her mouth, while she put the peanut butter cup into her vest pocket.

"Thank you so much."

"Don't you worry honey I'll walk with you until you're ready to run again...you're doing awesome. I used to run but not like you gals today. When I ran they thought it was bad for our health, Ha

Kathrine Switzer showed them. You keep up the calling young lady."

With the last bites of the PB and J still in her mouth and a big gulp of Coke, Candy turned to hug her new friend, although she had no idea of her name.

"I'm Candy, Thank you so much…what's your name?"

"Laura…it's been my pleasure honey."

After a quick hug, the two parted each other's company Candy 30-miles away from her goal and Laura 30-yards away from helping someone else.

With revitalized legs and a lifted-up spirit she set off to chew up another small section of the trail. Without dwelling on it Candy was very happy her legs came back to life but also fearful that they might fail her again. In 7-miles, she would see her crew, that became her sole focus along with following the 8/2 interval that Jim had prescribed.

One benefit about interval running was that once into the rhythm and flow of running, 8-minutes and walking for 2-minutes, it was easy to simply forget about the largeness of the day. The intervals broke down the challenge into bite-sized sections in comparison to the mammoth-sized task. Miles ran together, aid stations passed, runners passed her and Candy passed others all to the repetitive nature of 8-minutes on and 2 off. Her legs continued to rebound and move her forward. The only drawback was that her per mile pace dropped to around eleven minutes per mile.

Running mostly alone on the Towpath, except a few nods and smiles to passing runners, she felt the familiar beckoning of the long-distance runner. The calling of solitude, the state of isolation and the feeling of being truly alone in the world could be relaxing or haunting. With only the sound of your breathing and the tone of your shoes hitting the ground to keep you company your internal motivation could be challenged.

The gravity of the day hit her hard when at one-point pain crept in and her spirit turned weak. Some were undertaking this race to capstone a running career, others to celebrate a significant achievement and others as a milestone toward loftier goals. Candy ran this race to pay tribute to the love of her life. A wave of depression hit her hard when she realized that this race and her participation in it signified the end of a relationship that she hoped would last forever. A relationship she hoped would fill her soul. In Kyle, Candy envisioned a life where she would become whole. A partnership that could forgive and correct any misgiving from the past and open new doors to love, security and acceptance far greater than she had never known.

In the time since his passing, she had consciously dealt with his absence from her life. The race offered a continuing tie to him, a chance to finish his business. The routine of training maintained a connection to him. It hit her hard when she realized that as she drew closer to completing the JFK 50, this chapter of her life's story would be closed. That thought began to weigh heavy on her heart. Approaching the Antietam Aqueduct, Candy desperately needed the motivational shot in the arm that her crew would provide.

Mile 27.3

A quarter mile down the Towpath a familiar face stood along the side of the trail.

"Candy... Candy." JT beckoned.

The sound of his voice broke her from the state of isolation.

Candy lifted her eyes from the trail, wiped her face removing a layer of trail dust from her cheeks. As the palm of her hand passed close to her eyes something caught her attention. Her cheeks were stained with tears.

“Are you okay Candy, you look like you have been crying?” JT asked.

“It’s hard JT, it’s hard.” She collected her emotions and wiped her face again as the pair ran slowly toward Jim who had her personal aid station set up again just off the trail at the back of his car.

“What do you need Candy?” Jim asked.

"The same as before please, fill my bottle and something light to eat. I feel good just had some low times mentally, but I’m okay. Seeing you guys helps. It’s hard you know.”

“No doubt Candy it is difficult but you’re tough, you’re resilient, focused. You’ve got this! Don’t give into the tough times, don’t feed the trolls of despair…do not write your own obituary. Focus on the next mile and that’s all.”

Candy took a bite out of the sandwich and a quick shallow of her favorite drink. The cold diet Dew tasted so good.

“Oh, that is good…”

“What else do you need? Shoes, socks, do you have any rocks in your shoes? Can we do anything to help you?”

“I’m good Jim, just some mental stuff, I’m tired and it all adds up. It gets to me.” Candy paused as her voice trailed off. “It’s just…you know. I miss him.”

Jim also felt Kyle’s loss. The two had become very close. He never said as much to anyone, but the young man was much like a son. Jim also knew that in some fashion the end of this race was the end of his relationship with Kyle as well. The young man would always be a part of his life, but the preparation for the JFK 50 kept his presence in their world alive. Jim feared that at the end of this day Kyle would be just another memory not unlike that of other deceased friends and family. He painfully knew very well just what she meant.

As comforting as it may have been to stop running for a few seconds. As much as it lifted her spirits to see Jim and JT. Candy knew that she had to get moving. For every second she stood there talking to her crew, relishing in the comfort they provided, it became harder and harder to get back on the trail.

For some, the Did Not Finish status started with the ease at which you could find comfort among family and friends. Good intentions could easily entrap a tired, worn out, overworked soul to accept the easy way out. Alibis came easy when supporters unknowingly open doors that lead to failure with their good intended comments. “It’s okay, were proud of you. 27-miles is really a long way, you don’t have to keep running. We are proud of what you have done.” Candy was struggling but she was not going to accept anything but completing the 23-miles between her and finishing this race for her love.

The “Canal” section of the 50-mile race is almost totally flat, an unpaved dirt and gravel surface free of all vehicle traffic from mile-15.5 through mile-41.8. Running club sponsored aid stations were staggered along the canal portion of the course. These high spirited pitstops have grown in popularity and complexity over the years. These aid stations have become as much an attraction to the event as they help in providing a major supporting role to the runners.

One aid station featured a Star Wars theme complete with a dancing Wookie. Another built their theme around the movie “Miracle on 34th Street” named so appropriately for mile 34 of the race. This aid station was complete with Kris Kringle and a flock of helpers who cheered on those who passed by this southern location of Santa’s workshop. Their food table was stocked with plenty of homemade Christmas cookies along with a full array of sports drinks, salty snacks and the traditional ultra-smorgasbord of easy to consume trail food.

Mile 38 at Taylors Landing featured the aid station better known as "38 Special."

It would be a hard act to follow but Candy would see her crew right after Taylors Landing.

Candy's two men and a schnauzer gang set up shop 30 minutes before her estimated arrival time. Her two guys hung out, made small talk with other crew members and volunteers while they repeatedly glanced at their watches. The only one not too concerned with the time of day was Carly, she found a spot in the grass that received direct sunlight and sniffed at the ground as she circled endlessly to find the perfect sleeping spot. JT watched with a crooked smiled on his face as Carly finally settled down and fell asleep.

"Crazy dog," JT commented out loud. Then he glanced at his watch again. He silently reasoned that Candy was late.

A few yards down the Towpath, Jim stood with a handful of members of a local running club. Like him, they were there to support one of their own who was also a first-timer. He was the first one to see Candy. Her appearance shocked him. Candy was moving fine, as she made her way into the aid zone. A few minutes behind schedule, moving at a slower tempo than he had hoped for, was not what concerned him. Something deeper appeared to be brewing.

"Candy are you okay?" Jim called out. "How are you feeling?"

"I'm fine Jim, really just tired. I got a little behind on my nutrition I'm running on fumes. I'll be okay. I just need a kick in the butt. There's a lot of lonely miles out there. I get down some. The fatigue makes me think too much. This is hard. Life is hard and I miss him so much. Maybe this wasn't such a good idea."

Jim grabbed Candy by her shoulders, he moved in front of her and pulled her in close. In a comforting tone, he spoke into her ear, "You are right, life is tough. You…we got dealt a tough blow.

We all miss him. Don't feed that negativity out on the course. When depressing thoughts or ideas jump on your back, refuse to entertain them, refuse to acknowledge them. Okay?" Before she could nod in acknowledgment, Jim called back to the makeshift table telling JT she was coming and to be ready to refill her bottles.

"I know Jim, I do but it's just so hard. I loved him...I really did. I began to see my life with him. Kyle was my future and now." Candy paused and labored to take a depth breath. She wiped her eyes. "There's so much more."

"I know, let's get you fixed up. Stay positive, stay focused on what you're doing today, honoring his life. Today is all that matters, the next mile is all that matters. The next step is ALL that matters. Let's finish this, you can finish this."

The pair walked to her aid station that JT was tending too. Carly instantly jumped to life and barked a few times before walking up to Candy as she tried to remove some garbage from her pack.

"Oh, hi girl, it sure is nice to see you. You always bring a smile to my face. This is hard Carly...can you run a few miles for me?"

Carly jumped up and pawed at Candy's hand. "Awe girl, I love you. You been a good girl for the guys?"

As beat up physically as Candy was, she found it within herself to bend over and wrestle Carly's face next to hers. Carly for her part gave her friend a face full of wet doggie kiss.

"That's what I needed girl...thank you."

Jim fired off some commands as it was time to get back to business.

"JT make sure she drinks some but not too much. Can't lose your stomach now."

"My stomach is good, my feet hurt some, I'm just tired. I feel in decent shape, just low on gas. I need some high-octane fuel."

Jim reached into a clear Tupperware container with an off color green lid. "I got just what you need. Here, take this but don't eat it all at once, a few little bits here and there."

"Oh, you are the best, Jim."

In Candy's hand was a slice of Red Velvet Cake acquired earlier in the day from one of the 38 Special aid station volunteers. For years Jim had heard about the special JFK 50 cake and wanted some for himself. Setting up shop at Taylor's Landing he had crossed paths with a volunteer who had some set aside for fellow volunteers and crew members. When Jim told her that he had always wanted a slice for his own, that he had a weakness for cake, that red velvet was his absolute favorite, she cut him an oversized slice of his own.

Seeing Candy in dire shape he knew that his secret stash had a higher calling. His treat would be just the kick in the running shorts that she needed.

JT took care of all the "maintenance" that was needed. He filled her water bottles, placed them back in her running vest and wiped her face with a cool rag. He also made sure she had some extra snacks to take out on the trail tucked into her vest pockets. There were no limits of what he would do for her that day.

At a previous stop when Candy complained about a rock in her shoe JT sat on the ground and put Candy's foot in his lap. Like a well-timed NASCAR pit crew he untied her shoe, cleaned out the rocks, brushed off the bottom of her foot and put everything back together again ready for more miles in less than a minute.

"Oh man, this cake is so good." Candy called out.

Jim had handed her a fork but in true ultramarathon style Candy was feeding herself by hand.

“Thank you, so much.”

“It’s okay but you owe me one when you finish this race. Are you feeling better? You looked pretty down coming into here.”

“I do Jim. I’m ready to head back out there. Love you, Carly…”

“Do you have everything?” JT asked.

Candy looked down at her vest, inventoried everything out loud. “Water bottles, GUs, a snack or two, sunglasses, hat, no rocks in my shoes…I think I’m good.” Another big bite of cake muffled part of her reply.

“Great let’s get you back out on the course.”

JT walked beside her about 20 yards down the trail as she left Taylor’s Landing. In front laid the final 4-miles of the Towpath and 8-miles of rolling country roads.

“Go get it.” JT smiled as Candy turned her attention to the open path in front of her.

With hours of running behind her, she made her way toward the closing section of the race. Before the right-hand turn which took runners off the towpath and on to country roads, runners partake in one final JFK tradition or as some view it one final burden.

For those that arrive at the end of the Towpath before the magic hour of 3 p.m., there is no hoopla, no reward and no celebration. For racers gifted with quick feet they make a simple right-hand turn off the C&O Canal Towpath joining up with the Dam Number 4 Road and the final 8-mile challenge of the day. For those reaching this point after the witching hour of 3 p.m. the odds of finishing before sunset go down significantly. For this group equipped with steady progress and relentless determination, the race organizers provided a temporary yet unique gift for each runner passing the 40-mile marker after 3 p.m. A reflective traffic safety vest, better known humorously in the JFK circle as the

"Vest of shame." Although rebranded the “Vest of Fame” by the glass half full crew.

Candy was unphased when a race official asked her if he could place the vest on her just before the turn for the country roads leading to Williamsport.

“You bet…this means I’m still in this game.” Candy motored on with only a slight loss of time to adjust her new running accessory.

Once on her own, she silently wondered, “only 8 miles to go…how hard can this be?”

JFK 50 - Rolling Hills to a New Life Beyond

Chapter 28

The JFK 50 route leaves the Chesapeake & Ohio (C&O) Canal Towpath at Dam #4 and begins an uphill climb from the river basin to the farmlands of Maryland. This final 8-mile section signals the approaching end of the race which began some 40-miles away. Along the Towpath the aid stations helped count down the remaining miles, along the country roads strategically placed roadside mile markers help to remind and motivate participates that the end was drawing near. For some this added fuel to the fire propelling them to a strong finish. For others, the slow arduous mile by mile countdown sucked the last remaining wind from their sails.

"8 more miles to go." Candy spoke to herself again.

Over the course of the day, the field of participants which started off in Boonsboro as a tightly packed group standing together on main street had spread out over the length of the course. If gifted with a bird's eye view one would have been able to see groups of runners racing to the finish line while others struggled to stay in the game slogging their way along the Towpath. Candy had run most of the miles from Taylor's Landing alone. Over that time, she was pleasantly surprised no one caught her from behind and had accepted the fact that she could not track down anyone who was out in front of her.

The more traditional marathon runner has “the wall” that physically and emotionally challenges them from completing the race. It's at this point the body runs out of fuel, muscles grow fatigued and mentally people break down. For the ultra-runner, the length of their race being longer than the traditional 26.2-mile distance, this sect pushes past this traditional breaking point. For some, they face this wall multiple times during an ultramarathon event. The ultrarunner trains and conditions themselves to run extreme distances. They learn how to fuel their bodies on the go. and they discover ways to manage and overcome physical pain.

One thing that both groups have in common is that endurance athletes face extreme mental fatigue late in a race. Mental fatigue erodes their resolve, deludes their conviction and worse it tends to bring out their demons. For many those ghosts hunkered away deep in the hidden recess of their personal history are what many are trying to outrun.

Candy did not see the attack coming.

Along the side of the road as she crested one of the many rolling inclines, a young family of three stood and watched as the field of athletes passed by. A middle-aged couple from the tail end of the baby-boomer generation stood holding hands with a young girl sandwiched between them. As the three-some cheered on the approaching runners, Candy’s gaze became fixated on this simple scene as she approached their vantage point. She concluded, the little girl who swung back and forth holding on to her parents’ arms must have been their daughter. Behind them stood a traditionally styled white 2 story farm home with large windows and a wraparound porch. The scene was perfect Americana.

The father figure called out. “You’re all doing awesome, keep up the good work, only a few more miles to go.”

The young girl, was about six years old. She was outfitted in a yellow sundress and white "pretty" shoes. Standing proudly with her parents she wore a big smile, freckled cheeks, her near red hair parted in the middle with two big bows and ponytails. As the runners passed in front of this little girl, full of excitement and energy, she echoed her father's encouraging words.

"Good job! Runners."

Cresting the hill Candy who transitioned from a slow run to her hiking pace found herself caught up in the All-American scene that played out along the side of the course. Transfixed on the three figures, so simple, so pure, so much of what every young girl wanted when they grew up. A pretty house set on a hill with a deep green lawn and a white picket fence. A handsome doting husband and a beautiful young child. Within this scene, Candy saw the life she had envisioned with Kyle before that heartbreaking day.

She dreamed that one day her life would include Kyle, Carly and maybe a little girl of her own. She dreamed her name would be Jessica. She would have thick wavy blonde hair and blue eyes like her daddy. Her smile would light up a room, she would dance, sing songs and she would enjoy nature. Jessica would be easy to talk to and very curious. Carly and Jessica would be best friends. She would love animals, flowers and would live a life full of love and acceptance. A life which was safe, secure and surrounded by her loving parents. The life Candy had lived if only for a fleeting time and the very life that escaped her that summer in the park.

Waves of anxiety set in as her rhythmic breathing fell apart as the crushing realization that that dream could never become reality. She felt short of breath. Out of nowhere a bout of nausea overcame her. She could not regain control of her mind, her body or her thoughts. She tried to push on.

Overwhelmed with her deteriorating condition her paced slowed. Her breathing became erratic. Her feet began to feel heavy and labored. Tears filled her eyes as an already elevated heart rate worsened. For 45+ miles she held it all together. The pain of running, the physical turmoil of constant movement and the desire to simply be still. For much of the day, Candy had been in charge and determined. Sure, there were a few low spots but she was proud of herself for soldiering on and moving forward no matter the temporary discomfort. This time she surrendered.

Candy stopped running, she took a few more labored steps and finally sat down along the side of the road. She was just out of sight of the little girl who she could still hear. Along the curb of the road Candy put her hands-on-her-knees and lowered her head. Her eyes overflowing, her cheeks stained by tears completely broke down and she cried out loud. Mixed between her labored breath she carried on a conversation between herself and some imaginary figure.

"Why? Why me Kyle?" Her voice rang out with the tenor of anger and grief. "Why did you have to love me? Why did we have to meet...why am I the one that must live alone, without you? Why did you leave, ME?" Her breathing became worse as the very raw emotions took over. Her voice cracked, her words became distorted with emotion leaving them almost unrecognizable.

"I can't do this! I can't live without you and I can't..."

As Candy sat on the roadside Andrea, a slim but muscular girl whose gait kept her up on her toes approached. Dressed in a pair of black three-quarters length capris, a navy-blue tank top with *IRONMAN* Chattanooga emblazoned across the front and a Detroit Tigers ball cap worn squarely on her head. The mid-30-year-old runner wore a determined look as she scaled the small hill in front of the young family Candy had previously hiked passed. Moving progressively up through the pack all day, Andrea had her eyes set on catching Candy when the pair arrived on the blacktop road after leaving the Towpath. As Candy crested the small hill, Andrea thought she had lost contact with her rival.

Once over the small hill herself, Andrea noticed a figure sitting among the mixture of dirt, small rocks and shaggy grass along the side of the road. At first, she was happy to have finally caught up with the girl she had been trying to run down for the better part of a half-a-mile. Then a degree of fear set in as she wondered if something was seriously wrong. Why was the girl she had chased during the closing stages of the C&O suddenly stopped along the roadside? Had some overtaxed body part failed, did an overuse injury creep up or had her will to continue simply been broken?

Andrea maintained her steady pace as she drew nearer to the motionless and hunched over figure. The unmistakable sound of someone crying intermixed with a distressed and soft-spoken voice became audible. Some of the dialogue was clear and understandable, other parts muffled, distorted and were for the most part unrecognizable. Concerned, she stopped running and slowly closed the remaining distance between the two. Within an arm's reach, she cleared her throat to try gain the broken runners' attention.

"Are you okay?" There was no response. Andrea grew worried.

"Excuse me, Can I help?" Candy was unaware that another runner had approached her.

With no response, Andrea bent over and lightly placed her hand on Candy's shoulder.

"Excuse me are you okay? I heard that last part of your sentence. If you're not broken YOU can do this girl."

The physical contact and the sound of another voice combined to jolt Candy back into the reality that she was in the latter stages of a 50-mile race, sitting along the side of the road crying and talking to herself. Exposed, she quickly became embarrassed.

"Oh what, I'm sorry." Hastily she tried to dry her eyes and gain some composure. "I'm really, really, sorry you had to find me like this. I'm okay, just..."

"Hey, girlfriend...I get it. I'm tired too. Trust me. I want to sit down right there next to you and eat a plate of cupcakes. But we are tougher than that. Right?" Andrea extended her hand to help the distressed runner back to her feet.

The two now stood along the side of the road a steadying arm still on Candy's shoulder in case she needed some help with her balance. Andrea looked straight into her eyes, "you're going to be okay." Candy worked hard to maintain her composure and get herself back together again.

A more confident voice spoke up. "Hi, I'm Candy, thank you for stopping. I don't want to mess up your day or slow you down. I'm dealing with some things. Mental things, you know. Emotions, I mean…I'm not crazy." She chuckled.

Quickly snapping back Andrea replied, "Listen we're running 50-miles for a shiny metal disc on a red, white and blue ribbon...we are all a little batshit crazy."

"I guess when you put it like that we are a little nuts." The pair began a slow walk along the road towards Williamsport.

"For me, it's not just about the medal, or a challenge, or to say I can do this." Candy paused. "I lost someone recently and. He was." Her eyes again filled with tears and her voice once again sounded vulnerable. "We were, are going to..."

Andrea interrupted once she noted that this line of conversation was going to get Candy back into a place of not being able to maintain her composure.

"Oh my, I'm so sorry. Life is tough, we all have some story that very few people truly understand. Dang girl I had no way."

"I understand, really no one does. I have not told many people, I'm running with his bib today." Candy motioned to the bib pinned on her shorts. "His name was Kyle Richardson. He planned to run this race. He was a great guy and a world-class marathoner.

He tried to make the Olympic team last year. He came up just short, top ten. He was really a great guy, I loved him. We were in *love*." With such an emotional emphasis on the word love, Andrea knew instantly the depth of the young couple's connection. "His life had so many parts left incomplete. Including our relationship, I wanted us to get married and." Candy paused.

"He wanted to accomplish so much more. I want to finish this for him and for us."

"That's awesome, and one heck of a way to honor him. I'm here to help."

Andrea knew that a simple conversation at the right time in life can recharge someone's spirit. Likewise, in a race when things looked bleak, Andrea knew that a kind word with someone along the trail could help them battle through a low point of the day. She also knew that a few moments spent encouraging someone could propel them to overcome the mental, physical and endurance challenges that seemed insurmountable alone. The two walked briskly as they faced another of the many rolling hills.

"None of life's challenges can stop us unless we let them. Girl, you have the power to overcome and tackle anything placed in your way. Always remember that. When I started running these crazy races, I thought the marathon was going to kill me. Would you believe it, in front of you is a wife, a mother of two, a self-confessed cupcake addict and a state record holder? If I can do this, then you, my dear, can do anything."

With a new piece of information added to the storyline, Candy stopped along the road again. "What? A state record holder?"

"Ah it's nothing, I run this 24-hour cancer benefit race in Hampton, Virginia. It's how I got into ultrarunning in the first place. At the end of the day, they told me I was the new, get this." Andrea made the air quotes motion with her hands as Candy watched spellbound. "The new female, 35-40-year-old, Virginia State record holder for the 24-hour run with 92-miles."

“Well hot dog, Andrea…that is an accomplishment, I’m honored to run with you.” The pair started to move again, a slow trot at first then into a comfortable running pace where they could talk and run.

"Really, Andrea. That is awesome. Be proud and thank you so much for helping me work past that low point. Just having someone to talk to, to not be alone for a few minutes seems to have made everything look not so overwhelming. I’m good now. Out of danger, I’m able to keep moving on my own if you want to go on. At the end of the day I have a lot of good people in my life to help me, help me carry on and to help me with the future. All is not lost. I'll finish this for Kyle, and for…" The last part of Candy’s declaration she spoke so softly that it went unnoticed.

“my family…”

"Anytime. I'll see you at the finish. We only have two miles to go. It’s not that far considering. I'm going to put the hammer down and roll. Run for your life...and the life you shared with Kyle."

Unable to match Andrea's faster pace this late in the day Candy relented but was determined to keep her new friend in sight for as long as she could. Her road angle helped her regain her focus on the journey and her purpose which enabled her to reconnect with why she was running this race in the first place. Focused on finishing strong she was resolved to run the final miles without yielding to tired legs, overtaxed lungs or a mentally weak moment.

She made the final turn of the day, the 49th mile of her run, onto the slight incline of E. Sunset Ave. With the end of the day so near new life shot through her veins. Where once she was fatigued and desperately trying to hold on in this last push for home her stride quickened among the ranch style homes and the tree lined streets. Her ears filled with motivating cheers from locals on all sides of the road. Her smile widened as volunteers and Law enforcement officials who lined the course attempted to give her a high five and offer encouragement. Young kids came off their front porches waving wildly while attempting to run alongside the finishers. For a moment, she forgot about everything and simply enjoyed the run. Candy knew she finally understood the joy Kyle felt as all her pain, grief, regrets and problems seemingly melted away.

With less than a quarter mile to go, Candy dug deep into her personal pain cave and mustered up everything she had left to finish. As the crowd along the final yards of the course grew to a blur and the finish line came into view, Candy ran as fast and as hard as she ever had. With the inflatable red arch that spanned one lane of the blacktop road in front of Springfield Middle school in front of her, Candy made her final push.

There was no ribbon to break. No photo finishes. There was no live telecast beamed around the world. Yet Candy crossed the finish line with her arms raised proudly, her fists pumping into the air and with overwhelming joy on her face. Candy finished in the same fashion she believed Kyle would have run at the Olympics, if his life had not been cut short.

In the 9 hours 36 minutes and 10 seconds since the gun went off in Boonsboro, Maryland Candy experienced so much. She went into the race wanting to finish something for the man she loved. She wanted to provide a finishing statement for a life that was too short. To author a chapter to a life that was unfinished and for the potential of a new life. She finished the race in a way that would have made everyone and especially Kyle proud. At the end of the day, she was ready to begin the rest of her journey.

Jim and JT with Carly in tow ran to meet Candy as she exited the finishing area.

Exhausted and staggering, Candy found her way out of the finishing chute with a shiny medal on a red, white and blue ribbon draped around her neck. Heavier in the moment was that she had fulfilled the vow of finishing this race for the one person she truly loved. She finished for Kyle.

Jim was the first one to reach her, although Carly's barks were the first echoes from her personal cheering section. Candy smiled as her eyes filled with tears. She could hardly breath when she fell into Jim's outreached arms.

Her voice was dry, coarse and riddled with emotions. "Jim, you know how much Kyle meant to me, I loved him. And I know." She paused multiple times trying to force the words out between labored breaths and soul defining emotions.

"I know how..." She paused again as tears continued to roll down her cheeks. "that Kyle was like a son. He cared deeply for you, Jim." She paused and between the tears she smiled, "Jim you're going to be a grandfather."

The End

Brian Burk prior to running the Grand Canyon Rim 2 Rim 2 Rim

ABOUT THE AUTHOR:

Brian is presently a Mechanical Skills Instructor with a fortune 100 company living and working out of North Carolina and Virginia. Prior to his present position, he retired from the United States Air Force after serving as a Senior Noncommissioned Officer (SMSgt). During a 20-year military career, he served state side, and tours overseas including a remote tour to Thule, Greenland and a combat tour in Northern Iraq. Originally from Erie, Pa.

Not a natural runner Brian found his passion for running in his 30s. Since then his running career has seen him complete race distances from 5k to 100-miles in length.

Likewise, writing also came later in life. Brian could tell a gripping story but found it hard to get it onto paper. Unfinished is his third book. His other works include, **Running to Leadville**, his first novel and **26.2 Tips to run your best MARATHON**. He has also been published in national running publications, running theme blogs and his blog at http://briansrunningadventures.com

Follow Brian on Twitter and Instagram @cledawgs or like his Facebook page.

Running to
LEADVILLE

Life, Love, Loss and a 100-Mile Ultra Marathon Through the Colorado Rockies

The town of Leadville, Colorado. When you envision the hardscrabble towns that dotted the mountain regions of the wild west your mind draws a picture of a town like Leadville. When tales of fast fortune, expansive wealth, and hard labor of the gold boom period come to mind, communities like Leadville are at the forefront.

Leadville, Colorado is a town birthed out of the very ground, labor and mineral wealth of the land on which it was settled. Established when miners who struck out on finding gold found something else. These miners failed to find the treasure they sought after because of a strange heavy black sand that was clogging up the gold mining operations. Nearly giving up on the area, a few prospectors traced the black sand, aka Cerussite, to its source. In 1876 several silver-lead deposits were discovered and the town of Leadville was born.

Early mining operations brought unimaginable wealth to the area, the town, and the people who invested their lives there. Leadville quickly became the largest mining operation in the world. The population of the town exploded with numbers climbing as high as 15,000 producing gold, silver, and lead. This mining industry brought in nearly 15 million dollars annually.

Leadville is also a colorful town with an exciting past. Great wealth brings great personalities, talent and discovery. Home to several celebrities including the one and only lawman Doc Holiday, gunfighters Frank and Jesse James, from RMS Titanic "the unsinkable" Molly Brown, and Oscar Wilde to name a few.

As fast as Leadville prospered collapse came almost as fast. With a depressed demand, the mines were no longer running at full capacity. Before long the major mining operations stopped, in 1982 nearly 3,000 good paying mining jobs were lost.

A man named Ken Chlouber had an idea...

The race known as the Race Across the Sky.

A man cut from the very fabric of the mines, an avid marathon runner, Ken conceived of a 100-mile trail race to bring prosperity back to community. Chlouber knew that if he could stage the toughest Ultra-marathon in the world the race would bring visitors and money back to Leadville. Ken approached a local hospital administrator about his idea.

The administrator had a very simple reply.

"You're crazy! You'll kill someone!"

Chlouber responded, "Well, then we will be famous, won't we?"

The first addition of the race was run in 1983, the Leadville Trail 100-mile foot race starts at 6th & Harrison street in the center of town. A challenging start as Leadville is the highest incorporated city in the United States at around 10,200 feet above sea level.

The race takes runners on a 50-mile out and back course to the ghost town of Winfield, Co. On the way to Winfield the field travels over dirt roads, asphalt, uneven hiking trails, rough cut power line access roads and a double crossing of Hope Pass at 12,620 feet.

Running to Leadville is about so much more than a race or a town, the tale is about life on the run.

A tale of life, love, and loss. Running to Leadville is more than a technical manual on how to run. It's more than a collection of articles detailing the proper selection of gear, race strategies, or logistics to be successful. Running to Leadville is a story which will entertain, inspire and motivate you to live life to the fullest.

This tale set on the ultra-marathon stage is about life. A life that did not fit into the cookie cutter prototypical American dream. This story is about a young life derailed after the breakdown of his family and the seemingly lost relationship with his father. A narrative about a young adult life that seemed less than valued when his father chose other interests over being present. A existence that felt empty, unwanted, and rejected by the very figure he wanted to be accepted by.

Running to Leadville is about finally finding love. With love and running, collectively his life finally had meaning. He loved life and life had finally loved him back. He also loved her.

The haunting sounds of metallic chaos would forever be etched into his life song.

He was entrapped in a world he no longer wanted to be part of. Entangled in anger, hopelessness and misery he became desperate.

Running to Leadville could motivate you to start running or challenge you to run a 100-mile race.

Running to Leadville will forever change your outlook on life.

Reviews of Running to Leadville

"I've been reading Running to Leadville, thanks for sending it along. You are clearly a passionate and devoted individual and I applaud your grit and perseverance. Please never stop!"
Dean Karnazes – the ultra-marathon man

"Top 5 trail running novels, summer 2017"
Trail Runner Magazine

"The details in every chapter will draw you in and make you feel like you're walking in his footsteps."
Josh D - JFK 50 finisher.

"This book is about running, but also about how running shaped a person. A great read, I could not put it down until I finished it."
Betty Ann - Adventurer

"I absolutely loved this book! Being ultra-marathon runner it was easy to be completely captivated from the very first page."
Melinda H – Ultra-runner

"This book pulls you right in from the beginning. I had to keep reading to find out what happened." Amazon Customer

26.2

Tips to run your best MARATHON

(or any race for that matter)

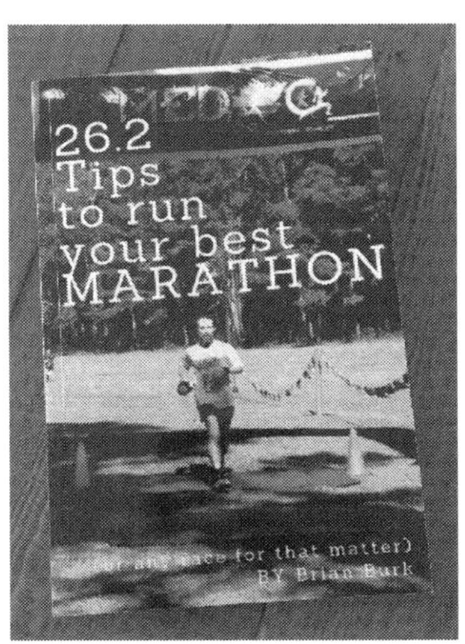

26.2 Tips to run your best MARATHON, is perfect for the first-time marathon runner and the veteran racer who is looking to improve their finishing times and race day experiences.

This book bridges the gap between training and racing in the real world. Not a training guide or a technical manual on how to get into marathon shape. The book does not contain training plans and or diets to get you into racing form. 26.2 Tips offers the reader valuable lessons learned and a look at race strategies to help you improve your finishing times, set new Personal records, or maybe even earn a Boston Qualifying time. This book also helps you capitalize on the race day experience.

I share with you my race day experiences with anecdotal stories where things have gone as planned and examples where I learned costly lessons when my plans fell apart. I also share with you what has worked and enabled me to shave nearly an hour off my marathon time.

A collection of strategies and tactics ideal for anyone looking to post their best marathon finishing time or the first-time marathon runner who is looking to uncover some of the mystery around race day. **26.2 Tips to run your best MARATHON** will capitalize on the small and often forgotten details that cost you large amounts of time on race day.

This book is also great for those who only want the best marathon "experience" they can have.

All of Brian's books are available on Amazon and his blog //

https://www.amazon.com/Brian-Burk/e/B01N3L87M0/

www.briansrunningadventures.com

Unfinished

Made in the USA
Columbia, SC
08 November 2019

82938881R00150